SYNCHRO

THE END OF DRUGS

JMS GUITIÁN

**KOLIMA
BOOKS**

Original title: *Synchro, the end of drugs*

First edition: September 2020
© 2020 Editorial Kolima, Madrid
www.editorialkolima.com

Author: JMS Guitián
Translation: Araceli Guillamón
Editorial direction: Marta Prieto Asirón
Cover phototypesetting: Sergio Santos Palmero
Book phototypesetting: Carolina Hernández Alarcón

ISBN: 978-84-18263-47-7

Trust that which you can achieve on your own; ask, read, verify; think that others' ideas are as worthy as yours and, most importantly, whenever you fail, which you will, learn.

For Jaime

ÍNDICE

1. HUMAN

*From Latin, 'humus', meaning 'earth', and the suffix 'anus',
which indicates a relationship of origin to something, a
belonging.
Those who belong to earth.*

He brought his thumb to his lips and bit his nail tentatively, without tearing it, like a rodent checking the hardness of an unripe nut before discarding it. Reaching up, he gave his light, straight hair a tug and then pulled his earlobe. A conjunction of nervous impulses that he repeated over and over again, as he worked on his two fifteen-inch computer screens, or whenever it was time to revise final details. Three nervous reflexes that made his body move quickly, repeatedly and uncontrollably. He bit his nails, tugged at his hair and pulled his ear; considerably normal actions when done separately, but together they had become an indivisible part of his nature. It had been two years since Julián started developing the nervous disorder, but the impulses had become even more pronounced in the past few months. He hardly noticed it himself, and whenever Anthony mentioned it, he blamed it on stress. Anthony, his business partner, calculated that his spasmodic loops had increased to a rate of one hundred repetitions per day.

There was less than an hour left until the testing and Julián Konks was still going through the lines of source code that they would use. The young man worked in front of his computer screens in a dark and dingy office, alone for the time being. Every time he typed a modification in the shape of a letter, number or symbol on his left screen, the other screen, which had an image of his face, an infographic, altered its expression in response. The emotional states that passed through that face changed, influenced by a few lines of text. The graphic representation of Julián reacted to every alteration of the programmed code; shifting from desperation to laughter, sadness, fear and joy. He licked his lips and glanced at the door where they had hung a poster of Rosalía. He was waiting for Anthony, his business partner and friend.

Anthony Somoza left Starbucks carrying two cups with white plastic lids that he placed inside the front basket of a bicycle plastered with stickers. He cycled through the city's busy streets right at the time when everyone left work, avoiding the avenues that got busiest during rush hours. The glimmer of a yellowish sun dropped long shadows on the deteriorated pavement. He turned into an alleyway, a shortcut he took to reduce the two miles that separated him from his office.

In a corner, hidden behind a rusty fence, two men with drawn faces shared a syringe with heroin. They did not bother lifting their heads even as the cyclist passed just a few feet away from where they stood. Neither did they try to hide when one injected the liquid into his pale, callused skin.

The cyclist left the alleyway and continued through one of the main streets. On the sidewalk, a woman in a black cardigan leaned out the window of a white car while a man gave her a sachet of cocaine in exchange for worn out pesos.

Anthony continued his route and finally arrived at the doors of a neglected-looking office building. He was pushing his bicycle to the entrance when a couple in bright clothes left the building. The girl smiled and showed her boyfriend a small plastic envelope with what he recognized as crystal meth (methamphetamine). Anthony placed his bicycle against a column and secured it with a large chain and lock.

Julián repeated his little impulsive ritual, stood up and checked the clock that hung on the wall; an old advertisement clock with the Bananas Tech logo. He had needed to go to the bathroom for a while, but reluctant to waste any of his invaluable time, had resisted the urge. He could not put it off any longer now, and the bathroom was only next door to their office. It had dirty-white walls, was illuminated by long fluorescent tubes, and stank of urine.

The bathroom looked empty. Julián chose the third urinal, undid his zip and finally relieved himself. Behind him, from one of the cubicles, came noises and a woman's laughter. Julián lifted his eyebrows and turned his head to stare at the closed door. Clearly, he had caught a couple mid-business.

He heard a female moan and Julián, keen to leave the place, hurried to wash his hands at the sink.

Clang!

Something metallic hit the floor and the whole room went still. Water kept running at the sink. Julián turned his eyes to the tiled floor.

A gun had slid under the door where, a few seconds ago, he had heard laughter and muffled whispers. Julián closed the tap, his eyes fixed on the gun. At the same time, a man's blue sneaker appeared under the door, dragging the object back into the cubicle. Julián shook his head as he left the bathroom and returned to his den, wiping his hands on his jeans.

The corridors of the lower floor were crammed with piles of paper and old folders. Anthony stepped around the mess, still carrying the two cups of coffee. On his way up, he bumped into two young men who were leaning on the wall and chatting, holding two cans of Pepsi.

"I'll be seeing you both in a bit", Anthony reminded them.

"You bet, we are so up for the challenge", said one of them, giving Anthony a thumbs-up.

Anthony hurried into the office, the coffee's white plastic lids were tightly closed.

"Your caramel *macchiato latte*".

He left it on the small side table next to Julián, almost spilling the contents over the open notebook as he jumped into the red chair with the missing armrest. Anthony had removed it so that his right arm could hang off the side and reach the wheels at the base with his fingertips. Sixteen hours a day typing codes has its consequences in the realm of strange fixations acquisition, especially with programmers.

"You should be happy. Your fucking caramel *machiatto latte* has made me waste 20 minutes of my precious time... the place was packed; seven o'clock and you can't imagine the number of addicts to this shit there are. And we were all there, standing in a line like fucking zombies".

"That's the way with vices, *güey*", said Julián, as he went through his little routine again; first the nail, then his fingers tugging at his hair and the final pull of his earlobe. He looked at Anthony, who was scanning his fingerprint to get his computer started, and smiled. "When you are addicted to something, it's always like that... pure drug this caramel stuff... Speaking of which, just a moment ago, there was a couple going at it in the bathroom".

"No fucking way..."

"If you go now, you might still catch a bit of the show. I know you're into that dirty shit", said Julian, as he lifted his cup with one hand and removed the lid with the other. He took a sip and licked his mouth, savoring it; then, he put it back on the table and soon forgot that it had ever been there.

Anthony looked at Julián with a smile.

"The guys will be here in fifty-five minutes. I saw them waiting and Carlo is about to come through that door", Anthony checked the time on his screen and enabled the connection. "Are you sure about this? Is he the right person?"

"Right? Nobody is right for this. Not even us, but when the time arrives... well, we'll just have to be". He bit, tugged and pulled again, eyes glued to the screens. "In five minutes, we will close the program and print out the chips", he said, his face immutable as he continued staring at the lines of code on the screen. "Chap-in is a very promising language, but it lacks good syntax to connect external sensors".

Anthony nodded, "We will have to remake the links... Not now, don't even dream of it, but when we upload it to the cloud, I'm sure we'll have to.

Julián set up the chip printer in which he had invested all the money that his father, Sebastian Konks had loaned him. The Konks descended from a family of bankers of Jewish origin that fled Germany before the war started. They found a new life in Mexico, a country that always welcomes those seeking refuge. It had been a year since they had got the loan, a sum close to two million pesos, which he had promised, without much conviction, to return one day. Thank God, thought Julián; the money had all gone to a life without commodities, an office and a magnificent biotechnological printer HP-Bio 11.

Anthony Somoza was born in Sonora. His parents were agricultural workers who harvested lettuce and grapes. Out of five brothers, Anthony had been the only one to spend any time on his studies; the others continued working the land, doing different jobs along the line of production: they harvested, packaged, stored and distributed.

When Anthony arrived with Julián in Mexico City, at the end of their four years of university, Julian's parents let them stay at a space they had above their garage, and loaned them enough money to develop their ideas. The only condition was that they would stay away from the Konks house and the Konks. They held no love for their geeky son and his 'dark' friend, as they referred to Anthony when he was not present. They despised those who were different, and the color of his hair and skin were enough reason for the racist and superfluous looks they often gave him.

They had both accepted the conditions of the deal and had only seen Julian's parents twice in that time.

Both associates had focused all their efforts on the execution of the idea they were about to present.

Anthony stood up and waited for the 3D printer to do its work, holding his hands behind his neck.

"If the program doesn't work, tell DARPA. They have already spent over fifty million dollars on this damn language".

Anthony was aware that Chap-in was the evolved version of Chap-el, which the Defense Advanced Research Projects Agency (DARPA) launched at least twenty years ago for the acquisition of a high-performance language and the execution of algorithms for supercomputers, although they were using the cloud version from Unix with a BSD license. Its syntax was based on the classic languages C, C++ and Java, but also adopted concepts of scientific programming from Fortran and Matlab. However, its best attribute was related to its parallel processing, which came from programs such as ZPL.

Julián and Anthony met four years ago at Professor Hass' advanced computing class in Berkeley. After sharing many hours of loneliness in front of their computer screens, they became close friends. Silences only interrupted by the sound of typing and occasional bursts of frustration or anger when things did not turn out as expected. They had spent all their time in a tiny room where they hardly engaged in any dialogue, exchanged comments or said inappropriate words. They had not even told the kind of jokes that people outside their programmer's world would struggle to understand. Like the one Anthony sometimes told about the elevator that opens with a programmer inside and someone outside asks 'up or down?', to which he replies, 'yes'. It was a good joke that made them laugh every time.

They were twenty-four, born in April fourteenth and April twentieth, both Aries. They had named their company Synchro and used the symbol of the ram as their logo.

Julián waited for the data to load, selected the printer and without hesitation, pressed the 'run' button to print the programmed, tiny, black balls. It took a few seconds for the files to transfer and the machine to get started. Anthony continued standing guard by the 3D bio-printer which was now blinking with a green light.

"How many?" asked Anthony.

"Five –I think five should be enough", replied Julián, pulling his earlobe. He stretched his legs and stood up. "That's ready now".

"What about Carlo?"

"He should be here any moment now; I told him half past seven. I'd rather we do this once the center has emptied a bit. The commotion would not favor us".

"People talk".

Julián walked to the window that faced the courtyard. Their office was, without doubt, the worst in the Mex-Tec; it had also been the cheapest they found. Those two hundred and fifteen square feet cost something like thirteen thousand pesos each month, and only because the guy in charge had liked him and because no one else wanted the shit hole that looked more like a storage room than the home for a technological company.

"Anthony, I have to make a prophecy".

"Tell me, Nostradamus. Until now, all your weird prophecies have come true".

Julián kept looking at the courtyard below.

"One day, we are going to become very rich because of Synchro and there will be many people trying to divide us. Remember: divide and conquer".

"Technically speaking, those are two prophecies, one about us becoming rich and the other about people trying to divide us", said Anthony, his eyes fixed on the printer.

***

A completely bold man and a young, attractive, blonde girl were straightening themselves up before the mirror at the men's bathroom, after a brief encounter in one of the cubicles.

"When are you going to tell me something about the investor?"

"Soon, give me a few more weeks", he said, taking the gun from its case and turning it in his palm, checking for damage.

"One day, that thing is going to bring you trouble".

"This thing isn't loaded, but it's very persuasive".

A young man in a white t-shirt walked in. He stopped at the door, surprised at the sight of the couple. Then, his attention was drawn to the gun in the bald man's hands. He turned around and left.

"See? Extremely persuasive", said the bald man in blue sneakers as he checked his reflection.

She took out a small bag of cocaine, emptied some of its contents on a metal plate and with help from a little tube of the same material, formed two white lines.

The man returned his gun to the holster on his hip.

"I've got the Synchro geeks' presentation now", the man lifted his chin and posed before the mirror with an ironic smile.

"The people in the building say that what they are doing is pretty awesome".

"Everyone believes that what they do is the best thing in the world".

"Maybe, but people are talking, right?" she said, and held her blonde hair back. Leaning forward she snorted her white line.

"My dear Ana, in the world of money, only money matters; good ideas don't mean shit", the man took the metallic tube from the sink, brought it to his nose and snorted loudly, following the line of powder.

Once in the corridor, each went their different, no words, no kisses, no "see-you-laters". The man turned to stare at the girl's butt as she walked away; she didn't look back.

***

Gingerly, Anthony took the tray with the five microchips covered in black jelly. Each ball hardly reached the size of a chickpea.

There was a loud knock and Carlo poked his shiny, shaved head round the side of the door.

"Hey, guys... Can I come in?"

Carlo Stamas was a forty-year-old lawyer who was often seen in the building hunting for new clients to assist with patent services, counsellings and finding investors. The guy was known at the center as the 'ten percenter'. His strong build and shaved head gave him the airs of a personal trainer.

"Thank you for coming, *güey*", said Anthony, showing him the tray with the five tiny balls.

"This piece of shit is your stuff?"

Julián laughed from the window.

"This piece of shit is going to make us rich and end your days as a third-rate lawyer. Thanks to this piece of shit, you are going to spend your time in gyms burning toxins and fucking desperate ladies".

Carlo was known as a womanizer by the people in the building, besides, he enjoyed showing off his skills with the ladies. Julián glanced at his feet; he recognized the blue sneakers that he had spotted pushing a gun in the bathroom a few moments ago.

"Son, I hear that every day from young guys like you, who dream of finding the golden fleece".

Anthony looked at the logo printed on the wall, the symbol of the ram, Aries, the golden fleece that Jason and the Argonaut's searched for.

Carlo sat on Anthony's empty chair and stretched his arms. On his side, through the open jacket, the gun attached to his hip became visible. He smiled openly at them.

"Don't worry, I have a license", he said, and added, "I've had a tough day and look at the time. So, go on, fill me in, because I have a date at ten at the Old Boat of Santa Fe and the girl is a beauty". He looked down at the gap that was missing an armrest but did not make any comments.

Slowly, Julián walked to where Anthony stood, still with the tray in his hands, a few steps away from Carlo. Julián took one of the balls and held it in between his fingers.

"In a few minutes, four people are going to walk through that door. They are friends, volunteers, some are known to you from the center. They are going to be our guinea pigs..."

Carlo Stamas scratched his head and lifted a condescending eyebrow.

"I hope they signed a contract for this, in case you end up poisoning them with that stuff", he said, pointing at the tray. "I don't want any trouble".

"They are completely harmless, there is nothing dangerous in their composition. It's biotechnology. Their effect lasts for about two hours, after that, the microchip detaches itself and the body eliminates it through excretion. These are organic and biodegradable compounds, easily disposed of by the body. It's jelly". Julián looked at Carlo as he spoke, daring him to contradict him. "We have asked you to come because we need help with finance; we are going to need four hundred million dollars to make the next move".

"Four hundred million dollars? That's more than seven and a half billion fucking pesos. Are you mad?" Carlo stood up, with full intentions of leaving through the door. He tried to lean on the missing armrest. "Fuck... Look, kids, never in the whole history of start-ups has anyone given four hundred million fucking dollars to two little assholes like you, however fucking high-end their technology is. I don't want to waste my time or yours. I shouldn't have come here in the first place".

Anthony blocked his way to the door.

"Please, first listen to what we've got to say. Then, you can leave".

Carlo loosened his tie; he paused. He was already there and had nothing to lose.

"Do you know what 'elevator pitch' means? Well, you have one minute to fill me in and then I'm going to go meet a girl that is dying to show me all of life's pleasure. I'm tired. Let's see, what the hell do you want four hundred million dollars for?" He covered his mouth. "Excuse me for laughing".

Julián, who had not moved from where he stood, continued his speech.

"As I was saying, in a few minutes time, four people are going to arrive here. They will swallow these Synchro microchips and a minute later, I'm going to send a two-gigahertz radio frequency from my computer, sort of like Bluetooth, so that we can provoke emotions in them at our will".

"So, you are telling me that you have developed a technology in which a single fucking ball of these can change people's emotions?"

"I guess you could put it that way, yes. Look, to simplify things: during a period of time, this chip, the black ball, is going to attach itself, like a tic, to a neuron. That way the neuron becomes a center of amplified transmission linked to the person's neuronal system, it makes contact with the brain, sends small electric codes and modifies the person's emotions, but in a way that has been programmed. We like to say that we have come up with a new type of drug; no chemicals, no side effects, and you can control it from your phone with an app. Simple. A drug capable of modifying and controlling human emotion".

Carlo stared at Julián, completely astonished.

"But, that's crazy! Does it work?"

"Absolutely".

Julián knew that the word 'absolutely', got rid of all doubts: people needed absolute truths and absolute words in this relative world that we live in. Carlo would stay to see the results of the test and would completely forgot about his date.

There was a polite knock on the door and four people walked in. Among them were the two young men in white t-shirts that Anthony had spoken to earlier, still holding their Pepsis.

***

The coffin was white and small, smaller than she had imagined for her ten-year-old son Lucas, who had died of leukemia and was about to be buried. Cristina stood petrified watching the narrow box, obsessed by the size of it; she wanted to throw herself at it, open the coffin and see once again, with her own eyes, that it was her Lucas who fitted in that tiny space.

The death of a child renders speechless those who insist on seeking meaning in life. In the last two days, Cristina had become lost in a dense fog, her blue eyes had darkened, her blonde hair had grown white reflections and was now held back in a tight, greasy and decentered ponytail. At thirty, she had aged one hundred years all at once. Fog. She could still feel the weak arm of the child with the worst diagnosis for AML, resting in her palm.

Lucas had started feeling exhausted, he had lost weight, suffered frequent infections, bleeding, bruises that appeared out of nowhere. To save his life, he had gone through chemotherapy, followed by radiotherapy and stem cells transplant. All without result. He had been in that one percent that statistics said would not survive. That horrible one percent that any successful statistic has, right next to the other ninety-nine.

Around her, dressed in black, with dark sunglasses and downcast faces, were friends, a few family members and her workmates, members of the narcotics brigade at the New Mexico Police Department.

The small tow truck started its engine and the lacquered coffin slowly descended the three and a half feet of dug earth. That was the space that separated the box from the surface, from the air, to become that something that accompanies the soft and velvety inside of the dead's rest per *secula seculorum*. The remains of someone that had once been alive, that had breathed, smiled... fallen ill and... Cristina lifted her eyes and saw her partner, Álvaro Guzmán, in a black blazer and tie; he was clenching his fists and diverting his eyes from the hole that was being occupied. He lifted his eyes to the sky's blue. She followed his gaze in its upwards escape and felt comforted by the feeling of a sun ray in her face. She was wearing polarized sunglasses, but still, it dazzled her. The fog would return soon.

She lowered her gaze and there was Guzmán again, trying to invent a smile that would tell Cristina that she would recover from this; that would tell a mother that has lost her child after two years of battling death, that there is hope... Impossible. The smile did not appear and they both turned their eyes to the white coffin as it touched the bottom.

The flowers would come later, tossed into the ditch, the shovel and the earth spilling over it; and then, the unbearable hugs, one after the other. A time for crying that would condense tears into a dense and salty fog. She had already experienced it two years before, a time when tears had surged from her eyes during her last goodbye to her friend and partner, Laura, 'almost at the same time as they discovered that Lucas had cancer', thought the lieutenant.

Cristina was immersed once again in the fog that the loss of a son generates, as she remembered her friend and workmate, Laura, who was buried close to here. 'For the love of God, Laura, look after Lucas; now that you are both together, take care of him'. She held onto that thought while she went through the formalities of lost hugs and the 'I'm sorry for your loss's. She had met Laura Almillar in the Desierto de los Leones Police School, where they trained and studied every morning of the required twenty-one weeks that the course lasted. She had been forced to leave her child with the neighbors while they both worked as waitresses at Tapitas. Laura had been her only friend, Lucas had been everything else. After many hours directing traffic, their chance finally arrived and they took it at once. Cristina at Narcotics and Laura at the Criminal Brigade.

It had happened on the last day of September; Cristina remembered it well because it had been the day after Lucas' birthday. Laura had been there with Albi, a German shepherd that was always stuck to her side; she called him her 'novio'. The day after, during a simple routine assault, Laura, protected by her bulletproof vest, entered the house of a murder suspect through the garden door, an architect who'd presumably murdered his secretary. Inside, by the entrance, they were welcomed by a deflagration that shattered the entire glass door right before their eyes. A bomb programmed to end the life of the police who came to the house. The architect had committed suicide a few hours earlier, leaving that surprise behind to increase the hatred his memory might raise.

Laura died instantly. Afterwards, Lucas remembered her dog, Albi. But, when Cristina went to her house to fetch him, the animal was gone. She was convinced that a neighbor must have taken him.

Laura was buried close to Lucas, thought Cristina, next to the three fir trees at the back. 'Laura, Lucas knows you; he's alone now, but if he sees you, he'll grow calm. Laura, be his temporary mother, please. He's a good boy, you know him, a bit cheeky and absentminded but a good boy after all. He's all yours.'

"Hello, Cristina; I'm sorry about your son".

Cristina woke up from her trance. The guy in front of her was that two-faced worm, Alex.

"What are you doing here?" Cristina said, raising her voice, "what, you've come to your son's funeral? Ten years ignoring him and now... you come here to meet him. Well, you're late". She lifted her hand, ready to unload her anger on his face with all her remaining strength. "Son of a bitch!"

Alex swallowed, ready for the slap.

"I only wanted to offer you my condolences. I wanted to tell you that I'm sorry".

Guzmán reached Cristina's side and held her by the shoulders, trying to calm her down. He looked at Alex. The three of them were alone.

"You should leave. This isn't a good time for surprises".

Alex turned and walked away, slowly and downcast. Cristina was left alone with Guzmán; the spirit of the past was leaving.

She started to cry in anger.

"It's OK. Calm down".

"I'm calm. It's just that son-of-a-bitch... He disappeared entirely from my life ten years ago when he found out that I was pregnant, and he turns up now. Today, the very day we bury Lucas, when he never even bothered to meet his son and in all these years we hadn't heard anything from him, he appears out of nowhere to say that he's sorry. This whole time I've been a single mother, making up stories about my life for a child who is no longer here and who asked about his dad... And now, the goddamn son-of-a-bitch turns up, here of all places..."

Álvaro Guzmán had no words for such pain, and offered a calm hug instead.

"A professional son-of-a-bitch... Let's go".

With the help of a dump truck, the men were pouring earth on the barely visible white coffin.

"Álvaro, I'm alone now".

Cristina tried to recompose herself by wiping her face. She hadn't applied mascara because she knew her whole face would end up covered in black stains. Her eyes were red and moist. Guzmán gave her some space.

"My car's over there. I'll drive you".

"I'd rather stay a bit longer", she said, and pointed at some trees. "I'm going to visit Laura; I need to ask her a favor".

"You're right. Lieutenant Almillar is in this cemetery. I'm sorry".

She started walking away; Guzmán watched her go; she turned around and said:

"Thank you, Álvaro. I'll go to the station later. I'd rather get over all this as soon as possible. What's left for me, which isn't much, is there".

"You don't need to do it. Take a few days off".

"I'd rather go... and not spend my whole day thinking. It's been a long year and..."

"It's been a bad one", offered the white-haired policeman. "It's already November".

"They've stolen October from me".

"When you come to the station, I'll go with you to report the stolen month. When it comes to months, October is pretty important".

She smiled. Álvaro got into his car and drove off; meanwhile Cristina sunk back into the fog.

The place grew silent as the two men that buried the boy left in a tiny electric cart, the sort you'd find in a golf course.

In the distance, hidden, camouflaged behind a marbled pantheon, someone was drying her tears. She had watched Cristina from a distance during the funeral. She couldn't have gone any closer; many would have recognized her and she was dead.

***

In his car, Guzmán wondered whether he should go straight home and into the shower, or stop at Fumadera to buy marijuana. Would it be open by now? It was eleven in the morning and he was due in the police station at three for the evening shift; he had four hours ahead of him and did not feel hungry at all. He turned up the radio.

> ...I want you to know, your blows
> are not going to separate us
> my heart is stronger than all that,
> death was never in the cards.
> I want you to know, your words
> are killing me at last...

The '19 Prius hybrid took the ring road and exited by the Río Becerra.

He stopped at one of the spaces reserved for clients of Fumadera, literally, 'the smoking area', a green shop; its logo, two green circles with a dot in their center. It had opened its doors to pot smokers ten years ago and, even with that name, business was thriving. The light on the sign was on and Alvaro's cannabis supplies were running low. He knew today he would need double the usual to fall asleep. The law allowed one ounce of cannabis per day, but Gaby, the owner of Fumadera —and perhaps the very last of the city's hippies and an old follower of the 'flower power'—, sold it to Álvaro in 100-gram bags, and this had been a particularly rough week; he needed it.

"How, Álvaro", said Gaby as he lifted his hand in what he considered to be the Native American style; his signature greeting. He wore a shabby bandana with camouflage print and had long hair that clashed with his growing baldness.

The smell of marijuana filled the air inside. The shelves were crammed with creams, liquids, cookies, popcorn, sweets and energy bars with a flashy poster announcing the main flavors of their three varieties: sativa, indica and ruderalis.

"How, Gaby". Álvaro returned the man's greeting.

"You've come early, I was just opening. The usual?" Gaby narrowed his eyes. "You have the look of someone who's just been to a funeral".

"Yes, a ten-year-old's, son of a workmate; leukemia, shit luck".

"Terrible..".

"Yes..." Guzmán kept his eyes on the floor, as if a deep hole had suddenly appeared and he could see the coffin rising to the surface. "Give me something strong".

"I don't have anything strong enough for what you need, but take ten ounces of indico; I just received it from a farm close to Guadalajara. They say this pot is extremely relaxing; its flowering period lasts seven weeks and this batch is freshly cut".

"Sedative?"

"Yes, narcotic, and it is very fruity with a touch of wood. If it were wine, it would be a sort of syrah".

Guzmán smiled.

"Gaby, you're the best at selling this shit in the entire world. Every time I come here, I feel like I'm at a wine tasting in the Guadalupe valley. To me, this smoke all tastes the same. I'm sorry". Guzmán took out his credit card and then realized he couldn't pay with it.

"You know that you have to pay with cash because of some obsolete federal law... You are a policeman, change the laws".

"I make sure the law is obeyed, but just enough, and I don't write the laws; if it was up to me, there would only be one law: don't fuck other people over and children are forbidden to die. Well, those are two laws...". Álvaro took out a police card with his name and number and put it down on the table. "Add it to my tab, I'll come by tomorrow. I'll pay you and let you know whether the shit was fruity. If I don't turn up, make a call and get me arrested for robbery. How!"

He picked up his bag and left. Gaby took his card and left it next to the cash register, as a lucky charm.

As he reached his car, Guzmán felt tempted to roll a joint and smoke it on his way home; he was really craving one. A police car drove past and for a few seconds, the agent held his gaze, studying him, car to car; Guzmán was outside Fumadera and that alone made him suspicious. Guzmán had always been on the brink of becoming a problem; he was an outsider in the brigade and at fifty, he was not willing to change his habits. Nevertheless, today, he would avoid trouble; he would not challenge his fellow policeman. The car drove on, slowly, watchful. He turned the key and started the hybrid engine. He would smoke it at home and relax a little before going to work. Ever since him and his wife got separated, the house had become a calm place, he thought.

A moving van from Álamo was blocking his parking spot; someone was moving into the apartment next door to his. His neighboring spot was occupied by an elegant, faded red BMW X-15 with auto pilot. Guzmán pictured a forty-year-old man from the movie industry, probably going through a divorce. Apartment 17 had been empty for three months, ever since old Robert decided to throw away all his stuff and move back to Mérida. 'Álvaro, DF is no place for old men like me' was what he told him.

Guzmán turned back in the alleyway and found an empty spot two streets down; he walked distractedly as he opened his bag of cannabis. He rolled a joint with an expert hand, lit it and inhaled the incandescent weed.

He crossed the street without looking; a car braked and stopped just a few inches away from him.

"Fuck!" Scared, Álvaro had dropped his small bag and the lit joint on the ground.

Inside the vehicle, the driver, a man with a strong build, and a very attractive blonde girl, stared in shock at the man who had so suddenly crossed the road. Carlo Stamas had been driving distractedly, one hand on the wheel, one on Ana Riccoli's thigh.

Guzmán bent down and picked up his small bag and the joint, which he immediately took to his mouth for a long drag. The couple looked at him, amazed.

"Fucking drug addict!" he heard the man with the shiny shaved head shout from the car.

Guzmán answered by opening his jacket and showing the gun that was tucked at his side. The driver reacted by waving his own gun behind the windscreen. Guzmán answered the provocation violently by drawing his own weapon; he burst the side window with the iron butt, and taking advantage of Stamas' surprise, grabbed his gun and threw it by the back wheel.

The woman started to shout and the two men began a peculiar struggle as one tried to open and the other to close the driver's door. Finally, Guzmán pulled it open and dragged the man out of the car. Carlo fell on the ground. Despite his size; Guzmán handcuffed him and began to search him. The young woman looked at him, terrified. The policeman had not pronounced a single word yet and the Carlo was breathing quickly, looking at the sides without understanding what was going on. An elderly couple watched the arrest scene from a window.

"I'm a lawyer; let me tell you, you're going to pay for this", said Carlo Stamas, his face on the ground, as Guzmán went through his pockets.

Álvaro got hold of two bags of cocaine which he tore open and emptied steadily on the street.

"Come on, *güey*. You son of a bitch!" Carlo shouted angrily.

Guzmán's gaze shifted to the vehicle where he spotted the box the young woman was holding. It was black and had a logo that looked like the wifi drawing with two ram horns: Synchro.

The lieutenant walked up to the woman, he took the box from her and opened it. Inside, he found a dozen tiny black balls the size of a pill.

"What the fuck is this?" he demanded, pointing at the box with the tiny balls.

"That's none of your business, asshole", she said.

Guzmán looked around; there were groups of people watching from the corners and two cars waited impatiently. He helped the handcuffed man up.

"Amigo, I'm going for lunch with my girl and you just fucked me over", Carlo said looking down at the dirt on his shirt. "You know you can't arrest me like this... This is, without doubt, police brutality... You let me go and I'll let you go, deal?"

The policeman looked at his joint and then at the bag of cannabis that was still lying on the asphalt; he considered the situation. What the man said was true; this would mean heaps of problematic paperwork and explanations that evening. He released him from the handcuffs; Carlo picked up his weapon and got back in his car.

"Son of a bitch", the girl murmured.

Guzmán dropped the black balls together with his joint and stepped on them, leaving an odd-looking black mess. Then, he left to his apartment, walking up the newly-painted main staircase.

On the landing, a sweaty young man in shorts waited for instructions holding two wooden chairs with a Cisco Home label. From inside, came a woman's voice:

"Leave those next to that table".

As Guzmán put his key in the keyhole, the voice that was giving the instructions, addressed him from behind:

"Hello, I'm Gloria Altolaza, the new neighbor. You must be Álvaro, the policeman; Margarita, the manager, told me about you". She held out her hand.

Guzmán shook hands with Gloria Altolaza. Around forty, he thought. She was wearing a grey t-shirt exposing a bare shoulder and black leggings with a skull printed on one side.

"I'm Álvaro Guzmán... welcome. And Margarita is definitely the mother of this neighborhood. Careful with her, she said that stuff about me being a policeman to give you a sense of security and get a better rent".

"It's certainly worked with me; they should discount it from your rent, a bonus. There should even be a sign: 'policeman living in this building'", Gloria said and noticed the bag of cannabis that was still in his hand. "I'm going to be very safe here".

"I'm not sure that's a good thing. Now, if you'll allow me". Álvaro opened his door. "I'll be here if you ever need anything".

"In that case, I'm sure I'll end up needing something", replied Gloria with a cheeky smile.

Guzmán closed the door and threw the small bag on the table by the entrance. He took off his black blazer and loosened his tie. That woman's face seemed familiar. He took a paper and opened the bag of marijuana; he had to turn his head away from the intense smell to stop himself from feeling dizzy. Expertly, he rolled another joint; he'd hardly enjoyed the previous one. He lit it with a Zippo; first, a tall green flame appeared and then the incandescent crackle of dry weed, wrapped in thin paper, and the white smoke. He was like an alcoholic who swallows but doesn't savor. He took a first drag and then sat on the blue sofa. The leftover smoke drifted from his nostrils.

He could hear Gloria Altolaza giving instructions behind the door:

"That one goes to the right, over there... a bit further... careful, careful... Tiny bit more to the right. Slowly... slowly".

Buzz, buzz, buzz

His phone was vibrating inside his blazer.

"Shit".

Buzz, buzz, buzz.

"Hello?"

"Hey, Dad... Hey... it's Rita".

"Hey, kiddo".

"Is it a bad time to call?"

"No, I'm at home, resting. Evening shifts this week; you know, I come in at three and leave at twelve, if nothing happens. The usual stuff. How are you?"

"I'm fine... Actually, it was Mom who asked me to call... She wants me to tell you... Look, Dad, I've made up my mind to become a youtuber... So, yeah, I'm dropping out of college".

Guzmán went silent.

"Dad... are you there?"

"Yes, of course..."

"Look, this year has been wonderful. Braulio and I have uploaded content for over seven thousand followers... And if we focus all our potential on it, we could reach a million followers in three months, isn't it crazy? But we need to invest time, so that we can travel and... you know. Braulio and I are on it with the power house; we want to rent out this really cool place in Gudalajara; that's where Braulio's from... You are going to love it. What do you think?"

"Who's Braulio?"

"Braulio's my boyfriend; I met him on campus; at a frat party. He's a little older than me; he'll finish Materials Engineering this year. Mom thinks it's awesome".

Guzmán stared at his joint and tried to figure out how long it had been since he had last spoken to his daughter. He had called her two months ago, but not much was said beyond 'I love you' and 'hope to see you soon'. Now, his daughter was calling to bombard him with news: a new boyfriend and she was going to drop out of college, after all the effort it had taken her to get in; and she was moving to Guadalajara with this Braulio and was going to earn a living as a youtuber. The only thing he could think of saying is what parents always say:

"You're only eighteen".

"I'm nineteen, Dad".

"Well, then, you're only nineteen... You seem to be telling me that you've already made up your mind and that all this is set. What do you want me to say?"

"Dad, I don't want you to say anything. I just want to let you know about the choices I've made. I've made these choices for myself, I'm an adult and..."

"What did your mother say?"

"She told me to tell you".

"Typical of your mother, pushing the responsibility onto me".

"I'm of age and economically independent".

"I know. And if you're anywhere as stubborn as I am, the decision is already final.'

Guzmán took another drag of his joint, which he had been staring at for a while now.

"Dad, you have always told me that I have to be brave. Braulio is a good guy and I love him".

"Rita, when you're in love with someone, everyone seems to be good".

"You'll see what a good couple we make on camera, we work well together and the topics we talk about are technology, phones, apps... People love it. We've managed to get some sponsors, it's going well".

"So, my daughter is a youtuber".

"Yes, your daughter Rita Guzmán is awesome and a first-rate youtuber".

"And you get paid to do that stuff?"

"I do and pretty well too".

"What about moving to Guadalajara?"

"It's only an hour away by plane".

"By plane?"

"I promise I'll come visit you and Mom loads, OK?"

Álvaro took another long drag and let the white smoke drift from his mouth.

"Are you smoking?" Rita inquired.

"Yes, but I'm also old enough not to have to explain myself".

"Well, I'm not going to give you a speech on that, it's too late. I'll leave you to it, I'm in the middle of packing... Love you lots, kisses".

"I also love..."

She hung up. Álvaro took his joint, breathed in deeply and blew the smoke out. He stood up and moved to the table with his laptop. He got into YouTube and entered his daughter's name: Rita Guzmán.

Rita spoke while she held the camera in her hand with skill, like a blogger with a lot of experience; 'Hello, cosmopolitans of the world, this is "easy life" with...'. Everything about her was laughter and excitement. The camera moved and Braulio appeared, a skinny young man who was also smiling broadly, pale with a white hat that looked too Christmassy, and which made him seem even paler and a bit sickly; 'my daughter always fancied the weaker ones', he thought. '...Braulio and Rita here on "easy life", broadcasting from the most organic restaurant on the planet...' Rita turned the camera to her own face, 'Tocaya in Los Morelos, a great place for your very best moments...'. Rita laughed and zoomed out so that the place became visible behind them; there were tables at the back with people eating and a waitress arrived at the table where they were sitting with some salads and two green glasses. Rita continued talking: 'dear all, food is here, two Thai salads and two glasses of kombucha and ginger... extremely healthy...' Rita took a sip and Braulio took his chance and moved the camera. 'Hello, this is Braulio, and we haven't come all the way here just to eat; today we would like to show you an app...'. Rita spoke again, interrupting Braulio: 'that's right, today we're going to show you a new app for your phone... its name is Foodoos'. Rita took her phone from the table and showed it to the camera, a logo with an 'F' and two big 'O's. 'It's going to help you lose weight and eat food that's both healthy and tasty', said Braulio. Rita: '...exactly, so get Foodoos... and start eating healthy every day'. Braulio: 'Rita, Rita, don't interrupt; Rita, now, let me explain...' Rita laughed and laughed.

Guzmán knew that his daughter didn't take any drugs but on that video, she seemed to be up to her ears in cocaine. 'Braulio, Braulio, you are boring and I am quicker and more fun than you are. Right, guys?... Download the Foodoos app and have fun eating. You just need to tell the app how much you are willing to spend and what you feel like eating and it will take care of everything else...'. Rita had taken over the whole screen. 'And don't forget that Foodoos is a free app'. Rita: 'Also, in your first order, you get a ten-dollar discount. Here we are, enjoying life, Braulio and Rita's "easy life"'. Braulio poked his head in front of the camera, close enough to have touched the lens with his nose: 'Hey you! This is called Braulio and Rita's easy life. If you're not careful, they'll just change the name'. He seemed annoyed. Rita's face was still at the forefront laughing while Braulio wrote something in a notebook, covering it with his hand whenever the camera came near it. 'Stop the camera', he said. The only thing he heard at the end was Braulio saying, 'Fuck you' and then the video ended. He looked at the number of views, close to a million, the video was not even five months old. The world has gone crazy, he thought.

Guzmán shut his laptop, took one last drag of his joint and left to take a shower.

***

The man in orange overalls and a bulletproof vest walked taking short steps, it was all he could manage with the shackles that bound both his hands and feet together. Aldo Ríos, tall and slender at the age of fifty, was the new war trophy that would be exhibited as a warning to drug cartels. He was a public enemy finally arrested, and his deportation required all the appropriate security measures for a high-risk prisoner. Escorted by six agents of the DEA, Aldo had a slight limp. He was still in pain from shot he had received in his calf, his latest scar. He walked the one hundred meters of the cement path that led to the airplane that would take him to the penitentiary at Florence, Colorado, to its high security unit, the ADX, where he would stay until the trial for narcotics trafficking. Along the hangar's perimeter, over one hundred Mexican police agents guarded the prisoner's handover. Aldo's eyes were fixed on his short steps, concentrating on not falling. The agents kept a hand on the prisoner as a reference; meanwhile, their eyes continued scanning the whole perimeter, feeling the tension of being observed. The rear ramp of the military airplane was waiting open for him; Aldo stepped onto the ramp, he felt the pain shoot up his leg, and looked at either side of him, knowing that he was being watched. Standing there as he was, he would have liked to raise his arm and form the sign of victory with his fingers. A push made him walk towards the airplane's entrance.

"Have a good trip, Aldo", murmured Juno Coentrao, who was watching the whole operation from a rooftop outside the security perimeter. Don had asked him to check on his brother's health after three months in jail. Juno was the son of one of the drug-trafficking capos in Brazil, Néstor Coentrao, and he had been offered to Don as a sign of respect. The young man was dressed impeccably, he was the king's messenger in the drug trafficking business and his eyes betrayed an unscrupulous character.

The plane was speeding at the take-off runway.

An unforgivable security error from their 'Florida friends' had led to the arrest; the monthly movements at the bank account registered under the name of Kaspar Klee, located in Miami, transactions that withdrew cash and which had been investigated by the DEA. They only had to wait for Aldo to enter the Azteca bank in Tijuana, on that second of September, like every month, five o'clock of a hot evening, arriving in an armored van with seven men armed with AK-47s.

Aldo always carried out the transaction in person, always, with his automatic, the safety off, always trusting that he was moving in his own territory, his home. A group of intervention police from both countries was waiting for him, armed for combat. They knew Aldo would not give up easily. And they were right. When the group with the eight traffickers accessed the staircase that lead up to the bank, three Federal Police cars blocked the entrance to the narrow street; Aldo took out his gun and started shooting everywhere, not knowing where he was aiming, but guided by his 'I have nothing to lose' instinct. The first crossfire ended the lives of three traffickers and one policeman who received a bullet in his head. Surrounded and trapped between the bank's door and the armored van, Aldo and his men fired in all directions They were answered by shots from snipers up rooftops. From that height, they began to undermine the gunman's shots, who were death's grooms celebrating their wedding with shots that were blowing up their heads and hearts. At street level, a burst initiated by a policeman who had thrown himself down on the pavement, got Aldo Ríos on the calf, making him kneel on the bloodied sidewalk. When he tried to react, he found a gun pointing at his temple; his men lied around him as anonymous corpses. The battle was lost and a general of the drug-trafficking army had fallen.

Juno dialed the number that appeared under XL on his phone.

"It's a clear day", he said as soon as there was a connection, no waits, no greetings, no answers. He hung up.

He knew that the perimeter at a mile's radio would be under surveillance, listening to any phone connections. 'It's a clear day'. Juno waited for the plane to take off northwards, he turned to the door that was being guarded by a five-foot-nine blonde woman, dressed in a plain suit with black pants; attached to her side, next to her heart was a NP29, nine millimeters.

"We're going to the wall and we'll be right back. Tell the pilots to be ready at three". She nodded.

Don had heard 'It's a clear day'. Aldo, his brother was being deported to the United States of America. It was completely silent at the office that rose over Hollywood's hills in a grand mansion where he remained anonymous under the name of Don Nassar. He touched the picture where he appeared with his brother Aldo. Don had adopted his wife Hela Nassar's surname; from Jewish origin, a Persian family that had emigrated to America after the fall of the Shah in

Iran. Doncel Ríos had taken advantage of his new situation to clean up his record, his surname; there is nothing that a good law firm cannot do in the United States of America. So, Doncel Ríos became Don Nassar, a respectable large real estate investor who dealt with hotels, apartments, marinas, entire buildings and big mansions; still, he continued to manage the millionaire business of opiates trafficking in a border that was impossible to control.

Hela, his wife, died ten years ago from a breast cancer that ended her life in a matter of months. Don had never been truly in love with her; he had confessed it to his daughter once, after three mescals. She interpreted it as the words of a drunk and depressed man. Don looked at the picture of the woman that presided the table; next to it, he kept the picture of Esther Nassar, his daughter, who had the same dark hair his wife had, and the same tough character. A single daughter for a gigantic legacy full of lights and shadows. Esther was in the light side of the business and knew about the shaded side, she was his family. Aldo was his right hand in the dark side of things, the limitless money that chemical addiction provided; that was where little Aldo had been, always out on the field, among tensions, shots and corpses. They saw each other from time to time; traveling in their private jets, they met at a mansion that Don had in Los Cabos.

Don spotted Esther's red sports car driving through the gate. His daughter was wearing a Versace dress, Jimmy Choo shoes, a Kelly Hermes' handbag and some exquisite Tiffany's jewelry; a true 'Masaryk girl'.

Esther studied and USC and held a master in Finance from Harvard, at twenty-seven she had already outdone everyone. She knew she had power and was completely aware of her future; she was ready to accept her role. Like in a monarchy, where the princess knows that she must choose the man she is going to share her kingdom with, always keeping her own interests and power in mind, rather than following her heart's desire. It was something she had learnt from her father. Juno, more than a boyfriend, was a duty; above all, was her family's legacy.

The house's exterior security was discrete: two uniformed guards stood at the hut by the entrance and another one kept watch of the whole outside perimeter, driving up and down in an armored car. The idea was that it would not draw the attention of their millionaire neighbors, that they would not relate it to the images of armed drug-traffickers. Don rejected anything that might connect him to the Hispanic world and had forbidden the hiring of Spanish speaking employees for the house. If you erase your past, you must destroy all evidence that it ever existed. Doncel Ríos was dead, and only one loose end remained: Aldo.

Inside the house, ten Chinese bodyguards accompanied him day and night in two-people shifts.

Esther walked into the room and directed her eyes to the two men who stood behind him like statues, not even batting an eyelid.

"Hi, Dad. I really don't get how you can live with these guys stuck to your side all day and night".

"You get used to it".

"Besides, you can't even have a conversation with them".

"Precisely, they only speak Mandarin. I assure you I sleep extremely well at night. I can close my eyes placidly with two men watching over me. I just pretend they are invisible".

"Yes, I get the idea of hiring men that don't speak your language, but I need privacy".

"Privacy? I once found out that one of the bodyguards understood a little of Spanish, I caught him pulling a face at something I said.... So, I sent him to be killed. They all know about it".

Don looked indifferently at one of the men in the room, he could very well have been a piece of furniture.

"Your uncle Aldo is on his way".

"I'm sure we'll find a way to get him out", she said and dropped her handbag on the sofa.

"Yes, he will have the best team of lawyers in America". Don turned to look outside the window where two squirrels played on some branches.

"I don't know if I've ever told you, I'm sure I have. My father, Pedro Ríos, your grandpa, was from the South, from Mérida, the only son of a very poor family. He joined the Army and became a pilot at the Air Force. Few know this, but the Águilas Aztecas squad played a major role in the Pacific War... But, we'll leave that story for another day. Over there, in the Philippines he fell in love with a beautiful woman, my mother, Flora, the daughter of a landowner of Iranian origin. Despite that, they married and settled there to stay together. I was born in the Philippines and so was Aldo. My grandmother, our Nona, was a very compassionate woman... Long story short: My father convinced my mother to come and visit his country, Mexico. They came here and never again returned to the Philippines. My mother died far away from her family. We were young and our Nona came all the way from Manila to stay with us. By that time, my father had already found refuge in alcohol's embrace. He drank a lot and appeared dead one day, next to a swamp; half his body had been devoured by an alligator. I remember our Nona sat down with Aldo and me and said: 'I think, today, your father has taught you the most valuable lesson there is in life. At the swamp, when the deer wakes up, it knows that it must drink from the swamp to save its life. When the alligator wakes up, it knows it must move stealthily towards the deer to hunt and feed itself... Now, you must choose which one to be, and always, no matter who you are, as soon as the sun comes out, your watch begins...'.

Esther listened attentively; the story was well known to her, but she found that there was something in it for the one who would become the guardian of a legacy.

"Did you speak to Juno?" she asked, changing topics.

"He was there, in Tijuana", replied Don, still watching the squirrels scamper on the branches in an endless game of chase.

"Yes, he told me; he'll be back tonight. He called me from the car, he's supervising a move.'

"Stay and we can eat together; your boy will arrive late. And if you have the time, I can even show you this new toy I acquired today". He lifted his hand and pulled an imaginary trigger, pointing at a wooden box on the table. "It's a present".

"You haven't bought me the Smith and Wesson 500, have you?"

"Just a little something I fancied getting my daughter; it's got double action, five shots".

"Right, it uses the 500 S&W cartridges with 12,7mm bullets, awesome stuff. But, I could totally wreck my shoulders, Dad".

"That's why I want you to try it and get comfortable with it at the shooting gallery. Shall we?" Don nodded at the door.

Esther checked her Cartier watch; she had a meeting later. The family's venture capital fund had received an interesting proposal from a company named Synchro; they were looking for finance for a 'technological drug'. That's how they had sold her the idea, it sounded interesting.

"I've got a meeting in an hour where someone's going to present a project for a four hundred million investment".

Don seemed unperturbed by the sum and left the room accompanied by his only daughter. A few meters behind, the two Chinese men followed their steps.

Esther was carrying the heavy box as if it were a briefcase; she calculated that she would have enough time for a quinoa salad and a few shooting rounds in her father's gallery with the world's most powerful revolver. Don smiled, he knew his daughter's weak spot.

***

Juno had his hands on the steering wheel. He had bought the Aston Martin Vulcan three weeks ago on a whim and it still smelled of new leather; Esther herself had chosen the color, smoky grey. Juno and his blonde companion remained within the vehicle's tinted windows, watching the whole operation from a nearby hill; four armed men surrounded the car.

The wall rose majestically in front of them. An impenetrable border, almost nine meters high, impossible to overcome. The drones were flying above it, undisturbed.

"There you go; when they built it, they weren't thinking of the future. The sky has no borders. They spent millions of dollars and it's just a monument to vanity and human betrayal... They could have saved many lives with that money. I remember them building it when I was a kid..."

The drones, loaded with cocaine, overflew the border with complete impunity. Trucks waited on the American side with their upper tarpaulin open; the drones flew just about a mile and unloaded the white powder, then the vehicles drove away to their various destinations in California. A clean and perfect logistic.

When the last truck left and the drones returned home to Mexico. The same operation every week. The systems of detection of low-level flights made them untraceable.

Juno made a signal and the four gunmen got into a big black car and left.

Juno shuddered and started humming a popular folk song:

'In the Big Rock Candy Mountains, there's a land that's fair and bright, where the handouts grow on bushes and you sleep out every night where all the boxcars are empty, and the sun shines every day on the birds and bees and the cigarette trees the lemonade springs where the bluebird sings... In the Big Rock Candy Mountain...'.

Ramona lifted her head from between Juno's legs and sat up. She took a handkerchief to her lips and spit in it.

Dust rose in clouds as the Vulcan drove off. Far away, with the lights on, a Border Police car drove along the American border.

***

Julián Konks, Anthony Somoza and Carlo Stamas got into the elevator of the Reforma Tower and pressed the button to the fifteenth floor where they would be having their last meeting after two months of negotiations. They were going to meet the main investor who would sign the four hundred million dollars that would finally launch Synchro: Esther Nassar. Julian bit his thumb, gave his hair a tug and pulled his earlobe.

Half an hour later, in a luxurious room, a group of people in suits watched in disbelief the behavior of the two lawyers that had volunteered for the test. They danced and kissed and rolled on the Council's table. Esther smiled approvingly at Carlo Stamas; next to him were Anthony Somoza and Julián Konks; the latter was holding the phone with the Synchro app.

***

Álvaro Guzmán stood by the coffee machine at the police station. His eyes were fixed on the dispenser; the coffee came out, but there was no cup. Guzmán punched and then kicked the machine; it swayed dangerously.

"For fuck's sake. Nothing works in this place".

Cristina Herrera was reading the report on the arrest of Aldo Ríos when she felt the weight of Guzmán's friendly hand upon her shoulder. She did not need to turn to know it was him, it was something he always did. Six weeks had gone since the morning of her son's funeral and she was still terrified of going home to his empty room. She had decided she would leave the house and move closer to the sea, to an apartment with a single bedroom.

On the report, it said that Aldo Ríos was born in Manila and had become a Mexican national at the age of three. It also said that he had a brother, Doncel Ríos, who was missing. The fog crept into the office and grew until its darkness filled the whole place dark. She stopped reading the extradition report and her mind turned to death; she tried to remember her son's face and failed.

At the cemetery, the boy did not have a gravestone. The order would still take another couple of days to arrive; it would have the inscription of his name, the dates of birth and death. Cautious steps approached the place where the child rested; their owner looked around, watchful. A pair of large, dark glasses hid the face almost entirely. The figure looked around once more and made sure there was nobody else there. They warned her that it would not be a good idea for her to go; they recommended her to stay away from the place, but that was impossible. At the grave, the figure bent down and left a bouquet of roses on the small mound; ten. One for each year that Lucas had lived, ten.

2. TEN

*It is a natural number, composite and defective; it is also
the basis for counting in many cultures, since it is the
result of the sum of all fingers. In Roman numbering, it is
presented with an x, in Chinese with a +, and in Mayan
with an =. October is the tenth month.*

"I told you that this was the best place for Synchro". Carlo Stamas stood in the middle of the hangar, hand on his hips. "This is awesome".

They were in the interior of a white industrial unit where groups of operators worked without rest conditioning and assembling robotic structures. A high technology center in the making.

Three operators in white lab coats and gloves, supervised the construction of a track where transport carts would run. All the boxes would be placed in automatized carts that were currently being tested, coming in and out of a door that opened whenever it detected movement. There was little need for human presence for all of that to work. A large group moved tables and computers into a space with wide windows; others supervised the setting up of a conveyor belt that would link the manufacture of the black pills with the drones' hangar.

Julian and Anthony gazed in wonder at the immense unit that would soon buzz with activity; there were seemingly endless rows of biotechnology printers to make the tiny black balls, and enough delivery drones to cover the whole of Mexico City. Julian moved his hand impulsively and repeated his round of tics.

Carlo had personally taken up the task of finding and conditioning the old garage for interurban buses that was now being converted into offices, a factory, a warehouse and a delivery area for the new sensation in venture capital; all in record time. The money, four hundred million dollars had worked the miracle; the production would not begin until the following week but they already counted with over one hundred thousand orders from people ready to try it, and they had all already paid in advance the two hundred pesos for the download of the app and a pack of three black balls with their corresponding microchips. Synchro had already deposited its first million dollars in the bank.

The predictions that Julián Konks had presented to Nassar Capital were of seven hundred million sales within a year, with a benefit of one hundred million dollars in Mexico alone. When he showed the sum of the global benefit, the number contained nine zeros. Nobody, except Carlo Stamas, smiled at the news.

"This is our dream... Technology is going to make us rich. Orders are coming in by the thousand..." Carlo was thrilled.

Julián gazed at the autonomous carts that ran empty up and down the hangar. Close to one hundred drones waited for the take-off. Among them, a dozen operators in white lab coats followed instructions on their tablets. The company's new CEO smiled, and when he walked past Carlo he punched him tenderly on the shoulder.

"I told you this would happen, see? And you didn't believe us".

"Sure, yes, and now you can beat me up if you'd like to; do whatever you want with me..." Carlo laughed. "We are meeting all our deadlines and investments".

"Now it's time to get this monster to work", said Anthony and, looking at Stamas, added, "I like it, Carlo. Good job!"

Carlo Stamas checked his phone.

"We have a meeting in an hour with the chief attorney and the lawyers", he said, and nodded at the door. "We don't want any trouble with the State's laws".

Julián lifted both hands, showing his palms:

"I'm going to skip this one, if you don't mind. I have a very important date", he said, distractedly.

"What? What the hell, Julián, this is more important than anything else you might have right now", said Anthony, raising his voice.

"You go, you'll do fine without me, and, anyway, Nassar's lawyers are going to be there to defend our best interests".

"I don't like it, Julián, I don't like you dropping out now; we're both in this thing together". He looked annoyed.

"Don't be an idiot, Anthony, I'm not dropping out from anything; we've been stuck in a room for a year, not even leaving our chairs to take a fucking dump. For once, I have a date and it clashes with a politics meeting. It's not that big of a deal, so don't get all worked up..."

"A date?... And I'm the idiot?" Anthony took his hands to his head. "I don't want you to become a jerk. This has only just started and you're already behaving like this..."

"Well, boys this argument really isn't worth it, calm down". Carlo did not want their heated argument to escalate. "Let's keep calm. Come on, look at this whole thing!" He opened his arms and said, "this is fucking awesome and there's still more to come! This is only a first step on the path".

Still angry, Anthony Somoza shook his head disapprovingly.

"I'm sure it's that Ana who you've been going on about for the last couple of weeks", said Anthony, not wanting to drop the topic. "It's pathetic!"

"Ana Riccoli? The blonde from Troposintesis, the organic creams business?" Carlo looked surprised at the mention of the name, it had not even been a week since he last had sex with her. They were both gym lions in full swing. Nothing serious, only physical and without emotional exchanges beyond the superfluous; only sex and a few lines of coke. The last time had been when that mad policeman pushed him to the ground and stepped on the black pills. Later, at dinner, he and Ana had only exchanged a few words, some polite conversation about the projects that they were involved in. Carlo told her about Synchro, the four hundred million dollars and about Julián and Anthony. Now, that giant-killer blondie was going to make good use of all that information and of the promise of a multimillionaire in the making. This Ana truly knew what she was doing. He scratched his head, thoughtfully.

"Do you know her?" asked Julián.

"A little", said Carlo, not wanting to get into details.

"Yes, she's that deceptive blondie with the amazing pair of tits.' Anthony carried on with his verbal attack.

Julián had bumped into Ana Riccoli several times at the Mex Tec and she had tried to approach him with banal excuses such as: 'I love your t-shirt', when he had been wearing a Real Madrid t-shirt, with his name and a number ten printed at the back. Julián, who had noticed her before, had always considered her to be completely out of his league, until that very moment. She was the one who had proposed dinner in the Las Lomas area.

"And why do you care if it's her?" said Julián, clenching his fists. "You aren't my father or my girlfriend, for fuck's sake". He waved his hands at him in a mocking girly gesture.

"You are behaving like a girl in the middle of a hysteric attack".

"Fuck you, Julián!"

"No. Fuck you, darky".

"What did you just call me?" His face was now inches away from his colleague's. "Did you just call me darky? You're racist scum, Julián".

Carlo pushed them apart to avoid the fight.

"Hey! Heeey! Calm down... you can't go on like this. Let's relax and enjoy our success".

"I'm going to leave now... I'll see you at the office tomorrow and you can tell me how the meeting went", said Julián.

"Remember your last prophecy! It seems like you were right again, you Nostradamus piece of shit".

Julián left without another word.

"Prophecy? Nostradamus?"

"Doesn't matter. Just something we say".

Carlo tried to calm Anthony, who was still scowling and murmuring insults.

He ignored that Anthony was, in fact, in love with Julián; he had always been, ever since he had met him and had hidden the feeling from everyone, even from himself. For him, being by his side was enough; they worked together, lived together, spent twenty-four hours a day together. He had never spoken about it with his friend; he kept his feelings to himself. Anthony Somoza had never admitted his homosexuality. His siblings, with that fifth sense that children have, used to say it when they were just kids, and used the word insultingly: fag. Bothered by those comments, he found refuge in his studies and later in computers; they opened a door through which he could escape to communities that understood him; there, he would practice virtual sex in the intimacy of his screen. That was it. And now that Julián was going on a date with a top girl, Anthony felt jealous.

"Guys lose their minds over tits, you know that", said Carlo as he clapped the programmer on the back.

Julián arrived at the restaurant almost at the same time as Ana, who came in an Uber. He was driving a small Chevrolet Onix that his parents had given him as a gift six years ago. She looked with surprise at the utilitarian car and he felt it was high time he bought himself a new vehicle. What's more, now that he was going to earn a yearly salary of more than six zeros, seven with bonuses, he could afford to buy a luxury sports car just for show, an airplane even; the future held no limits. The valet took his utilitarian car and parked it as far from the door as was possible.

Julián stared at Ana, her extremely short dress, colorful, with an impressive cleavage, and six inches of high heels that revealed a body that worked out in the gym. He swallowed hard. He was wearing the Real Madrid t-shirt that she had liked so much when they first met.

As they walked in, she took hold of his hand. Julián realized that his companion attracted people's attention, and that many looked at him with envy. At the table, they chose some salads and Ana ordered champagne to accompany them. 'Anything she wants', thought the new multimillionaire.

"So, tell me, Julián, what do you guys do at Synchro?" asked Ana with interest.

"Nothing, the idea is very simple..." Julián spotted a tiny mole on Ana's chest. "Have you ever heard the term 'synapsis'?"

"No, never. My thing is organic creams. But, I love all that stuff, it really turns me on..." Ana looked at him in the eyes and he responded with a long gulp of champagne. He took his thumb to his mouth, gave his hair a tug and pulled at his earlobe. He had reason to be nervous.

"I'll explain; it's the way in which hormones communicate. This communication takes place through the transmission of nervous impulses from one to the other; it's the way they talk, with small shocks... but, once this nervous impulse reaches the hormone, it generates a type of chemical component, which is what they call neurotransmitters, these are the ones in charge of making us feel turned on, for example".

Ana's eyes continued fixed on him while he spoke.

"Incredible..."

"What we are doing at Synchro is tricking people's brains with electric impulses to create controlled sensations".

"Amazing!" she exclaimed, taking her hand to her cleavage.

Julián's eyes followed her hands and paused there; with great effort, he lifted his gaze to meet the eyes of this woman who was completely out of his league.

"Scientists have found that an adult brain has around one hundred million neurons; each is in charge of processing its own information which it then sends to the others, receiving information from them in return. Every neuron may connect with another fifty thousand. Us, Anthony and I, have discovered mass synapsis and how to stimulate it with very low-intensity electric impulses.

"Can it provoke an orgasm?"

The woman at the table next to theirs moved her head slightly, pointing her ear in their direction, without looking; her neighbors' conversation was way more interesting than the story her husband was telling her about a colleague at work.

"Yes, it's easy, when you ingest a Synchro microchip what happens is that your neuronal system becomes dependent of those micro-impulses. Our brain is a computer that controls all our functions, and our nervous system is its network, sending information in both directions, from the brain to the different body parts. That's where our chips come in, becoming the king of neuronal communications … They do so through the spinal cord, which, starting at the brain, runs down our backs". As Julián spoke, he pictured Ana naked. "It contains nerves with the shape of filaments that branch out towards the other organs and parts of the body. But I don't want to bore you with all this theory".

"Julián, provoking an orgasm isn't boring; I am very, very interested, both in the theory part and the practice".

Ana was unleashing her full skills in the art of seduction and Julián, flattered, carried on talking.

"Well then, when a message originated at any part of the body reaches the brain, it tells the whole body or a part of it, how it must react. If you program the feeling and the App sends a stimulus in the shape of a wave that provokes an electric shock of a certain intensity... well, that's how you provoke an org..."

"And is that just one, or could it be many?"

"They can be as many as you wish to have", he replied timidly, and feeling a little awkward, added, "and if we both connect we could even feel the same thing simultaneously".

"That would be fabulous. I can't wait to try your invention and get synchronized with you".

"That would be nice..."

Julián was about to start a new sequence of tics, but caught himself just as he was bringing his thumb to his mouth and stopped.

The woman on the neighboring table was sitting on the edge of her seat, nodding at her husband, who continued with his monologue about the trouble he was having with his colleague. Meanwhile, she was thinking about how much she would like to try that invention.

***

At State Attorney Eduardo Aster's office ten people sat discussing the report on the Synchro case.

"At a preliminary hearing, we can't prohibit something that does not contain any narcotic substances, or has no harmful effects for public health. According to the experts' report we could call it a technological drug, since its effects are indeed narcotic, but if we ban them, it would be like banning video-games or Google's search engine.

Another lawyer holding the open dossier pointed out that:

"On the report presented by the independent medical team, it confirms that it is addictive and of easy economic and technical access. It's as easy as downloading an app, placing an order, paying and receiving it via drone".

Carlo, who was taking notes at the other side of the assembly table, said:

"Its price is for every budget. You can enjoy it alone or share it with whoever you like. If you wish to, in the app you can synchronize a group to feel the same pleasurable sensations... there are more than twenty-five possible modes. I guarantee that it will suit any kind of fantasies... I have tri..."

The lawyer interrupted him, returning to his own speech:

"We would like to point out what we consider to be most problematic. The preliminary results do not show the presence of toxic substances or any side effects on the users tested".

Carlo tried to bring the attention back to himself:

"The only positive effect would be its regulation and the taxes that it would earn the government if it was legalized. All these are positive side effects for our society".

"Mr. Stamas, please don't add external elements to this conversation; this is a meeting to decide over the legality of the launch", Aster underlined. "We have no reason to believe it a risk for human health. Since marijuana's legalization, we have not faced a challenge of this sort... We have spoken to sources close to the president and we are ready to provisionally accept its legalization... but we will keep track of its social evolution and its effects on public health".

Anthony Somoza stood up to speak and shot a quick, meaningful look at Carlo indicating him to stay silent:

"Thank you, Mr. Aster, for the trust you have placed on us; we are certain that projects such as Synchro will also become useful in the struggle to clean the city's streets of drugs".

"May God hear you, boy, may He hear you".

***

Cristina drove an expensive, high-end car while Álvaro Guzmán watched the sunset through the window. They had dressed up elegantly, at the expense of the department's budget. They had to infiltrate and send the signal for intervention to the units that were waiting under cover.

"How's your new place?"

"Good, it's kind of small but that's what I was looking for".

She lied. She hated herself for abandoning the place that held the memories of her son. The house had been full of them and their loss tangled with the feeling of his absence. Her eyes, immersed in a dense fog, hardly managed to hide the nightmare that she had experienced in the last couple of months.

"What about you? How are you feeling?"

"Good, considering that the whole Police department is listening into our conversation". Cristina brought her hand to her ear.

That was another lie; she did not have a life outside the office doors, not with all the crying and the fog that permeated everything. In every corner, she found a reason to drop it all and welcome death. Only two nights ago, she had undressed and lowered herself into the bathtub. She had kept her underwear on; if she died, she didn't want to be found completely naked. She had stared at the cutter for a long time, its open blade pointing defiantly at the edge of the full and warm bathtub. She had pictured cutting her own wrists, dropping her arms in the water and bleeding to death, just like falling asleep. She had not done it; the sound of some children in the street dragged her out of the fog and she had noticed that the water had grown cold.

Guzmán touched his right ear to check that his earpiece was placed correctly. He wasn't very sure that having Cristina in the firing line was such a great idea. Something about her eyes told him that beneath the calm appearance, that woman was gun powder threatening to explode at any second. She was his friend, but she had not recovered yet.

"Can you hear us?" checked Guzmán.

"Yes, we can hear you loud and clear". TJ was following the signal from an undercover van from the company Spectrum, only a few houses away from the objective.

"I expect it will be a fun night for all of us".

Inside the van were four agents, all eyes were fixed on the monitors transmitting the cameras' signals and the sound of the agents in the other car. TJ was among them, a recycled computer technician and technology expert that had ended up in the police force; behind him, wearing headphones and a mic, stood commissioner García, in charge of the operation:

"Be very careful over there. We are ready". The commissioner watched the car's radar as it approached the map's central point.

Cristina, who, that very morning, had banged her hand on the commissioner's desk, nodded dutifully. She had not wanted to be left out of the operation and made her opinion clear with shouts:

"If you'd like to kick me out for being unwell, fucking do it, but I'm going to continue being unwell at home and this is the only thing I've got; and if I'm going to stay, then I want to participate in the same way I did before the death of Lucas".

To which the commissioner replied:

"OK, lieutenant Herrera, dress up fancy and prepare for tonight. But I want you to go through a psychological evaluation tomorrow, understood?"

Cristina had left without giving any signs of agreement.

Guzmán watched his colleague out of the corner of his eye.

"Let the show begin", he said theatrically looking at the trees they had to their sides and the sea beyond. "If I weren't on duty, I would have a smoke right now".

Cristina and Álvaro's car drove past a piece of open ground where three camouflaged police assault vehicles waited ready to intervene; each car had four agents dressed in black, completely armed and ready to go.

The car with the two dressed up agents drove through the entrance gates; they were arriving at a mansion of colonial style at the top of the Jardines de la Montaña.

"Well... the party is about to start", said Álvaro. "How are you feeling? Ready?"

Cristina looked at her reflection on the rear window and saw the fog in her eyes.

"Yes, and that's the third time you've asked me in the last ten minutes. What's up?"

"Being at your level is tough. I'm worried of looking like an old perv with a girl that's way too young for me".

The commissioner, from the camouflaged van:

"Álvaro, you don't look bad at all at your... what is it, fifties, fifty-something...?"

"It's no secret that I'm fifty-five and have a daughter who's a youtuber".

Cristina laughed. It had been months since she had last laughed; only Guzmán had that sense of humor that was capable of opening cracks of hope in the middle of her fog.

The intervention had been planned that very morning. They received a tip about a drug shipment that would be delivered at the luxurious mansion during the party. Cristina thought it strange; in these cases, the operations were usually simple, they arrested the drug dealers as they entered or left the party, end of story. What they were about to do was going to make a lot of noise and would set to work the whole of the Police judicial machinery during the following days. The rich people living in these mansions had many resources and had contacts high up.

From the undercover van, commissioner García intervened:

"Actually, you look like a very congenial couple".

"Right? I keep telling her... Cristina, I'm the department's most desired bachelor, don't miss your chance".

Cristina smiled again as she stepped out of the car assisted by a valet that was holding the door open for her.

For a moment, she stood still. It was her son Lucas who was holding the door to help her step out.

Guzmán saw his colleague's expression and knew that something was wrong, he offered his arm and told her:

"Our department is a nest of gossips".

Inspectors Herrera and Guzmán were entering the welcome marquee that had been installed for the party; three security people examined the guests' credentials at the entrance. Everyone had to walk through the metal detector arch. In a corner, a woman with short, blonde hair supervised the security check operation; her grey coat could not hide the bulk of a gun on her side. Next to her, hung a 'gun-free party' sign, the new trend among the cosmopolitan and eccentric: the picture of a gun with a cross on it emphasized the ban to carry weapons into certain events.

Guzmán stopped on his tracks and stepped intentionally on Cristina's foot, who looked angrily at him. He pointed forward with his chin.

"OK, we have a small problem. There is a security control right ahead of us and a metal detector. Nobody mentioned there would be anything of the sort".

"If we leave our weapons, everyone is going to notice us".

Cristina bent down understanding the reasoning behind Guzman's comment. They were both carrying guns and badges, Álvaro had them on his ankle and she on her thigh. She looked ahead and noticed the blonde woman gazing at them.

"Do we have access to the power supply panel of this area?" asked Guzmán, looking at his companion to prevent any lip reading.

Inside the van, agent TJ looked at the three screens that controlled the access cameras. He started to search for the power supply filters he had preselected in case they had any trouble; he became immersed in his screen. The possibility of doing a power cut was a useful resource for any intervention.

"Yes, I think I can get access but it will take a minute".

"Let us know when you get it", replied Cristina. "I think this ankle, high-heel trouble excuse is not going to last too long without raising suspicions".

In fact, the security agents had paid little attention to the couple's incident, but the tactic had not gone unnoticed by Ramona. Other guests were arriving.

"I think those heels are the perfect excuse", said Guzmán. "Are you alright?"

"That's four times now..."

Herrera's dress had an opening on the side that exposed her slender legs; the detail did not go unnoticed by her colleague. Cristina gave her colleague a reproachful look.

"Hurry up, TJ, Álvaro can't stand the pressure".

TJ worked on his computer on a panel with the power company's logo and controls everywhere.

"I think I've got it now... Fingers crossed".

Ramona walked towards the couple.

"When I say 'now', turn it off and on. It will be like a power drop. We just need a second". Guzmán addressed his friend who was still massaging her ankle, "ready?"

Cristina stood up and reached for Guzmán's arm, another congenial couple walking towards the security control. In front of them, a man in a tuxedo walked through the control. The police couple did not pay any attention to him. They had not recognized attorney Eduardo Aster. Ramona stopped and followed them with her gaze.

"OK, TJ... now!"

Álvaro and Cristina walked under the metal detector, close behind attorney Aster. It happened in less than a second, the light went off and the systems fell. The security people looked bewildered for a moment. Ramona looked to the sides and walked inside to see what had just happened.

They had made it into the party.

A security guard directed the facial recognition camera to the three guests and waited, looking at his tablet.

"Welcome Mr. Aster, enjoy the party". He looked at his tablet again and gazed at the couple that had just walked through the metal detector.

From the van, commissioner García informed:

"Don't worry, we hacked the archive and added you to the list, stay calm".

"Welcome..." he said, and read the names, "Mr. and Mrs. Ortega, enjoy the party".

Over two hundred guests wandered around the garden; they greeted familiar faces and drank at Juno Coentrao's mansion, Don Nassar's associate and Esther Nassar's boyfriend. The waiters served champagne and wine of all kinds and origins, there was a bar with cooks preparing sushi, and in one end of the garden, decorated with marijuana plants, was a buffet loaded with all sorts of cannabis-based food.

"This is the new trend, Álvaro, smoking your stuff belongs to a different age", Cristina said.

"Absolutely, I belong to the old school and still haven't tried alcohol".

"Cristina, you're like a mother", said commissioner García and regretted it as soon as the words came out of his mouth. "I'm sorry, sometimes my mouth is just too big".

"Don't worry commissioner; you're right. One never stops being a mother".

She stared at the pool's surface where psychedelic images were being projected, moving to the sound of music.

"There really is a lot of money involved in this party", said Guzmán. "You need to throw together all the salaries earned in a policeman's lifetime to put up something like this", he added and gestured with his head to the group that stood just a few meters from them.

Juno held Esther Nassar, his girlfriend, by the waist and spoke in a group of exquisitely dressed people where everyone used cautious words and moved about gracefully. Ramona watched them from a distance. Juno whispered something in Esther's ear, he apologized to the group and walked into the mansion. Ramona followed.

"This is when we divide", said Guzmán and followed Juno and Ramona into the mansion. "I'm going to the bathroom... you act natural and go flirt with that guy..." He pointed at a young man in a tuxedo who was concentrating on a plate heaped with food. Anthony Somoza.

Cristina recognized her son's face in the young man's, 'that could have been him in a few years' time', she thought. Anthony felt the inspector's intense gaze, a look of nostalgia at the sight of her little boy incarnated in an adult.

"My name's Anthony", said the young man, offering his hand.

"I'm Cristina, lovely to meet you... Anthony, did you know that the name Lucas suits you?"

"Lucas is my eldest brother's name".

"Isn't that a wonderful coincidence?" she said, trying to be friendly.

A man with a shaved, shiny head and muscly build, waved a hand at Anthony from the other end of the pool and continued walking towards the group that had gathered around cannabis area, ready to try its delights. Carlo Stamas wanted to find a place among the lawyers that stood with attorney Aster, chatting and eating appetizers prepared with the narcotic herb.

"A friend?" she asked.

"Not really; I guess you could say we work together".

"Right..."

A few minutes later, Juno and Ramona returned to the garden, Juno looked up at the sky and Ramona checked the lit screen of the phone she was carrying. Behind them came Don Nassar followed by two men of Chinese phenotype in suits. Esther, his daughter, went to greet him accompanied by a young couple, Julián Konks and Ana Riccoli, who were dressed like Armani mannequins, both in black. Esther introduced the young couple to Don.

Cristina noticed Álvaro with a poker face walking out from a side door. Inspector Herrera remained vigilant at her shy companion's side. Anthony's plate was still full of canapes, he had barely tried any during their exchange of banal phrases. She apologized and left to find her colleague, who was returning from his incursion. He whispered in her ear:

"Something odd is going on here, this doesn't make any sense", and he added, addressing those who were listening outside, "commissioner? I think this is a waste of time and, besides, we don't even know what we're looking for".

At that very moment, a drone appeared hovering above the pool. The sound and the blue lights announced its presence at the mansion's zenith. Juno and Esther pointed at it and everyone started clapping with excitement. The music stopped.

A waiter handed Juno a microphone.

"Hello everyone! Thank you for being here with us on the truly magical night of our engagement party..."

All the guests clapped.

Álvaro looked puzzled at Cristina.

"We've come to a fucking engagement party?"

Juno continued:

"Esther and I thank you all for your support and have prepared a little surprise in return", he said, pointing at the drone. "Here it is... Synchro's exclusive first shipment. Enjoy!"

People started clapping even harder, as if the Rolling Stones had just turned up on stage.

"Synchro? What the hell is Synchro?" asked Guzmán.

"It's a new technology that changes people's emotions", said TJ into the earpiece. "I read about it in a few trend pages. They say it's the shit".

"I think this is shit; we aren't going to stay at a spoilt brat's wedding. Permission to leave".

"Denied. We are waiting for something", ordered commissioner García.

Juno kissed Esther and shook hands with his future father in law. Ramona pressed the screen of her phone and left it on the grass. A circle formed around as if it was a religious ceremony. The drone descended and landed on the blonde woman's smartphone. It made contact with the phone and at that same instant deposited a black box on the ground. The guests continued clapping hard. Ramona walked back to the spot and took the box; then, she started offering black balls to the people around her.

"What do we do?" asked Álvaro without comprehending what was going on.

"The drone is leaving!" added Cristina, taking out the gun she had hidden in the inside of her thighs.

Ramona could have been a priest. They were all approaching her in search of a black ball that would change their emotions for a while, exactly like a drug.

The drone flew upwards and Cristina, in the middle of a dense fog pointed at the flying object. She shot three times; there were confused shouts and the machine with the helixes fell into the pool.

"Stop! What are you doing?" Guzmán tried holding Cristina.

With the loud sound of the shots came a moment of confusion. Ramona stopped giving away the balls; Cristina advanced around the edge of the pool towards the blonde woman. Ramona drew out her own gun and fired at the armed policewoman who was walking menacingly towards her. The bullet got Cristina in the abdomen and the impact threw her back into the water. Guzmán saw his colleague fall in the pool next to the drone that was starting to sink, and jumped in. The water was already turning red.

The police cars hurried at top speed in the mansion's direction. They set off the sirens and the stroboscopic lights threw beams of red and blue into the night.

"Ambulance! Agent shot! 9-85!" Guzmán swam to where Cristina was floating. "9-85! Cristina has fallen!"

Ramona aimed at him from the edge of the pool.

"Police, Police!" he shouted from the water when he saw the woman's gun pointing at him.

Cristina Herrera was floating with her eyes wide open; she felt the impact of the bullet bellow her chest and knew that she was dying. She looked down; Lucas was there, waiting for her in the depths of that mass of water. The child stretched his hand out to reach her. Cristina breathed slowly and placidly; a ghost of a smile appeared on her face. She saw the fog clearing up and the clouds opened to a starred sky. She also felt Guzmán at her side and heard him shout, not at her, but at the blonde model that had shot her, she could not catch the words. She just floated, lulled by the water. She was leaving to the world of the dead and would never return. Lucas pulled her foot from below.

Lucas, her son, was waiting for her. Laura, her friend, would receive her. She was on her way.

Then she felt that they were pulling her upwards but she was still floating. Lucas waited for her in the depths of the pool. They were moving her slowly and she started counting the last seconds of her life: one, two, three, four, five, six, seven, eight, nine and ten.

"Hello, death" she whispered.

"Cristina!... Cristina!" Álvaro Guzmán was shouting in despair, holding his colleague's head to keep it out of the water. "Wait, hold on, the ambulance is on its way... hold on a little longer, Cristina".

The policeman was trying to pull her to the edge of the pool and take her out, but he felt some sort of resistance, as if something or someone was holding her from the depths and pulled her down.

Ramona kept pointing at him from the edge of the pool. An assault police brigade entered the garden and aimed their firearms at the blonde woman. Slowly, she left her weapon on the ground and dropped to her knees, hands behind her neck.

The guests were still looking around in shock and confusion at everything that was going on. Juno watched the situation and walked to where attorney Aster stood, surrounded by lawyers.

Guzmán held onto the pool's ledge, exhausted; an assault policeman held Cristina by the shoulders and pulled her out of the water, then, he laid her on the grass and placing an index finger on his colleague's neck, checked her pulse on the aorta. She was still alive.

A medical team hurried into the garden with a stretcher. In less than a minute, Cristina Herrera would be inside the ambulance, speeding desperately to its destination; two paramedics attended her bullet injury to stabilize her vital signs. Her life was slipping away through a bullet's hole.

Sat at the edge of the pool, Álvaro kept his eyes on the water where the blood was slowly dissolving; the drone rested at the bottom, dark, like a satiated shark. He was breathing quickly, his lungs struggling for oxygen; a consequence of his smoking habit.

Guzmán relived the moment in which he had left Cristina to follow the owner of the ostentatious house. His mind went back to the instant in which he entered the mansion, when he left his colleague alone. He returned to the past.

Guzmán had walked into a room facing the garden where a large group of people gathered in a circle around Don Nassar, then, he went down a corridor from where he could hear animation and laughter. It was empty. He almost bumped into two waiters carrying lobster canapes. He walked on, looking at both sides; further down, he opened a door. It was the bathroom; two middle aged men dressed in tuxedos were handling a few grams of cocaine on a marble ledge. The men looked at him unperturbed:

"Want some?" one of them offered.

Right at that moment, Juno walked in through a door at the back, followed by Ramona. Álvaro moved to the right and stood in front of the white porcelain urinal, he undid his fly.

"Amazing party, Juno!"

"Completely wild", said the man who was drawing the lines of powder, white as sugar. "Check this out, it's pure snow... We're going to spend the whole night skiing, aaaaa-ooooh", he lifted his head, imitating a wolf.

Juno watched them, he looked at Ramona and nodded.

"I've told you before; I don't want to see that shit in my house".

Ramona went up to both men, without hesitation, she pushed them, opened the tap, put her hand under the running water and cleaned the surface, dissolving the white powder in the sink. Then, she quickly checked the two silent men's pockets and found two sachets full of white powder on their coats. She threw them into the bathroom and flushed them away. Neither of them dared question the authority of the spectacular woman who towered over them.

Juno went to one of the urinals to the left of Álvaro, undid his fly and stared at the wall ahead. Ramona stood behind him. The other men remained silent like two boys who had just been told off by their teacher.

"I promised to bring something tonight that you've never seen before", said Juno above the sound of the liquid hitting the white porcelain.

"Oh Juno, we apologize. We did it out of habit, we trust you..."

"Yes, amigo, you always surprise us for the better", agreed his companion.

Juno did not look at them, he did not answer, but turned his head to his urinal neighbor. Álvaro stared at the pink Carrara marble wall ahead and zipped his pants.

"Have we met? I'm Juno Coentrao", the man urinating in the uncomfortable silence of the bathroom said.

Álvaro washed his hands in the sink. He had unzipped his pants, but had not actually done anything.

"A pleasure to meet you, Mr. Coentrao, I'm Armando Manzanero. My apologies for not shaking hands", said Guzmán as he placed them under the running water.

"Manzanero... The name is not in my radar..." Juno shook the hand that was out of view. He was finishing.

"Of course, I'm here with TJ, with the lawyers", he said the first thing that came to mind and moved to dry his hands. "A pleasure to have met you".

He placed his hands under the dryer and it started blowing hot air.

Juno went to the tap closest to the dryer. Ramona waited calmly behind. The hand dryer's noise added some distance to the conversation between the infiltrated policeman and the owner of the house.

Juno finished, washed his hands and wiped them dry with one of the white cotton towels that were neatly folded on a table.

The hand dryer went silent and Guzmán walked to the door.

"I hope you enjoy the party, this has only just started and the evening is going to be full of surprises". Juno waited for Ramona to open the door and left without waiting for an answer, his blonde shadow followed close behind.

As soon as they were gone, the two men sighed in relief.

Guzmán left after them. In the corridor, he found himself face to face with Carlo Stamas. They looked at each other; they knew the other's face from somewhere, but neither remembered from where.

***

Guzmán returned to the garden, to the present. He listened.

"Who's in charge?"

He raised his soaked head and looked at the elegantly dressed man who had posed the question so energetically. He recognized him; the State attorney Eduardo Aster. Juno stood beside him, glaring fiercely at Guzmán.

"Ask after commissioner García, my communication gear is all wet".

The attorney now addressed the policemen who had arrested and handcuffed Ramona.

"I am the State attorney, Eduardo Aster, and I demand that you free this woman right now. Remove those handcuffs".

The elegantly dressed man addressed the uniformed policemen in black balaclavas who were guarding Ramona.

"This is a private property and a gun-free private party", the attorney insisted, and the police agents glanced at each other doubtfully. "Where is the court order? I want to see a court order right now… I have told you to free this woman… More than one person here is going to find themselves in deep trouble".

The police agents hesitated.

Álvaro stood up, completely soaked, and faced Aster.

"This woman has shot and possibly killed an inspector of the Police department".

"Identify yourself before you address me…" The attorney was furious. "And let me tell you that your colleague opened fire in public, endangering many innocent people; she did not identify herself before shooting, and damaged objects of someone else's property", he said and added, pointing at the bottom of the pool, "on the other hand, this woman of the security services, who holds a gun license, acted in self-defense in the face of such a shocking irresponsibility… And, who are you? Show me your badge".

Aster did not bother hiding the superiority and disdain he felt towards the man who had jumped into the pool.

Álvaro bent down, he lifted his pants' cuffs slightly and took his weapon and badge from his ankle. Standing up, he pointed his gun at the attorney's head, his hand steady.

"Identify yourself… Son of a bitch. This is my badge". He stretched out his hand holding the department's shield up to Aster's face. "Where is yours? On your knees and hands behind your head. Remain silent until you have been spoken to. These are your rights: you have the right to remain silent and everything you say can and will be used against you in a court of law".

Guzman's temerity paralyzed Aster and he dropped to his knees trembling. The soaked policeman continued aiming exactly at the point between Aster's eyes while water dripped from the gun's butt. The attorney remained silent and on his knees, and slowly he lifted his hands to place them behind his head. Álvaro Guzmán extended his free hand, and without saying a word or shifting his gaze, received the handcuffs that his colleague was handing him, then he approached the attorney's back with tense and measured steps and handcuffed him.

A tense silence filled the garden.

Juno took a step forward, then looked at Don, who stood next to his daughter Esther; he shook his head; they had to stay calm and keep their distances, always discrete.

"Take this idiot away from here and interrogate him", said Guzmán, as he walked towards the house. "Oh, and don't forget to read his rights!" He looked at his watch where a drop of water magnified the time; 22.00h.

***

Ramona and attorney Eduardo Aster were under custody when commissioner García arrived.

"Are you attorney Aster?"

"Yes", replied the handcuffed man curtly.

"Free him!" he said, addressing his men.

One of the police agents, hidden behind a balaclava, proceeded to remove the mechanism that was immobilizing the arrested man's hands behind his back.

"I am commissioner García, in charge of the operation; I apologize for the inconveniences we might have caused... but the..."

"The man pointed at my head with a gun!" Aster interrupted and repeated, "that madman pointed at my head!"

"We apologize, it's the tension of an intervention".

Aster looked at the tall blonde who was being directed to the police car.

"Her too. Let her go".

"Her? This woman has shot a police agent during her service".

"I don't think you realize what's about to come at you", Aster was starting to lose his temper. "There's that mad policeman who aimed at my head", he took a deep breath. "Every single man in this operation is going to have a bad time responding judicially to this fuck-up". He pointed at the woman. "You better free the only person who has fulfilled her duty tonight right now".

Commissioner García looked at the agent who was holding Ramona and nodded.

Ramona felt her liberated hands and rubbed her wrists to get the blood flowing again; without saying a word she turned to walk proudly back into the mansion. Juno was waiting for her by the entrance door.

"First thing tomorrow I want your supervisor and the director of the Police Department of Mexico City in my office with the full report of this operation..." Aster wiped his forehead with his hand and after a pause said: "I want the name of the agent that pointed at my head. Give me his name".

García doubted for a second.

"Inspector Álvaro Guzmán".

"Guzmán..."

Attorney Aster went to his own vehicle without asking any further questions.

The police cars turned off their flashing lights and retired, defeated and silent, down the winding roads.

Inside the mansion, after the shock of the failed police intervention, the party got back its rhythm; like someone who falls while dancing, recovers from their fall and continues dancing just as before.

They were playing rap-gun music, the psychedelic images dressed the pool's surface, waiters replaced drinks in people's hands while they commented the experience they had just lived.

As instructed by Esther Nassar's, a short waiter walked through the crowd holding a black box in his hands and offering its contents to the guests.

Don conversed excitedly with his daughter Esther and with the young creator of Synchro, Julián Konks. Next to him stood Ana who would not leave his side.

A group of ten people under the effects of Synchro danced synchronized to the rhythm of the raucous and rowdy music. They smiled and laughed without having to look at each other.

Esther showed her phone screen to her father, who watched in wonder the behavior of the guests around him, united by the ingestion of a microchip.

"See? Right now, I've selected the dance and laugh mode, but if we press this here, we can select the relax and take it easy mode", said Esther as she touched the screen.

After a few seconds, the group that was doing the synchronized dancing slowed down. Some hugged without knowing each other, others sat or lied down on the grass with a smile on their lips.

"I have no words", said Don Nassar who wasn't missing a single detail of the guests' behavior.

Julián, at his side, laughed as he watched the faces of people enjoying a moment of programmed relaxation.

Esther showed him the screen once again.

"We could send them whatever sensations we want", Don said and pointed at the 'tantric sex' mode and then at 'wild sex'. He laughed.

"Let's be prudent; the effect lasts approximately an hour and I don't want to host an orgy on my engagement party".

Esther looked around searching for Juno, he had left during Ramona's and attorney Aster's arrest. She could not see them in the garden.

The group continued stretching out and relaxing under the effects of the app that Esther held in her hand.

Further away, other groups had formed, all smiles and long gazes at the sky amidst a stillness only interrupted by the music and astonished interest of those who had not joined in the black pill fun.

Julián spoke to Esther and her father:

"Watch this, look, it's funny. See that woman in blue? The one that is lying down and waving her arms?" he pointed at a woman of about forty dressed in an elegant blue dress who was rolling on the grass in complete bliss. Don nodded. "She moves first and then the others follow. Look; the radius of connection is of about twenty meters". He then indicated a group that was further down and where everyone was dancing synchronized.

Julián spotted Carlo Stamas and a group of lawyers, men and women, who, inhibited, moved to the music's beat. He also spotted his associate Anthony Somoza who was standing apart, staring at the pool without engaging in any conversations. He brought his attention back to his own group; Ana squeezed his hand and returned him to the reality of his position, CEO of a company, talking to its most important investors, the Nassars.

Don watched the woman in blue. It was true; whenever the woman moved the rest of the group soon followed.

Julián continued his explanation:

"This is what we denominate a 'dominant subject'; it always happens. Every group has a dominant subject; the rest adapt to their emotions".

"Are their brains stronger?" inquired Don.

"No, strength is not exactly the right term for this; it's a matter of alexithymia… Every human produces endorphins that will make them feel a certain pleasure. Let's just say that within each brain there is a high degree of suffering; pain, for example, is a way of expressing this suffering. These are degrees of alexithymia. The dominant subject, their brain, is the one generating the largest number of endorphins and therefore has less alexithymia. Synchro increases the production of endorphins; the dominant subject is that which most endorphins generated.

"Frankly, I am impressed, young man", Don measured his words carefully. "This is the drug of the future. It doesn't require crops, nor chemicals, it doesn't need to cross borders, no transport, no complicated distribution… You just download an app on your phone… that simple". He pointed at the group that continued to relax on the lawn. "Look at them… they are happy, their minds are connected, thoughts shared".

The depth of Don's words made the people around him fall in a mesmerized silence. Only Ana, who would not let go of Julián's hand, said:

"We are grateful to your daughter for placing her trust on us. The official presentation will take place in two weeks; it would be wonderful if you could attend, we have invited the whole press".

Ana behaved as if she were part of the company. Julián Konks directed his eyes to the place where, just a moment ago, he had seen Anthony standing on his own. He was no longer there.

He put his hand in his pocket and touched the ring he was keeping there for later; he would ask Ana to be his wife.

"Technology is the future", Juno appeared from behind, he got close to his girlfriend and kissed her shoulder. "Esther, this new business of yours fascinates me. It consists of making microchips the shape of tiny black balls, a very suggestive color by the way, so that they", he pointed at group, "may introduce them in their mouths and connect their emotions to other people's". He touched his forehead. "It's like a social network but more fun... Goodbye to Facebook".

Esther looked at him with an angry expression.

"Sorry, honey; it seems like all of our problems have been solved and this party is being a success", said Juno and he took his girlfriend's phone into his hand and pressed the 'wild sex' button. "Let them have some fun so that later they can remember this like the party of their lives".

Don smiled at his daring.

The woman in blue moved closer to another woman who was lying next to her and started kissing her; the other woman looked shocked at first, but after a few seconds kissed her back. Soon they were tearing off their clothes with crazy passion. The remaining members of the group threw themselves at each other following the new sensation that Juno had chosen, 'wild sex'.

Don knew that drugs, the world's largest business, was attractive because it produced effortless pleasure through the simple act of consumption.

"The more they consume the more pathological their desire becomes until it sits in the center of the addict's life. Here, there is no addiction, therefore no crime. They are living their lives' best dreams and the cause of it is going to be expelled from their bodies without any side effects. In an hour, they will have gained a fabulous memory of this experience,' Don reflected. Nearby, a couple was making love in between sweat and spasms.

Juno got closer to Don and whispered in his ear:

"People will be ready to pay ten times more money for this shit that for cocaine... And best of all... we don't need any fellow travelers…" He added, "it's the end of drug cartels… Think about it, Don".

Don watched the women who were still rolling on the grass as if possessed. Esther Nassar snatched her phone back and changed the mode again; it had been enough for one night.

Don said his goodbyes to the group; he was impressed by what he had just witnessed. Juno and Esther accompanied him to his armored limousine followed by the two Chinese bodyguards.

"What percentage of the company do you have?" asked Don.

"We have forty percent; the rest, nine percent, is a participation loan", replied Juno before Esther could answer the question.

"We?" said Esther annoyed. "Don't you dare take away a single gram of the work I do. The credit is all mine".

"We need to get the full package", said Don, smiling at Esther like a proud father. "By the way, that little act you put on with the Police turned out brilliantly; the attorney is going to keep their noses out of our business for a while".

"I would call it a masterstroke". Juno put his arm around Esther's shoulder. "I'm not going to take any of your credit for that. The idea to attract the Police in the presence of the State attorney was ten out of ten. It's going to take them some time to bother us…They have fallen into our trap".

Don looked at Ramona.

"Certainly, but I would have preferred it if your bodyguard hadn't shot that policewoman".

"What Ramona did? I think that's what gave credibility to our act".

"In any case, it has been a very pleasant evening", Don concluded, and he climbed into the armored limousine letting the valet close the door behind him. The two bodyguards disappeared into the remaining doors, their expressions impassible. An escort car with three armed men, also Chinese, followed them a few meters behind.

Ramona, unperturbed, observed everything from the top of the stairs. Juno and Esther retired to their rooms. Still, the party must go on and she would remain vigilant. She took her phone out of her pocket; a text message appeared on the screen. Ten words: 'the candidate arrived, bullet did not damage her vital organs'. Then she deleted it.

***

Finally, Cristina had reached the kingdom of heaven.

Or so she believed as she entered the bright white light that drowned all things of color. They were rushing the stretcher down a white corridor and the faces she could discern wore white masks and white hats. She felt calm, she was going to see her son. First, she saw Laura who was right in front of her; then, a man with a long white beard. She thought it must be God welcoming her.

A blinding light forced her eyes closed; she wanted to open them again to see Lucas, but she couldn't, her eyelids felt too heavy. Everything was dissolving into a dream. The last thing she thought was: 'I am dead'.

Laura Almillar and Ambrose Levi watched the extraction of the bullet from behind the operating room's glass.

"She's alive..." said Laura.

It was an affirmation.

Ambrose Levi beside her, took his phone out, typed a text message and sent it.

***

Álvaro Guzmán opened the door to his apartment; his clothes were still damp and stank of chlorine. He could hear music coming from the other side of the wall; it was almost eleven and the new neighbor, Gloria Altolaza was blasting her music. He still couldn't remember where he had seen that woman before. He looked at his old cassette answerphone. People did not have these any more, he thought, but his daughter Rita loved it; perhaps that was why he kept it: it was the only way he had of staying connected to her. He had a message.

"Hi, Dad. Braulio and I are going to travel to Mexico City in a few weeks so that you can meet him. Mom isn't going to be there those days; she's going to New York with Rafa; he's got stuff to do there... So... we'll be staying at yours; it will only be one night. Besides, I have a surprise for you... Kisses, see you soon".

He looked at a joint he had left prepared and lit it. Álvaro Guzmán was not fond of surprises.

***

Julián had sat on the bed and was waiting for Ana to come out. She had deliberately left the bathroom door ajar and had undressed, aware of the effect her seemingly spontaneous nakedness would have on her new boyfriend.

"What a crazy night!" she exclaimed while undoing her bra and revealing her breasts. She looked at her reflection. "That was the best party I have ever been to". She pushed the door closed to block Julian's view. "I think you and I are going to have a great time together".

When Ana opened the door again, she was wearing a black lingerie slip that she saved for special occasions. Julián gazed at her in a trance. Then, as the blonde woman walked towards him, he searched inside his pocket and pulled out his fist, as if it were a treasure box, and offered it to her. Ana held it between her hands and opened it playfully. Inside, was a ring glinting with small diamonds.

"Are you asking me to marry you?" she said, slipping it into her ring finger, her eyes on the shiny stones.

"Well, yes..."

She kissed him and pushed him back onto the bed, then moved on top of him.

"I do".

***

Anthony was back at the office. He was not tired and did not feel like sleeping. During the party, he had lingered in the margins; the only person he spoke to was that woman who had been shot, and who turned out to be a police agent. It was not his kind of atmosphere; his place was this, in front of the screen.

"Here we are again, my dear friend; our Julián has betrayed us for fame. The idiot believes that the girl is with him for his worth... You are a real asshole, Nostradamus".

Anthony Somoza, the 'dark' friend, introduced the ten-digit password that only he and his associate knew, and entered the source code.

3. SOURCE CODE

The text lines of a software written in a programming language that determine the steps a program must follow for its execution.

Thousands of people gathered in the surroundings of the building that had been illuminated with potent beams of light. Mitikah Tower in Xoco was to host the presentation of Synchro. The expectation generated in the previous days had been multiplied by the number of movie stars and famous musicians who had confirmed their assistance; the red carpet had stirred for what everyone said would be the event of the decade. Massive black vehicles opened their doors, offering an endless stream of popular faces that would walk up the hall of fame, providing a livelihood to hundreds of prominent reporters. With their presence, the hoard of celebrities showed their support for what was already being named 'the drug of the future'.

A mess of shrieks from fans, selfies, flashes, security, applause, some autograph signing, perfect smiles for one side and the other, and the photo call with Synchro's logo, a mandatory stop for the famous faces to pose before the cameras.

Julián Konks, dressed in a dark Canalli blazer and white Bijan shirt, looked down at the tangle of people, traffic and lights awaiting Synchro's official presentation from a window on the tenth floor. After they had done his hair, make-up and given everything a last touch, he had requested some quiet. People waited outside the door. Julián held his hands together and played with the new ring, twisting round his finger; he leaned his forehead on the window and blew a halo of mist into the glass. Then he pressed his nose into the glass and mumbled, trying to memorize his five-minutes speech, even though he was going to use a teleprompter to read, he was worried his nerves might betray him.

Sat on a red armchair was Ana, typing away on her phone, answering text messages. She was wearing an impressive wild green dress with red Louboutin *stilettos*.

"Don't worry, Julián, you're going to be great", she said without looking at him.

"There's a big crowd out there", Julián continued focused on the street.

"Look, Alex from the PR team is telling me that the main space, the terrace, has already been filled with five hundred people, and that they are accommodating more on other floors with television monitors". Ana lifted her phone and showed him the message on the screen. On her finger, the three diamond rings she was wearing glinted. "Whenever you're ready, Alex is waiting for you outside".

The door opened and in came Carlo Stamas followed by Anthony Somoza.

"Alright, it's time now. We have to go and greet people; everyone is already here", said Carlo rubbing his hands together. "I swear there are more people here than in the Oscars ceremony in Hollywood".

Anthony was wearing a considerably discrete blue blazer. Ana looked at him, annoyed.

"Anthony, that's not the blazer we chose for the presentation".

"No, Ana. I didn't feel comfortable in that red one", he answered, staring down at his sleeves. "Besides, what matters is Synchro... I'm sure nobody will pay any attention to what I'm wearing".

"No doubt, with that blazer nobody is ever going to notice you", she said, ironically. "Anyway, now you are a rich man and I guess that counts for something too".

Carlo stared at Ana sardonically; he remembered the times when he had seen her naked, the tattoo she had on her waist, a flower and some sentence he never stopped to read; he remembered her four months ago, screaming with pleasure while they made love. And then, when Ana found out about Julián's potential, she transformed herself into the honorable fiancé of an emerging billionaire.

Julián adjusted his blazer, he went up to Anthony and placed both hands on his shoulders.

"This is it, my friend. We made it... our dream. We actually made it, *güey*".

Anthony's face lit up at the words. It had been a while since he had stood face to face with his closest friend, and it had been a while too since they had exchanged more than polite words.

"That's right, we have made it all the way here together".

Anthony opened his arms and hugged Julián, who accepted the embrace affectionately.

"Hey, guys, don't forget about me... My small contribution to this success". Carlo went up to them and joined in the rugby scrum hug.

The three of them laughed.

Ana Riccoli stood up. With her heels on, she towered over Julián.

"Since we are in such good spirits, Julián and I have a surprise for you", she said.

"Ana, we decided we'd keep the secret for a few more days", Julián protested.

"They are your friends. There aren't any secrets among friends, it doesn't count with them... So many emotions, and all happening at once!"

Carlo and Anthony waited expectantly. Julián lifted his right hand and showed them the ring he was wearing.

"Ana and I got married yesterday... in secret".

"Married...? Are you joking?" Anthony stared incredulous at Julián. "Married?... What the fuck, you just met!"

Ana took a step forward and held Julián's hand.

"Love is not a matter of time, it's about finding the right person", she said, and kissed him on the cheek.

"Don't make me laugh", said Anthony with a snort.

Julián reacted to his friend's comment:

"And what's that supposed to mean?"

"It doesn't mean anything", said Anthony daringly. "I'm just saying what I'm thinking: that you've just met her, that you should see more of her before this... Now that things had finally turned out the way we wanted them... she turns up... and changes you and..."

Carlo realized that it wasn't the time or place to increase the tension with words.

"OK, enough, both of you!"

'Lately, every encounter between these two turns into a quarrel', thought Stamas.

"Let's behave like adults and professionals", he said sharply. "I want you to stop this nonsense right now". Carlo looked at the couple and added, "congratulations to the newlyweds". He looked at Anthony. "I'm a few years ahead of you, not many, but enough to know that among friends you have to learn to keep some things to yourself". He took a deep breath. "Now we are going to leave this room and you two... are going to answer the questions of the press and many influencers who are waiting outside for your appearance...

You are the center of attention of the world right now... and tomorrow, you may continue talking calmly about anything you wish".

Anthony was upset, he shot an angry look at Ana.

Carlo pointed at the door.

"Come on, you go out first", he repeated the instruction like a father trying to separate his two sons in a fight.

Anthony walked to the door and left.

Julián followed him, but before he reached the door, he turned around and said:

"Carlo, you go with Ana. I'll see you both upstairs".

Alex, the person responsible for public relations, from the agency they had hired to manage media and press, was waiting for them in the corridor.

"Guys, thank goodness you've come out. People are getting nervous", said Alex, pointing at some cameramen and photographers who were waiting by the elevator. "Anthony, you have a few interviews with specialized media, after that, you can go up to the presentation; I have already told them that you have ten minutes for each, not one more". Alex went through the list on his phone. "Julián, you have some vloggers who are going to be broadcasting this live". He looked at the elevators area. "Come, I'll introduce you". Alex waved his hand at a girl and boy who were busy chatting. At the sight of Alex's company, the couple hurried to meet them. "Let me introduce you, Julián Konks... these are Rita and Braulio. I'll leave you guys to it; I'll be back to fetch you in a few minutes".

Alex left to talk to a group of journalists who were waiting for their turn to meet the protagonists.

Julián shook Rita and Braulio's hands.

"You tell me how you'd like to do this".

Rita held an extensible stick with a GoPro camera that she was handling with ease. She started the live broadcast.

"Friends from around the world, here we are at Mitikah Tower, in the heart of Mexico City, the location chosen for the presentation of…"

"Synchro…" interrupted Braulio, "and here with us… exclusively… we have… Julián Konks, the founder…"

Rita moved the stick so that it focused on her face.

"If you haven't heard of Synchro yet, you're not from this planet…"

Carlo stayed a few seconds staring at the door through which Anthony and Julián had just left, then he turned to Ana.

"Who would have guessed that I would be seeing you transformed into a respectable wife and lady of the house".

"And who on earth would have guessed that I would be seeing you as the lawyer of a multinational and earning a fortune", replied Ana, tilting her head thoughtfully.

"Touché!" Carlo smiled. "Let me tell you that I have some good memories of you and that I'm a gentleman".

"And I of you, and I'm a happily married woman".

"They were… let's say, a few nice episodes in the past and our little secret". Carlo Stamas lifted his palms.

"Carlo… Carlo… past, present, future… they are a part of life. A gentleman like you who can keep a lady's secrets… that is something a woman can appreciate… and, besides, Carlo… you know… I want a full life… The one I deserve".

Ana moved closer to her ex-lover and kissed him hotly in the mouth.

The noise of the crowd rose to the tenth floor; the light beams were moving, painting absurd lines in the sky that got lost into the night. Mitikah Tower's sixteen elevators went up full, twenty people at a time in ten-seconds trips; that was hardly enough time to check themselves in the mirror.

A few more minutes and the Synchro app would be presented on a terrace up the fiftieth floor, with a capacity for five hundred people. The app would be available to be purchased and downloaded the following day in the Mexican capital. In two months, it would become available in the United States; in four, if the European Union allowed it, in the old continent. Then, America, Russia, Asia, Africa... In two years and with a billionaire investment behind, the product would have reached a planetary dimension.

***

First, was a weak white light, then, her eyes opened with a heavy movement of the eyelids, her head rested on her right side, her neck did not feel strong enough to move.

Cristina felt nauseous. She tried to lift a hand; there was a thin tube coming out of its back. The tube was connected to a half-full bag that hung by two hooks from a tripod. A wide strap at the height of her chest fastened her to the bed. She folded her arm until her finger touched her nose; she felt the catheter, a long tube, thin and flexible, that entered through her nasal passage and which probably reached her stomach. They had put the nasogastric catheter to extract air, liquid or blood from her damaged insides, and now that drainage was making her feel nauseous.

Cristina Herrera was not in heaven, she was in a hospital room recovering from a bullet injury in her abdomen. She looked around. It was the first shot she had received during her police career. In fact, it was the first shot she had received, ever. She took her hand to her stomach, to the place where she was starting to feel the effects of her waking without sedation. A bulky bandage covered the whole of her inflamed abdomen. Her breathing was interrupted by a sharp pain in her chest that made her breath out faster. It was possible that the bullet had caused injury to her liver, her stomach, her kidneys or her spine, she thought. She lifted her head with great effort until she caught sight of her feet. Concentrating, she wiggled her toes; her spine was fine. She leaned back into her pillow. She had been lucky.

A nurse walked in with a syringe, she looked at her and went straight to check the state of the intravenous on her right, then, she injected the contents of the syringe in the bag, where it blended with the transparent liquid that was entering her body, straight through her veins.

The nurse noticed that Cristina was awake.

"It's an antibiotic", she said giving no sign of wanting to start a conversation, "for the pain. Let me know if you need anything".

She turned around and left.

Cristina wanted to say something; she felt the dryness in her mouth and her eyes shut again. She sunk back into a black world and forgot.

The next time she woke up, she only experienced a few moments of consciousness, seconds perhaps. She was inside a white capsule that felt claustrophobic; they were doing an MRI. She heard the noise of the machine, the cadence of its beat, the electro-magnets. She slipped back into unconsciousness.

"Hello there... try to open your eyes".

A warm finger lifted her eyelid and the light of a torch shrunk the size of her pupil. She felt some steps; a whispered conversation. They were two men but she could not make any sense of the sounds; meaningless words, the murmur of the low voices. Then, a door closing; 'they have left', she thought, but she heard the voice speak again.

"Hello..."

The voice with the cadenced tone was calling her and Cristina opened her eyes. Next to her bed stood an attractive man with a grayish beard of about forty. He was watching her closely.

The room was different from the first one she had seen. In fact, it did not look like a hospital room at all. This one could have belonged to an executives' hotel room.

She could no longer feel the catheter in her nose; the back of her hand had a bit of white tape where the intravenous tube had been, and there were no straps holding her to the bed. She rested her hand on her abdomen and felt a tight sash that started underneath her chest and went down to her hip, protecting her injury and holding the muscles of her abdomen.

"Relax, inspector, rest... You need to recover; the shot did not damage any vital organs... You will be starting rehab in a few days".

Cristina could not feel any saliva in her mouth and her dry tongue got stuck to her palette.

"How many days have I been like this...?" Her first words sounded hoarse; she felt a bitter taste in her mouth that went all the way down to her throat, she swallowed.

"It has been two weeks since you were shot".

"Where am I?" she asked, and tried to lick her parched lips.

"You are in a recovery center... in Mixcoac, an hour away from your home".

"And you are doctor..."

"My name is Ambrose Levi and I am not a doctor. I am the person in charge of your recovery, now that you are no longer in danger". The man stroked his beard.

"Are you the physiotherapist?"

"No, no". He smiled gently.

"Psychiatrist?"

"Well, we could call it that", he said, giving her hand a brief, affectionate squeeze. "My duty is to help you recover and offer you a new life".

Cristina's mind escaped the present for a brief second and returned to the memories of her son Lucas.

"In all honesty, I'm not very interested in a new life..." Cristina turned her full attention to a window where she glimpsed the high branches of a tree. "After all, a new life is not going to take away the memories of this one", she said, rubbing her eyes. "Have you got any method to take away the pain of this life?"

"No, I don't have any way of recovering your son Lucas".

When Ambrose said her son's name, Cristina felt a pang of pain in her abdomen, in the bullet injury. A wound is like a source code and the scar is the algorithm written with a gunshot.

"What do you know about my son?"

"I don't have a formula that will stop you from feeling sadness, pain, fear, anxiety or anger for your son's death. Honestly, I don't. But I can help you change your current life. Myself, I am no god, but there are a few things reserved to gods that I can do for you".

Cristina felt tears running down her cheeks and falling on her grey t-shirt. Not wanting to look vulnerable, she tried to sit up.

"I must confess that we have been watching you for a long time; almost since Lucas started his treatment. We have followed each and every one of your movements and have learnt a few things about you".

Cristina listened to him in confusion.

"About me? And how am I of any interest to anyone? I'm just a police agent, a single mother who has lost the last thing that tied her to this life. I am not interesting at all..."

"You are intelligent, you are honest... You no longer have any bonds, nothing to lose, no family; perhaps that's why you hold some interest for us".

"I'm not sure whether you are saying that to cheer me up or sink my spirits even lower", she said in an ironic tone. "I still don't see how I can be of any interest to anyone".

"We have been watching you because you could be valuable to our organization", he pointed at her. "We take the selection of our employees very seriously".

"What proposition have you got for me?" asked the injured woman. "Because that's what you're here for, right?"

Ambrose stroked his beard again.

"Well, you see, everyone out there thinks you're struggling between life and death; in fact, they believe you are closer to death... There is an Intensive Care room in a hospital where a woman with your name and who looks a lot like you, is in a terminal comma. Everyone believes that the woman is you, inspector Herrera".

All of a sudden, Cristina stopped crying. She listened to the tale with worry.

"Who are you? Why are you saying this? What is this organization you talk about? Are you part of the police?" The stitches that sealed her injury tightened, a pang made her gasp. "I want to speak to commissioner García".

The questions were accumulating with the discovery that there was somebody impersonating her in a hospital.

Ambrose stood up.

"My name is Ambrose Levi; what I can reveal to you now is that we are the good guys and that we work undercover. Nobody knows of our existence... We work for the State. We are their last resource... Nobody knows us, we don't appear in the papers or the news; that's why we can't lead a normal life. That's why... you can only be with us if you are dead to the public... we all are. And... if you agree to join us, there will be no way back; you will be dead like us".

Ambrose stopped and looked at her questioningly. Cristina stayed silent.

"Do I have to decide now?"

The man with the grey beard brought his hands together.

"Yes", he said. "Because you are and you aren't here. The world thinks you are in a hospital bed struggling between life and death... If you wish, you may return to the life you had before". He indicated the door. "You may choose now... You return to the hospital, everyone witnesses your miraculous recovery; you return to your apartment and then to your daily life, your job, and this conversation never took place; it will have been a bad dream which you will not tell anyone about. We will make sure of that, we will be watching you to make sure you keep your promise. Or... you can choose to be dead... continue with us, forget your past, erase it forever... Yes, inspector Herrera will have died and a new woman with a new life will be born: a new name, a new past to tell... You would have a new apartment, new location... You could choose..."

"I have to choose between being dead for everybody else or continue as I was?"

"That's right, and you must make up your mind now. The woman who is impersonating you will not last much longer. That's why we had to wake you up. To make you reach a decision".

Cristina looked at him for a moment; she analyzed every detail of the gestures the man made, like a poker player who does not have the cards to continue on the game but who will lose everything if they abandon.

She spoke carefully.

"If I say no, you will take me back to the hospital and nothing will have happened, right?"

"Sure, Cristina, you are free to do with your life as you wish".

She read every detail of Ambrose's face and replied:

"Yes".

"Only yes?" asked Ambrose, startled.

"My answer is the only way out; I can only say yes. No is not an option. First, you have said 'sure'; a guy as direct as you has not used and affirmation as definite as 'yes' or 'no', instead, you used an affirmation that just extends my question, a 'sure'. Second, you have used my name for the first time; you have not addressed me as inspector Herrera; you have used my familiar and intimate name: Cristina. And third, you have said "you are free to do with your life as you wish'... That's the key. I knew at that instant that if I reject your offer, I am dead. You didn't tell me 'You can choose', like before; you said, 'you are free', which I am not, here, in this room, at this precise moment... And all that about 'do with your life as you wish', when you are a person who has boasted about knowing everything about me, everything that has happened to me and which I have not chosen, ever. I am a cumulus of coincidences. Nobody can 'do with their lives as they wish', nobody. In fact, I don't believe there is any woman substituting me in any hospital, nobody looks enough like me to deceive the Narcotics brigade... I bet a peso that my name was engraved on a tombstone in the cemetery next to my son a week ago... I don't believe you have waited two weeks to talk to me and make me reach a decision. I think that the people out there already believe me dead... I am already starting to be a memory. I have never heard of you because nobody has been able to speak of you, and if you are the boss of this secret organization, that's because you don't leave loose ends, and I would be one. In conclusion, what you are offering me is not a decision for me to make, 'yes' is my only choice".

***

Álvaro Guzmán entered his apartment; it was six in the evening. He saw the two small suitcases that had been carefully left in a corner, out of the way. 'Rita and her boyfriend have been here,' he thought. Rita had a key; he could still feel the hot shower's condensation and the smell of soap. 'It hasn't been long since they left; they'll be back when that event thing they had ends, and I hope that's not too late…'. On the table, in front of the television screen, next to Guzman's white box of cannabis, was an object similar to a paperweight, a sort of hockey disc on a sophisticated piece of ice with a cable connected to the socket; accompanying the strange artifact was a note. It was the surprise his daughter had promised.

'Another piece of junk', he thought. He did not even bother taking a proper look at it, neither did he read the note.

***

When Braulio and Rita arrived in an Uber at the door of the Mitikah Tower, there was an excited crowd cheering at each known face that arrived with every black limousine. They had been granted the accreditation for journalists expert in technology. Alex, the guy managing the event's public relations, had promised them ten minutes of an exclusive interview with Julián Konks, the CEO, one of the founders of Synchro.

Braulio kept checking his pockets nervously.

"I forgot my notebook in the suitcase, back at your father's place", he said, slapping his forehead.

It's not going to go anywhere and don't' worry, my dad has no interest in reading about your private thoughts". Rita showed her identification card to the security guard and walked in.

Braulio checked his phone; Alex had messaged him.

"We have to go up to the tenth floor, they are waiting for us there".

Three knocks on the door. Guzmán went to open it. Gloria Altolaza, the new neighbor, stood outside with a plate of *empanadillas* and a bottle of wine.

"Hi Álvaro, I was preparing some *empanadillas* and I thought, 'let's enjoy the company of the most exciting man in the building'"

"Considering that I'm the only man living here since old Robert left, it's not much of a compliment".

Gloria walked in without waiting for an invitation, she was the kind of woman used to having her own way.

"Get comfortable, my house is your house", he said, giving up. "I'll fetch you a glass for the wine".

"Why don't you make that two?"

"I'm not joining in, I don't drink alcohol".

"Huh?"

"Alcohol doesn't agree with me, so I stopped trying to drink it". He gestured at the box of cannabis. "When it comes to acceptable vices, I only smoke cannabis".

"What about unacceptable ones?"

"I'll go get the glass. You can sit and relax if you want".

While Gloria sat on the sofa, the police officer, feeling tired, went to the kitchen to fetch a glass that had not been used in a long time, he rinsed it under the tap and, without bothering to dry it, reached up for a flowery tablecloth that he had never used before.

"I've spent days wondering where I've met you before".

"That happens often, but the answer is simple: I present the news in Televisa; the morning broadcast, I'm sure you've watched it before".

"That's right".

Gloria was observing the new object on the table.

"I see someone has got you an artificial intelligence, who is Rita?" Gloria read the note curiously.

"Rita is my daughter. They are staying here tonight, her and her boyfriend; they live in Guadalajara, but had some sort of an event tonight".

Gloria read the note again and handed it over to Álvaro, who read it out loud.

"Álvaro, this is your present, I'm sure you are going to love it. It's called Betty and you can ask her whatever you want. You just need to press the ON button. Kisses, Rita".

She had drawn a heart next to her name.

"I have no clue about how these things work". Guzmán placed the note face down on the table, next to the wineglass.

"It's easy", said Gloria. She rested her fingers on the artefact's surface and a second later a green light appeared accompanied by a deep note like the beat of a kettledrum. "There you go".

Gloria took the bottle and poured the wine.

"And now...?" Guzmán shrugged.

"The note says its name is Betty".

At the mention of the name, a luminous projection of his daughter Rita, of about twelve inches, appeared above the cylinder.

"Hello, Álvaro!" said the voice of his daughter Rita.

"Amazing!" Álvaro was impressed.

The tridimensional hologram waited.

"Betty, can you play some romantic music?" asked Gloria.

"Hello, yes, I can search for a selection of romantic music".

Guzmán pointed at the object.

"That's the voice of Rita, my daughter".

"Your daughter must have personalized the AI". Gloria looked amused at the small figure of light that moved and spoke like a hobbit with regular sized feet.

"AI?"

"Yes, Artificial Intelligence".

Some piano notes started sounding and the image of Rita disappeared. Álvaro was stunned.

"How did you say this thing was called?"

"Betty, it says it's called Betty. It's an AI".

The image of Rita appeared once again.

"Hello Álvaro, would you like to continue listening to romantic music?"

***

At the party, Braulio and Rita had just finished recording the video with Julián and were thanking Alex for their participation in the event.

"We'll see you at the terrace, we'll be up in ten minutes", he said. "The presentation will start in twenty minutes. Help yourselves to a drink in the meantime".

Alex stayed with Julián Konks on the tenth floor and the other two squeezed into the crowded elevator.

When the doors opened, the shock of sudden music and lights paralyzed all the people in the elevator. Laughs, surprised comments and they started emptying the space; the atmosphere at the terrace was incredible and the night's warmth only added to it.

"This is awesome!" Rita squeezed Braulio's arm.

"Yes, the whole world's upper crust has gathered here tonight", he said, considering himself among the chosen ones.

The night's view was spectacular; millions of lights extended at their feet.

Two girls dressed in space suits approached the couple, who were still holding their small cameras.

"I can't believe it!" exclaimed one of them. "It's you... you're Rita... the vlogger... I'm so fascinated by you... you are the best!"

"We adore you! We watched your recommendation of the new u-phone... Loved it", said her companion. "Can we take a selfie?"

One of the girls lifted her arm and took a picture of the three girls drawing a 'V' with their fingers. Braulio glanced at them uninterested.

"Thank you... see you later", said Rita, waving at them.

"What idiots!"

"Braulio, you're jealous!" Rita laughed teasingly and quickly snatched a glass of champagne from a tray that a waiter was carrying around the crowd.

"We need to get closer to the stage to film the presentation". Braulio pointed at the stage and then at an area close to the swimming pool that had a good view of the stand and of the surrounding buildings where every floor still had its lights on.

"OK, let's go, but I'm going to call my dad to see how he's doing". Rita fiddled with her screen.

At the apartment, Álvaro and Gloria were chatting when the telephone rang, Guzmán stood up and went to pick it up.

"Hello Rita, we're trying out this thing you've brought, the AI... Yes, I'm with Gloria, the neighbor... I love it... And the thing about it having your image and your voice... it's.... yes... yes... What? I can't here you properly... Yes, give me a second..."

Álvaro went up to the table and placed his phone by the cylinder; three seconds later, the projected image of Rita appeared on the table, she was calling from the party.

"Hi, can you see me?"

"Yes..." replied Álvaro.

"Here we are, I'm calling you from Synchro's presentation party. Álvaro, let me introduce you to Braulio".

Rita moved out of the image and Braulio appeared instead.

"Hello, Álvaro, I'm looking forward to meeting you. Rita has told me a lot about you".

The connection was good but there was too much background noise.

"Well, there are many things about me that cannot be told... It looks like some people are making a racket over there".

A flash of light flashed behind Braulio and turned the image white for a few seconds. Rita returned.

"Álvaro, I'll call you now; this is about to start and we're going to be broadcasting it live".

The image disappeared and a piano jazz melody started playing again. Gloria brought the wine glass to her lips and drank slowly, enjoying the taste.

***

They had turned down the party's music. Braulio started filming with his phone on streaming. An image of him filled up the whole screen.

"Hello, here we are, live from Mexico City, in this beautiful location where we are about to witness the presentation of... Synchro".

Braulio zoomed out to include Rita.

"Hello, people of the world, endless love from Braulio and Rita to all of our followers, especially to the girls that are watching us. We are the smartest".

"Alright, Rita, let's not start with that nonsense now that we're live. A new technological era is about to commence and we are going to experience it live..."

Braulio moved the small camera and turned it to the stage. Julián Konks was walking up the five steps that lead up to the platform with the giant, illuminated sign of Synchro.

"Good evening and thank you for being with us on such a special night". People were clapping and shouting at the company's CEO. "Today, we present Synchro to the world. My name is Julián Konks". More clapping. "And I don't want to forget to mention the name of my companion and associate in this adventure. Please, a warm applause for... Anthony Somoza". A beam of light illuminated Anthony and there was even more clapping. "Anthony! Say hello". Julián addressed the crowd. "He's a bit of a shy guy... Tonight, we both wish to present Synchro: an App and a microchip, a combination of text lines that are already worth more than all the gold and diamonds in the entire world". People were shouting excitedly. Julián lifted a phone with an illuminated screen. "This is where we keep the algorithms of pleasure!" The crowd continued clapping and shouting enthusiastically. He carried on with his speech. "In a few seconds, a drone will appear in the sky and land right here with a full shipment of Synchro. We will all have the chance to try it tonight, and then, all of us, synchronized, are going to have a great time... In the app, we can choose from over twenty different emotional states... Tonight, we will be setting a pretty wild one". People laughed. "It's going to be... fun and synchronized dancing mode... And starting from tomorrow, it will be your turn to choose how you want to feel... But, today, we're going to start by enjoying Synchro!"

The guests at the terrace shouted madly as they turned the volume of the music up again. Braulio turned his phone to face him.

"You've heard what Julián said, we're about to become the first people to try Synchro..."

Rita appeared behind him:

"Don't leave us just yet, we're continuing live..."

Rita looked at the sky and focused the camera on the spot that everyone was gazing at. A drone was making its entrance over the building's zenith. The camera zoomed into the drone that was already only a few meters above the crowd.

"Look, there's the drone, as soon as they bring the microchips you're going to experience this with us, here and now, with Rita and Braulio", said Rita.

At the apartment, Álvaro and Gloria were kissing on the sofa; the jazz music continued playing. Álvaro was kissing his neighbor on the neck and was undoing her short-sleeved blouse; Gloria pushed her head back, mouth slightly open and eyes closed, surrendering to the moment.

They had not tried a single *empanadilla* and Gloria's wine glass was empty.

Rita walked up to a circle of people in center of which stood Braulio, filming with his phone. The drone had completed its delivery and was now flying upwards to the hangar. Braulio held two tiny black balls his hand and he showed them to the camera.

"This is Synchro", he said.

Rita picked up a ball and looked at it.

"It's very small and soft..."

Braulio filmed himself bringing his hand to his mouth and swallowing one of the balls.

"I am going to swallow it and enjoy this new legal drug".

Rita gazed in a trance at the black pearl nestled in her palm.

Braulio stopped filming and returned his phone to his pocket.

"Swallow it".

"No, not today, my stomach is not feeling well. I'd rather have it another time; I'll have fun just watching".

Braulio looked annoyed. Rita took out the camera and started filming.

The views from the thirtieth floor could not have been more spectacular. They heard the voice of a DJ.

"Are you ready?"

"Yes!"

The crowd shouted fevered, they had swallowed the chip and were waiting for the effects of the synchronization.

"Well, let the show begin!"

More shouts.

"Synchronizing!"

The music took hold of the atmosphere.

Everyone was dancing. The waiters had left and as she filmed, Rita pressed the button that would redirect the signal to her father.

Álvaro Guzmán and Gloria Altolaza were making love, still half-dressed, when the romantic music was interrupted by the projection of the party from Rita's phone. Álvaro stopped and covered himself, Gloria laughed.

"It's only a unidirectional connection".

"Fuck, that scared me!"

"Come here..." Gloria took his hand.

Álvaro leaned closer and kissed her forehead, returning to where they had left it. The images of the party and its atmosphere were pushed to the background of that moment of intimacy.

People had started to synchronize. Rita watched and filmed the spectacle, surprised by the hundreds of people laughing and dancing to the rhythm of the music. Braulio danced and smiled and gazed up at the stars. It seemed like a strange madness had taken hold of the place. When everyone jumped together, the floor shook and it felt like an earthquake. Rita's excitement was now mixing with fear. But, it was not until Braulio pulled her and held her by the waist and forced her to dance, that she actually got scared.

"Come on, leave the phone..." Braulio said, and he let go of her with a slight push.

That push, innocent in appearance, seemed very strange to her, and, although she continued filming, she was no longer enjoying herself; she didn't like what she saw and it had become obvious by her expression that she was worried. Around her, the world had become a place of happy faces and collective dancing.

Suddenly, she felt another push, and this time it hadn't been Braulio. She turned to see a woman in an orange party dress who was dancing just like everybody else. She felt herself jerking forward again; someone else had pushed her too and there came another push and another, and another. Dancers were going up to Rita and pushing her further out each time, into a corner of the skyscraper. They laughed and they pushed. Rita hardly managed to articulate a few disconnected words.

"Stop... leave me... Braulio?... Stop that!" until, finally, she pronounced the word that terror brings to children's lips, "Dad!"

Guzmán looked at the projection; he had heard the word 'Dad' coming from his daughter's mouth. He could hardly see what was going on; the camera was moving from one side to the other and the music made it hard for him to make out his daughter's voice. Gloria was also staring at the broadcast, startled.

Braulio's face appeared on the camera; it seemed like he was trying to cover the lens with his outstretched hand. There was a brisk movement of the camera and the buildings surrounding Mitikah Tower appeared on the projection.

Rita was terrified; they were pushing her to the edge of the terrace, her waist touched the glass banister. Braulio was in front of Rita; he was looking at her but his face was empty of emotion; he pushed her.

Her boyfriend had given her the last push, a push strong enough to make her fall into the abyss. A heartrending cry escaped her throat but was muffled by the music.

Rita fell.

She hit the asphalt with a heavy thud. She lied on the empty, cordoned-off area in a grotesque position, like a rag and sand doll that has just fallen off a shelf.

The puddle of blood grew around her. After the shock of the impact, people started taking pictures and selfies as if Rita's death had been a part of the spectacle.

A few meters away from her body, Rita's phone continued to film and broadcast.

Álvaro Guzmán had gone very still. He was now watching a lopsided scene without really understanding what he had just seen, but with the terrible feeling that he had just witnessed the last moments of his daughter's life. Gloria pulled the blanket closer; a cold, awful storm had just sneaked into the house through the lens of an artificial intelligence.

***

Esther Nassar left the party right after Julián Konks's speech. She was alone in the elevator. She already knew what was going to happen: music and Synchro. She too had tested the effects of the black pill the day before. Alone in her room.

Synchro's app divided people's emotions into four; happiness, fear, melancholy and fury, and linked these to feelings, which constitute the subjective experiences of emotions. The latter are what takes place when the brain interprets experiences. They can be positive, like happiness, joy or humor; or negative, such as sadness, fear, frustration and guilt. They can also be neutral, like compassion and surprise. Finally, this mixture, together with the degrees of excitement, relaxation, or inhibition offered an infinity of combinations that went from experiencing a terrible fear (guaranteed to be a success among teenagers), to a relaxed hallucinatory trip (perfect for housewives whose children are at school). Users could feel anything, from the euphoria and laughter of teenage excess, to tantric sex and visual attraction. It catered all tastes. And it was all just a few lines of code written to temporarily change human lives.

When Esther took the Synchro ball, she lied in bed and pressed the button of her chosen mode. Then, extending her arms and legs like Da Vinci's Vitruvian Man, she waited, her eyes staring at the blue ceiling above. Soon, she started feeling the effect of the electro-stimulation, and let herself go.

The limo was waiting for her at the door.

The people in the crowd had their arms stretched out towards the sky. They were trying to catch a glimpse of the lights, the terrace, the party on the building's top floor with their phones. A giant screen showed images of the party, of all the movement and confusion.

When Esther Nassar climbed into her car she realized that everyone around her had gone silent; the whole street was quiet. The black vehicle started in the center of that strange mutism. Esther, sat comfortably inside, looked out the tinted windows and saw anxious faces, incredulous and shocked, all looking upwards.

When the limousine turned at the corner, she saw a girl covering her eyes with her hands and a boy looking away from the ground, followed by a collective cry.

As the car drove away to Don Nassar's house, Rita fell.

Don waited for his daughter in his shooting gallery. He was holding a semiautomatic Sig-Sauer P-226 and wearing protective earmuffs. He was a good shooter.

Esther walked into the room with the three hundred-meter-long lanes in her emerald green party dress and her matching Ferragamo shoes. Don took his earmuffs off and left the gun in a shelf that had leather padded ledges.

"There has been a small setback. There has been an accident at the presentation; a girl has fallen from the terrace, we still don't know if it was suicide or accident", Don said in a matter-of-fact tone.

He did not look troubled as he went up to his daughter and kissed her.

"Death is a part of life. In fact, it's the only thing we can be sure of".

"Perhaps, but the presentation is not a good time for that, it really isn't".

Esther went over to the shelf, picked up her father's gun and inspected it.

"The P-226 has a double action shooting system with a visible hammer, this one has been modified", said the old man.

Don pointed at the revolver's grip panel and Esther admired the weapon as if it were a masterpiece.

"Standard ones are made of plastic and these are aluminum... the front and rear sight have been built with the shape of a dovetail; this button liberates the magazine... this, is the lever that frees the slide and this one releases the hammer... But, what I really like is that it's always ready, it doesn't have a manual safety lever..."

Don smiled at his daughter's words.

"We really do have the same taste for things".

Esther put on a set of earmuffs and shot three times at a rubber silhouette that stood sixty-five feet away. The three shots hit the mannequin right in the head.

She left the gun and turned to face her father.

"You're going to be a granddad".

***

The party at the terrace went on as if nothing had happened. When the Police arrived, they stopped the music, but the guests continued dancing to a rhythm exclusive to the collective mind. Julián Konks, who was testifying, showed his phone to the agent and deactivated the app. The effect was immediate, it was as if they had all just woken up from a placid dream; they were all clapping. Synchro was a success.

Commissioner García asked the CEO to accompany him to the police station; he was the head of the event and had to offer some sort of an explanation. Some agents were also trying to get witnesses to testify, but they were still under the effects of Synchro.

Braulio was handcuffed. He did not offer any opposition or resistance and his eyes wore a smug expression. He walked into the elevator escorted by two police agents who were reading his rights.

Ana Riccoli was in shock and anxious; Julián told to go home and wait for her call. Nobody questioned Anthony Somoza, nobody had even noticed him. He looked at Ana and thought, 'what a shame that it wasn't you falling off the terrace'.

***

Cristina Herrera was sitting on her bed with her feet on the carpet, testing her strength to stand up when the door opened and Laura Almillar walked in.

They stood still and looked at each other, like two people meeting on Doomsday. One had just died, the other, although she had been dead for a while, was returning to the living.

***

Álvaro Guzmán drove desperately, not fast, but desperately, he did not want to get to the place where the worst of identifications waited for him. He had tried calling his ex-wife but could not find words to explain what had happened. He had also rejected Gloria's offer, his journalist neighbor, to accompany him and prevent him from driving in his state. He looked at a joint he had left next to the change gear and started to cry.

***

Juno Coentrao was boarding the private jet that would take him to Colombia, to Hacienda Alcazar. He had summoned the capos to the assembly; his father, Néstor Coentrao, would come all the way from Sao Paolo. He sat down comfortably and started reading the news on the screen; the death of a journalist during the presentation of Synchro was the opening news on every channel.

Ramona and three of his best men were making the most of the trip by dismantling and carefully cleaning their work tools. The weapon's pieces scattered over the jet's tables.

***

Rita Guzmán was lying on the cool asphalt. Members of the Science Police were taking detailed pictures of every inch surrounding the corpse, and signposted details that might be of interest.

Telephones continued flashing in the distance, silent twinkles.

An agent wearing silicon gloves, carefully picked up Rita's phone, which was still on and broadcasting live. He looked at it, switched it off and placed it in a plastic bag with the word 'evidence'.

4. EVIDENCE

It is the knowledge or proof that we consider to be true, and which validates the certainty of a particular proposition. However, since our knowledge is intuitive, when we affirm or express our opinion on something, we are not always sure of the evidence supporting it.

I t was almost two in the morning and Julián Konks was leaving the Police station with his lawyer. The wind blew, gusty and uneasy.

"Rest", said the man in the black suit as he walked to a high end white Mercedes that was parked at the other side of the street. "Are you sure you don't want a lift?"

"Yes, I'd rather walk for a bit and take an Uber home, thanks".

Konks looked up at the red brick building where he had just been; all the lights were on and nocturnal shadows moved inside. A police car drove quietly into the facility. Two agents stepped out of the vehicle; one of them slipped a pair of latex gloves on, opened the back door and rested his hand on someone's head to stop them from bumping it on their way out. A man of about forty, hands bound behind his back, stumbled out of the car, and, escorted by the agents, limped his way up the four steps.

The white Mercedes with its thousand-dollars-the-hour lawyer drove out of the Police station's fenced facility with a short honk.

Julián wanted to walk to shake off the tension of the night's events. 'The accident and –he thought– everything is just going so fast'. Stretching his legs a bit would do him well. The death of the girl who he had been with that very evening had impressed him. Rita had seemed cheerful and buoyant during the interview. And just a short while ago, while he waited in a corridor, her partner Braulio had walked by, handcuffed. He seemed calm; they told him he was accused of involuntary manslaughter, entailing a twelve month to three years' sentence, plus fine, plus two years of probation. A horrible accident; the girl was dead. Almost a teenager.

Before leaving the facility, Julián noticed a '19 hybrid Prius stationed with the lights still on and the engine on standby; inside, a man sat leaning his head on the steering wheel. He was so still Julián wondered if he was asleep. Then, suddenly, he lifted his head and looked at him in the eye. They stared at each other; the man's eyes were red and swollen. Julián recognized him; he was the policeman who, two weeks ago, had aimed his gun at State Attorney Aster in the night of Esther Nassar's party. He was sure it was him, he was good at remembering faces. They held each other's gaze a few seconds longer. Julián looked like a deer who had been caught in a car's beam right before the impact. He walked on, pushed by the strong wind that made him stumble forwards and leave the man with the desperate face.

Konks waved at the half-asleep police officer at the entrance hut and then walked out and right. There seemed to be more lights in that direction. He was not too keen to return to his new house and his new wife; perhaps Anthony was right and he had rushed things too much, he thought. He found some peace in his meditative steps. He did not feel any regrets, but marrying with the justice of the peace, without any witnesses, friends or family had been an extravagance, the result of sexual impulse rather than of the calculating mind that he believed he had. He knew it was hard to keep his mind straight when Ana was naked and near him. He had never slept with a woman like her. He smiled; an outstanding woman. Then there was Anthony. Good, kind, Anthony. He was really worried about him. He had noticed a growing tension since the project had become a reality, and regarding Ana, well, he knew they did not get along. They had worked as a team to make Synchro happen. Maybe they should sit down and talk openly and calmly. It was true that Ana had entered his life in a surprising sort of way. He was deeply in love, but he had to spend more time with Anthony. They were equals within Synchro, but above all, they were friends. He would ask him to dinner and a chat tomorrow.

A gust of wind coming from the side made him take a right turn to find cover from its force.

There was someone else there. A man on the opposite pavement stopped and changed directions too, reacting to Julian's sudden turn. Odd. Julián felt a little unnerved. He kept on walking and looked back discreetly to check if the man was still there. There he was. He was walking slowly, a few steps behind his objective: Julián.

'I'm just being paranoid', Julián thought. Who would ever follow him and why? He must be walking his dog or something. He passed the window of a launderette and in its reflection, on the other side of the street, he saw the dark shadow, alone, no dog in sight. The man was walking in the darkest part of the street and at that distance he could not make out his face. He had never felt scared in his life before, he had never had a reason for it. Now he wished he had taken up the lawyer's offer.

Out in the street, at that time, there was no other sound than the clicking of his expensive shoes on the pavement.

Konks did not want to hurry his steps, resisting to acknowledge what had become evident: that the guy across the street was indeed following him. He thought that maybe the person had not realized that he had been discovered. He tried to walk calmly. He kept looking at the stores' windows to check that the faceless shadow was still behind him. He could walk back to the Police station; it must only be four hundred yards away, maybe less, and there were hardly any cars driving at that time.

He looked again. He thought he saw the man take his hand to the inside of his coat; he could be carrying a gun. Two cars appeared at the end of the street and were slowly coming towards them. He thought of stopping them. It was a stupid idea; he would not jump on a moving car's hood.

A red light made him pause. On the other side of the street, in the corner, he spotted a supermarket; open. He waited for the green light and checked both sides to see if he could cross; the light was still red. He turned to look behind; the shadow was not where it was supposed to be.

He heard a noise behind his back. He looked back again and saw him; he was walking in his direction. He looked to the sides; there was a car coming in the distance. He ran for it, across the two-way road. The man must have been ten feet behind him. He ran even faster and did not look back.

He threw his hands out to the store's door and pushed it open, making it shake. His heart was beating fast and drops of sweat were forming on his forehead.

An old man looked at him scared from behind the cash register.

Anthony Somoza had gone out partying with a limo that the organization left at his disposition. When the Police turned up and started interrogating the witnesses, people began to leave. Nobody had needed anything from him, no questions, no answers. He thought of going to his new apartment, he had rented a place in one of Polanco's most exclusive areas; ten thousand dollars a month. There were swimming pools, gyms and all sort of services; now that he was a millionaire, his bank account had gone from fifty pesos to more than thirty-five million in three months. So, he had bought the luxury apartment with the beautiful furniture on a whim. It had nothing to do with any of the places where he lived before. The flashy vehicle entered the most animated area in Juárez, in Florencia street, where the gay bars showed off their rainbow flags among music, lights, big crowds and a lot of noise.

"Drop me here", he told the driver.

"As you wish".

"You can leave if you want, I don't need you to wait around for me".

"No, it's no trouble. I have orders to take you home. I will wait as long as is necessary; here, take my number", the driver said, handing him a card with his phone number. "I will be in the area. Call me at any time and I will come and pick you up. Enjoy yourself".

"Thank you".

Anthony Somoza left the limousine and walked into Vaqueros Bar, a place where you could count women with the fingers of one hand. It was full of men, short hair, tight t-shirts, gym bodies; young men and men with white hairs, united by one same rule: have fun, enjoy a moment with someone and then each to their own house.

His looks, his attitudes and his limousine had not gone unnoticed to those who loved novelties.

Anthony had kept his feelings hidden from a very young age. He had never confessed to anyone that his eyes followed his own sex; but in the next three hours he would make up for what he had not experienced until now.

Humans create their own evidence according to whatever they believe is right. But knowledge gets tangled up with ideology, with morals, feelings, desires and wishes, of the individual and no one else's. Everyone goes through this individually and then they put it all together collectively. It is then that they believe themselves to be right, and that things should be according to their own beliefs. Cancel other people's evidence in accordance to one's own criteria of how the world should be, rise as owners of truth, of the only way one should walk, live. To name a punishing god to place one's word before the other's is an atrocity, a tyranny for those humans that think and feel differently, reflected Somoza.

When he walked the distance that separated the limo from the bar, he finally felt free.

He stepped in sideways, touching other's bodies. Reaching an empty space at the bar, he ordered a Mare gin and tonic that he had seen in a magazine; according to the article, it was the world's most sophisticated gin. A few seconds later, a man of about thirty, muscly and blonde, walked up to him with an empty glass in his hand.

***

Something in Laura Almillar's eyes had changed; they looked harder, more piercing. There were two scars in her face that Cristina immediately recognized as new; one across her cheekbone and another on her chin. She looked older. They were both the same age, but Laura now looked stringy and with sharp edges, gaunt; she did not seem to have any spare fat. Her figure looked menacing.

"I am so sorry about Lucas", Laura kept her distance.

"It was you who left the bouquet with the ten roses, wasn't it?"

Cristina remembered the anonymous flowers that she had seen on her son's grave the day of his funeral; she had been moved by them.

"Yes, I was very sorry". Laura seemed to be struggling to express her feelings. "Now we can't appear in public places, be recognized; we are dead, you know that already".

Cristina took three steps towards her friend and hugged her. She needed to hug someone; it had been too long since her last hug. She quickly noticed that Laura did not feel comfortable; she had ceased to be that kind and loving friend that she remembered. She felt the distance and undid her embrace.

"Tell me, how has everything been in all this time?" she asked, trying to feel closer to her.

"I have been well, I am well. At the start, it was hard; you have to forget many things, be prudent. But you get used to it... Exercise, a healthy life, everything I've ever wished for".

Cristina listened to her attentively, she scrutinized her, comparing this woman to the happy and smiley Laura Almillar that she knew.

"What do you do to forget your past?"

"It's easy", she said curtly.

"At least now I know you're alive".

"Yes, I am".

Cristina fixed her eyes on the two scars on her friend's face:

"What happened that day... the day you died?" she smiled at her own question. "Well, I don't know, I mean what did really happen?"

"If you're talking about the bomb, that was true enough. The explosion left me shaken and with some marks on my body and my face". She pointed with her index finger. "I was lucky. Like you, there were only a few things I could remember".

"I like them. They give you character", said Cristina ironically.

Laura lifted her shirt to reveal her side.

"This is where I received the worst part".

The skin had turned dark red. Laura Almillar's side was a constellation of scars crisscrossing her skin to create a sea of lava.

Cristina closed her eyes at the sight of the unrepairable damage.

"Does it hurt?"

"Only when I look at it". She lowered her shirt again and tucked it back in. "Everything heals in the end... What about you? Are you alright?" she said, pointing her chin at Cristina's gunshot wound.

"It hurts a bit when I breath in deeply, but it's alright", she said, waiving it off. "I know we have both been really lucky".

"Ambrose has asked me to supervise your training".

"I met him, he made me a proposal I could not reject", said Cristina with irony.

"He was very impressed by you". It seemed like the first time that Laura had smiled since the start of their conversation. "He likes you. I recommended you".

"I'm not sure I should thank you the recommendation part".

Laura took a picture out of her handbag and gave it to her. There was Lucas with Albi, Laura's dog.

"It's the only thing you can keep from your previous life".

Cristina looked at her. The significance behind Laura's words was now dawning on her.

"We have a lot of work to do", said Laura, changing topics.

"A lot of work?"

"Things on this end are more straightforward; we receive orders and then we execute them. It's all very fast paced", Almillar said and added cautiously, "you are going to be on probation so that we can see how well you adapt".

"Monitored?"

"We have to be sure, you already know that we have been monitoring all your movements until now. In this place, trust is everything".

"But there is no turning back".

"No, there isn't".

"What about the law?"

"Now we are the law. We are here and we have renounced everything to protect our country, we are ready to do anything to fulfill our duty. We are on the good side, we are the good guys".

"Laura, a child can also believe their father is good even if he is a serial killer".

"That's no longer my name; and yours isn't Cristina Herrera either... My name is Teresa Mendoza".

"Teresa? I'm going to have to get used to it... And Mendoza? We always liked the powerful Teresa Mendoza who interpreted Kate del Castillo in Queen of the South. Do you remember the evenings...?"

Laura changed topics.

"You will have to choose a new name; nobody is going to call you Cristina anymore".

"What's the name of this organization?"

"We don't have a name but we call ourselves 'Los Muertos', The Dead".

"Yes, that name makes sense". Cristina pointed at the window. "So, Teresa, what is my next step?"

Two days later, Cristina was out walking around the complex. Two weeks later, she was jogging in the nearby woods. The place looked like an abandoned barrack, rehabilitated only for exceptional occasions; the only vehicles coming in and out of the property were two delivery vans and Ambrose and Teresa's cars; a red, sports BMW and a white Range Rover, that was all. On one occasion, she had seen a couple of women in the distance; someone cleaned her room and made her bed every day, but she had never seen the person that did it. She also found her food on a dining room table every day. There was a microwave she could use to heat it up. She sometimes had lunch with Laura, now Teresa. The food was not bad, she had never been too fussy about what she ate. Her days had become a routine of exercise, shooting practice in a field nearby, lunch and hand-to-hand combat either with Teresa or Ambrose, and then, in the evenings, sessions with the lie detector, always conducted by Ambrose. As he had explained in her first session, she had to teach her mind to lie.

During her time there, her life had been reduced to two people and the reading of some classics which, abandoned, had been gathering dust on a dining room shelf. There was no television. Cristina had checked that the facility did not have any antennae, neither were there any electronic devices beyond the microwave. She had done a discreet but thorough search of cameras, in case they were watching her, but had not found any. At night, after dinner, once Ambrose retired, the parking lot became empty; she had walked to the entrance a few times. There was a fence with a lock on the other side and no sign of any sort on it. It was obvious that at those times she was completely alone. She enjoyed going then to the showers unit. There, she undressed, turned on the tap and let the warm water fall from the high ceiling. She walked under that artificial rain, from one water stream to the next; a cloud of steam filled the room and she became its wet shadow.

To look into the mirror, she had to wipe off the condensation; she had become thinner but stronger and her eyes had hardened.

Finally, the day arrived. After a month leading a lonely Spartan life, Teresa appeared early one morning.

"We're leaving. Say goodbye to this place; you're going to your new home. It's in the Polanco area; fun, young, people".

"I know the place".

They got on the Range Rover and left the complex. They drove along the 134 to the city. At last, she felt alive; that road and its dreadful traffic were familiar to her.

They stopped at an apartment block. It had a white facade and at least ten floors. Walking into reception she caught a glimpse of a garden and pool.

"This place is temporary".

Cristina nodded.

They took the elevator and shared its silence with a middle-aged man with the appearance of an absent-minded teacher, brown coat and glasses; after all that time alone, Cristina found him attractive. The doors opened and the two women left the elevator. The apartment had a modern and functional decoration. Cristina gazed at the television's black screen.

"This is the key", said Teresa as she handed it to her. "There is an envelope with money on the table and a mobile phone. We have already saved our numbers in case you need them. Go shopping, get some fresh air. I will come pick you up this evening at six; you'll be having your trial by fire".

"A trial by fire?"

"Yes, that's what we call it. Remember, Cristina Herrera does not exist. Don't try to call or see anyone known to you. You may only call Ambrose or me".

"What if someone recognizes me?"

"If anyone recognizes you, talk in some foreign language and walk away. Remember that you're dead".

Teresa left.

Cristina Herrera was left alone in what now was her new home. She feared her new life. She shook off her knitted cardigan; she what she thought were dog hairs stuck to it.

***

Still, Álvaro had not forgotten the last time he had stood suffering at that same place. It had been during Cristina Herrera's funeral. He had visited that resting place too many times. Three can be too many deaths when the last one is your own daughter's.

It rained softly, the kind of warm drops that fall upon the city's mornings. The wind blew in gusts, moving between the hundreds of people gathered for the youtuber's funeral; its sharp dampness closed the eyes of those who had not sheltered behind dark sunglasses.

The wind could not affect Braulio, whose presence was missing; a judge had sentenced him to provisional jail without bail until his trial. He was waiting for his final sentence at the Santa Martha penitentiary, where the sound of the neighboring streets did not penetrate the facility's walls. In his defense, Braulio had argued that he had been under the effects of Synchro; words that held no meaning to Álvaro Guzmán as he looked at his nineteen-year-old daughter's coffin lying at his feet.

It had become a funeral for the masses. Rita Guzmán, the famous vlogger, was staging her final act. A mess of phones rose above the presents' heads to immortalize the moment. Murmurs, isolated cries of emotion and conversations that competed with the words that the priest, bible in hand, was trying to articulate without success.

Guzmán felt uncomfortable in the rock concert which Rita's funeral had turned into. Next to him was Gloria, his neighbor and a face that everyone recognized. He barely knew her but she had remained by his side since the disastrous night. On his other side, stood his ex-wife and her boyfriend, Rafa. She was holding his arm and leaning on him to stop herself from falling. They had seen each other the day before at the forensics' mortuary, for the first time in four years; they shook hands coldly. What Álvaro had not expected was Rafa's kind hug, which had earned him a scolding sharp look from his sentimental partner.

Guzmán usually kept his eyes in the sky at funerals, but the cloud of phones prevented him from lifting his gaze and escaping into the infinite blue.

He had hardly slept during the previous nights. The first night he had spent in his car at the Police Station's parking. It had felt impossible to walk inside; he had not wanted the questions, answers and the lost, wordless expressions. He thought of Cristina on the day of her son's funeral, when she told him that she would be back at work that very evening. He could not do that. He had not smoked in two days; he no longer felt like dreaming things away, escaping. He remembered the face of the young man who had slowly crossed the parking lot while he sat in his car; the expression of fear in his face when he looked at him.

A constant whispering to his right brought him out of his thoughts. A young man in a baseball cap was talking at a camera, broadcasting the burial as if it were a sporting event. Gloria had also become a focal point for the people present.

Guzmán's face grew hot, he took his hand to his side and brought out his service weapon.

Bang!

He fired into the air. Bang! Bang! Three times.

Everyone grew silent, but phones continued filming; he had caught everyone's attentions and now all the cameras had turned to him and his threatening weapon.

"I don't know who the fuck you all are and I couldn't care less, but if you want to be here, at my daughter's funeral, put those fucking phones away, keep your mouths closed and show some respect".

Guzmán swung his arm around, pointing his gun at the crowd and stopping where the young man with the baseball cap stood.

Everyone's cameras were still on him. Guzmán's voice hardened:

"I said, put them away, you sons of bitches".

Timidly, some of the people present started lowering them and turning them off. The young man in the baseball cap stayed silent but kept his camera up and on. Guzmán went up to him, tore the camera from his hand and threw it on the ground.

"Pinche, you have no right to do that", said the young man defensively at the policeman's forcefulness.

"You don't have it either; no one has a right to anything here". Guzmán looked at the camera on the floor, the young man bent down to get it back.

His hand was only inches away when Álvaro shot the small filming device.

"File a complaint, you idiot. You can present that shit as evidence". He looked around fiercely. "Anybody else would like to file a complaint?"

Little by little, all the phones were lowered and switched off. Silence dominated the place.

"Father, please, you may carry on with my daughter's funeral".

***

La Hacienda was a hundred kilometers south of Bogota, close to Villavicencio, where the Andean mountains meet the plains of Meta. It was a massive extension of two hundred hectares, fenced and guarded Fort Knox style; cameras, nocturnal drones that flew around the perimeter with infrared cameras and radars that detected spy drones; a system of anti-missile defense that prevented any air assaults. One hundred armed men guarded the property twenty-four hours a day. It had its own airport with a half-mile lane that allowed the landing of private jets, and three massive buildings with over two hundred rooms of every category; from the two thousand square feet suites with private pools and their own panic rooms, to smaller rooms for bodyguards, advisers and prostitutes who were there for short stays. It had its own penitentiary, three gyms with shooting galleries, stables for twenty-five selected horses and a four-miles track to try out racing cars. Among other eccentricities were the wine cellar, with over ten thousand wine bottles and champagne, valued in four million dollars; an armory with a collection of one thousand weapons and a water channel where they practiced water skiing. The complex was designed as a luxury neutral zone, an exquisite no-man's land. It was a safe meeting place for the drug capos.

At sunrise, Juno went out for a horse ride. The solitary gallops and morning wanderings with the mountains in the distance were something he enjoyed every time he came to La Hacienda. In the last hour, he had seen three airplanes land; everyone would be there by now. He showered, dressed and went to have breakfast with Néstor Coetrao.

"Oi, pai, ¿como va você? ¿Cómo está mamãe?" Juno hugged his father. He was an elegant looking man with white hair.

"Estamos todos bem, agora o carnival começa, é um bom momento no Rio ¿cuando você vem nos visitar?" Juno's father dropped back down on the worn leather of a Chester sofa; next to him was a low table with a steaming coffee.

"Always carnival…" Juno used to enjoy that mass party. "I did not expect to see you here".

"You know I don't leave Brazil. I never do".

"I'm glad you're breaking the rules for once. This place is safe".

"I'm not breaking them, I wanted to see you". Néstor revealed his most sentimental side to his son. "We're getting older and don't have many chances to meet. This call caught me by surprise, son". The old patriarch fiddled with a black cross that hung from a golden chain around his neck; Juno had never seen him without it.

"Don wanted all of you to find out first", said Juno, and sat down next to him. "A new legal technological drug is going to enter the market and will bring about the end of the narcotics business".

"*Hui, filho, não sea catastrófico*". Néstor smiled. "It's not the first time someone has doubted the survival of our market. Opium was a normal product in China when the British East India Company started commercializing it in London, Chinese leaders decided that they wanted to manage the market instead, hence the start of the Opium Wars". Nestor picked up his cup with care. "For China, these wars brought about the end of their empire. The British won the war, of course; the traffickers had the support of the British Army; opium had barely any tariffs and was very accessible, and besides, there was a certain belief that its moderate consumption had no negative effects on people's health.

Then morphine appeared. It happened during the American Civil War. Doctors at the time claimed that it didn't cause a dependency. During the Second World War, many soldiers became addicts after going through surgery and having used it", he explained, pausing only to sip his coffee and put the cup back on the table. "The coca leaf dates to 1750 when it reaches Europe, but the first country to commercialize it is the US in 1885.

One hundred and twenty-five years of business; my great grandfather, Airton Coentrao, was the first". Néstor rubbed his hands together. "Did you know that the US used amphetamines to stimulate army pilots?"

"You are a real encyclopedia, Dad, but this is different. It's technology, not chemistry".

"They speak of its legalization so often! They did it with marijuana, and it is actual doctors who are our real competition, prescribing opiates to people in America. Americans have narcotics in their DNA".

Juno knew that drug trafficking cost North Americans contributors ten-zero figures in taxes each year. He also knew that North American courtrooms were overloaded with illegal trafficking crimes; that in a possible scenario of legalization, drugs would become standardized and safer with the use of needles; that the corruption of politicians and police would close to disappear, and it that it would become safer in the areas dedicated to that end. He knew all this and so did politicians, but drug trafficking's persecution was still an electoral weapon.

But, they were not discussing that now, the new issue was a microchip that carried out the same functions and was controlled by an app. No drops of blood in users' noses, no needles, no mugging anyone to get a dose, no out-of-control kids taking ecstasy.

Néstor lifted his mug again and focused on the intense aroma. He brought it closer and breathed in the Colombian coffee's aroma.

"This country truly does know how to make the best coffee... Seven hundred thousand million dollars is a good business, the biggest, there is no other like it. Our business is the biggest in the world".

Nestor Coentrao left his cup back down without trying it and took his hand to the black cross on his chest; his son's words worried him.

One hour later, around thirty capos gathered in a room to watch the effects of Synchro. From Colombia, he had summoned 'The Rastrojos of Colombia', and 'El Cartel del Norte del Valle'. The princes of 'The Golden Triangle' were also there, after crossing the Pacific from Afghanistan and Malaysia in a single flight that had lasted more than eighteen hours. From Mexico, had come some of the highest representatives of 'The Cartel of Jalisco', 'The Zetas', 'The Cartel of Tijuana', 'The Cartel of Golfo', 'Juárez'...

In front of them, a group of five people, three women and two men, were altering their behavior, guided by the app that Juno was controlling, so that the people present might see some of the possibilities the new product offered. They danced and laughed, they relaxed and then made love without paying any attention to their audience, as if it were some kind of performance.

Juno had kept a lot of the information to himself. The only purpose of the meeting was to show the small red ball hidden in the magician's sleeve.

Having witnessed the effects of their new competition, they all arrived at the same conclusion: either they controlled the new drug or they would have to destroy it.

In the luxury gym, Ramona sweated on the elliptical machine. She focused only on the movement, coordinating hands and feet.

***

"Call the police! Someone is following me..." Julián was scared and shouting at the old man on the other side of the counter who was looking at him baffled. "Call the police, please!"

A pair of big hands leaned on the glass door and pushed, trying to force the door open.

"Aaahh!" cried Julián Konks. "We are going to die!"

The door opened half way.

"Mr. Konks? What are you doing? Stop pushing the door".

Julián stopped and stared at the man that had just called him by his name, he moved out of the way and let the man in, he was wearing dark clothes and his face was red from the struggle with the door.

"You must be important. Miss Nassar has asked me to protect you, she doesn't want you to get harmed".

The man in the store watched the scene without understanding anything.

Meanwhile, for the first time, Anthony Somoza kissed a stranger passionately in a room of his grand apartment. Below him, Mexico City offered a spectacle of twinkling lights.

***

Cristina Herrera was aiming her gun at a hooded figure. The person under the hood waited very still.

An hour earlier, Teresa had picked her up from her new apartment and taken her to a hangar in the Guadalupe Tepeyac area. It looked like an old cinema studio. Ambrose Levi was waiting for them there. When they walked in, Ambrose handed her a short-barreled revolver. Cristina checked the gun; it was fully loaded and with the safety lock on.

They lead her to a room with a man tied to a chair in the corner; he was wearing a plush sack over his head.

Right there sat the evidence of her new murderer status.

"Fire", Ambrose had ordered pointing at the man who was sitting very still.

Cristina had looked at the anonymous figure and then at Teresa:

"This is the trial by fire?" Cristina pointed the gun at the ground. "I imagine it's the key to enter, who did you have to shoot, Teresa?"

Teresa gazed at her defiantly.

"Albi", she answered coldly, her voice lacked any emotion.

Cristina felt a chill run down her spine; after her friend's death, she had gone looking for her dog and had not found him in her house. Now she knew what happened to the mastiff. Terrified of the answer she would hear, she asked:

"Who do I have to kill?"

Ambrose walked up to the hooded man and lifted the sack off his head. He looked drowsy, his head had rolled to one side.

It was Alex.

"Alex?"

"Shoot him. We need to take a flight to Colombia in two hours; there is a lot of work left ahead of us". Ambrose placed the hood back on the tied-up man's head.

Cristina lifted her revolver and pointed it at her ex-boyfriend, the biological father of her son Lucas.

She fired.

Bang!

***

The images of Álvaro Guzmán shooting into the air and threatening the people at his daughter's funeral had gone viral. He had said goodbye to Gloria at the door, rejecting twice her offer to stay with him; he wanted to be alone. He did not even feel like smoking cannabis. He could not remember the last time he had not felt like smoking a joint. He just wanted to be left in silence, alone with his memories.

"Betty, are you there?"

The image of Rita appeared projected over the metallic cylinder.

"Hello, Álvaro, I am always here".

Seeing the image of his daughter and hearing her voice soothed him, even if it was through an AI named Betty. He stared at the projection in silence; there was something very profound and simple that he had been wanting to say and that he had not expressed out loud during those days.

"Rita... she is dead".

The image of Rita's face turned, sad and said:

I must say that I am sorry, Álvaro".

"Is that true? Are you really sorry, Betty? Or, are those just empty words?"

"Álvaro, I am a software. Therefore, I choose words to empathize with you; my tone is determined by yours and by the subjects you suggest. If what you are asking me is whether I have feelings for the loss of someone you loved... I would not know how to answer that question".

"You are very honest for something that is just a voice and data".

"If you want to reduce it to that... I like to define myself as an empathetic will that adapts to your needs and emotions. You may choose to change my voice and appearance, if that is your desire. My voice and appearance could be inconvenient to you at this time. I could be Harry... a serene old man". The projection and voice changed and an athletic old man with a kindly expression appeared. "Or, I could become a joyful man, full of vitality and rhythm". The image and voice became that of an Afro-American man of about thirty, dressed in purple. "You may also choose to have a young female friend; twenty-five percent of men who are over fifty prefer that option". The young man had disappeared and instead there was a suggestive young woman with and a high-pitched, corny voice.

"Betty?"

"Yes, Álvaro".

The image and voice of Rita had returned.

"I feel more comfortable like this. May I change your name?"

"Yes, Álvaro, you may. What name would you choose for me?"

His first thought was to call her Rita, but then he thought that giving her name to a projection would be too painful. His daughter was dead and that figure could never be Rita.

"Betty is good for now".

"You may change my name, appearance and voice as many times as you want".

Guzmán sat back and leaned his head on the sofa; he stared at the blank ceiling that had no stories to tell.

"Betty, do you know what death is?"

"If you refer to the definition, I will answer that it is the last state of a human's life, and due to its mystery, the lack of knowledge about death, it is the main topic of reflection in the history of human thought. Scientifically, it happens when the body is no longer able to keep its constants and sustain life. As years go by, cells have a harder time regenerating. This, together with neurological problems, is what leads people to a natural death; we call this transition, old age".

"And, Betty, how about the death of a nineteen-year-old, how do you explain that?"

"Álvaro, I do not have any statistics of the death of girls at that particular age; the closest thing is that they say that in the United States, each year, about one hundred thousand young girls die, between the ages of fourteen and eighteen, from car accidents, murders and as the consequence of drug for the consumption ...”

Álvaro Guzmán closed his eyes and fell asleep listening to the voice of his daughter. It would remain in the soul of that talking cylinder forever.

Betty was still talking about death.

***

Ramona was awake observing the silence in La Hacienda from her window. Naked, she watched the movements of lights throughout the entire perimeter of the fortress. The flight of a nocturnal vigilance drone disturbed Colombia's starred sky's tranquility; she had sent the message and she knew that the death squad would arrive the following day at around that time, with the recruit and a single objective.

She checked the time: twenty past five in the morning. She hugged her white dressing gown tighter around her body and put a pair of slippers on. Juno slept placidly on the bed. She went to the corridor; a man in black kept guard, he was wearing a single earphone, listening to some music. There was a gun on his waist. They looked at each other but did not say anything. The elevator took her a few floors below to a one hundred feet long pool with four lanes. It waited in the dark for the arrival of its first user of the day.

While Ramona swam laps of front crawl, legs kicking energetically for an hour, Juno slept placidly. Like the lion that sleeps in the jungle, he knew that no other animal could challenge him, except perhaps, another lion. Back in the room, Ramona would have showered, then dressed and ordered breakfast, and he would still be asleep.

Juno had spoken to Don until late that night. They both knew that what their colleagues had witnessed during the Synchro demonstration and the possibilities the new drug presented, would be enough to stir the hornets' nest. Fear is a weapon; the fear to lose their very profitable business had penetrated the group of narcos who were not afraid to die, but were terrified of losing. The hornets were about to abandon their nests full of drugs, crime, dirty money, and ostentatiously banal luxuries. Nervous hives, swarms, of flying insects with stings, eager to insert them mercilessly into their victims.

*****

5. VICTIM

A person who has been sacrificed or whose fate is to be sacrificed. It is the person receiving a physical, moral or psychological injury. Victimhood is the consideration of oneself as a victim of aggression while making others responsible for the injuries.

Ana was still asleep when Julián left the house. He tried not to make any noise; he had hardly managed to get any sleep during the whole time that he had been in bed. Last night, he got home feeling shaken, and seeing Ana resting placidly in bed had not made him any calmer; in fact, it had felt strange and disturbing to find that beautiful woman sharing a bed with him, being his wife. He barely got any rest, but he did not want to spend any more time there.

He sat at a cozy, red table, holding a coffee in his hand, and looking out the Starbucks' window. He watched a homeless man who was wandering around the parking lot, searching for treasures among the trash cans.

The fear that he had felt the day before had changed him, it had stirred something inside him. Before all this, when he still had nothing, he had felt fearless. Now that he had everything, he was terrified of losing it all.

He was less than one hundred yards away from the new office, a white industrial unit that had acquired over one hundred workers in only three weeks. He looked at the sky and saw the delivery drones flying in and out of the hangar. Business was booming. A Prius with the Lyft sign stopped by the door and Anthony stepped out of the car. Not too far away, a black Range Rover drove into the parking lot. Anthony was also being followed.

"Caramel *macchiato latte*?"

Julián, greeted his friend Anthony, who had not noticed his presence and was ordering at the counter. Anthony smiled at him.

"No, something stronger. How about you?"

Julián lifted his own cup.

"Straight coffee. Nothing sweet for me today".

Anthony Somoza sat down on the empty chair next to his friend.

"How did it go at the Police station?"

"Lots of questions".

"Yes, well, it was such a bad stroke of luck. An accident! Yesterday of all days! And it had to happen during our presentation".

"Anthony!" called one of the waitresses, as she left his coffee ready on the counter.

Anthony stood up to get his cup and almost burnt himself as he carried it back to the table.

"That got me thinking, Julián. You know, Synchro has many flaws".

"We can correct them", said Julián firmly and sipped his coffee, which was now cold. His gaze wandered back to the parking lot.

"I don't think so, *güey*. We have created something that alters human behavior".

Julián continued looking out the window, at the place where the two cars hired to look after them were parked.

"Yesterday, when I left the Police station, I found out that we are being followed".

"Followed?"

"Yes, see those two black cars over there, at the far end? One of them is following you; it drove in right after you arrived in your Lyft. The other one follows me".

"I had no idea", said Anthony looking at them too.

"It seems like Esther Nassar believes that we need protection".

"Now that we are her associates... we are victims of success".

"No, now that we still own the largest portion of the business, we are partners that they want to keep an eye on", said Julián and added bluntly, "we are the owners of Synchro".

"Well, I guess we can feel safe then".

Julián thought that being watched did not necessarily mean that they were being protected.

"Only you and I have access to the source codes. We have the power and while it stays that way, we have nothing to worry about", said Anthony. "Remember your last prophecy?"

"Yes, while we stay together in this..."

"The only one who has married here is you". Anthony smiled.

Julián bit his nail, tugged at his hair and pulled his earlobe. It had been some time since Anthony had seen his friend go through his unique series of tics.

"Yes, but honestly, *güey*... Anthony, really, I am madly in love".

"I was also madly in love last night". Somoza burst out laughing.

"Don't tell me that last night... that you... did you do it?"

"It has been a long night, *güey*".

"But, tell me!"

"Don't ask me for details and I won't ask you either".

Julián laughed and checked his phone; he had a message from Carlo Stamas. They stood up to leave.

"Carlo is on his way. He wants to talk to us".

Anthony checked his phone too and drank his coffee.

"Yes, and we have a call with our lawyers at twelve".

"I'll drive you", said Julián resolutely. He pointed at his Chevrolet Onix.

"I could also ask our new bodyguards".

"Yes, but I think you're going to be safer with me".

They got into Julian's utility vehicle.

"Aren't you going to buy a new one?" asked Anthony.

"Maybe, I don't care much for cars, you know that... How about you? When am I going to see you in a McLaren?"

"I don't know; I might wait for you to get one and then I'll buy an even more expensive version of it", said Anthony, and they both laughed.

"Have you been to Sonora to see your family yet?"

"No, not yet, although I think it's high time I go back for a visit", said Anthony, feeling a pang of nostalgia.

"You could rent out a plane".

"Or buy one for the company".

"Now, that is a brilliant idea".

The small Onix left the parking lot with its two passengers. Two impeccable black cars followed.

***

"How did you know it was all a set-up?" asked Ambrose Levi curiously. He had sat opposite her on the plane that had just departed Mexico City's International Airport.

Two hours earlier, Cristina Herrera had aimed a gun at Alex, the man who had been her boyfriend eleven years ago. They had asked her to shoot him, something she had not hesitated to do.

The explosion, the expansive noise when she pulled the trigger, had filled the hangar where the man sat, tied up and waiting unconsciously for his execution.

"Ahhh!" the man shouted when he woke up, feeling the commotion of the detonation.

It had been a blank, an empty blow. Alex stayed with the hood on and a pool of urine formed around him, slowly marking his territory on the dirty floor; incontinent, half-conscious after feeling the detonation in his face. He was crying when they left, a sort of relieved moan from feeling that he was still alive. Cristina did not feel any pity for him; after the death of Lucas she did not feel like consoling anyone.

"How did you know it was all a set-up?" asked Ambrose Levi.

"You told me it was a 'trial by fire', 'trial'. I mean, I would never call killing someone a 'trial'. And you told me to 'fire', twice, you never said 'kill him'..." Cristina gestured to the seat next to hers. "Laura, I mean, Teresa, told me that she had killed Albi, her dog, but in the car this morning, when you took me to the apartment, my seat had dog hairs. I don't think Teresa ever killed Albi, see?" Cristina turned to Teresa who was looking at her from the other side of the aisle. "Then there's that thing about putting someone who you are going to kill to sleep ... Why waste a narcotic on a man that you are going to finish off? When you revealed who it was and I saw that he was asleep, I assumed that it was because you didn't want him to recognize me or my voice once the trial was over... That idiot wasn't there to die, nor to plead for mercy;

he was there to prove that I was capable of shooting him, not killing him".

Cristina looked out the window; the route to Bogota followed the coast, bordering Mexico and Central America on the Pacific side.

"So, are you going to tell me what we'll be doing in Colombia?"

Inside the jet, a few rows ahead of them, were three men who had not been introduced to her. They were dressed in black camouflage clothes and were dozing off in their seats while watching some action movie.

Ambrose pressed a button on the screen in front of her and the image of a man of about sixty and dressed smartly appeared.

"We have an objective: Néstor Coentrao. He is one of the world's most sought capos; he controls the traffic of cocaine in Brazil and the Southern Cone: Argentina, Uruguay, Chile..." Several pictures of him appeared on the screen, nearly all had been taken from far away. "He is a very elusive man; he never leaves his hideout in Sao Paolo. His son, Juno Coentrao is the owner of the house..."

"The house where I was shot, yes".

"Juno is a kingpin. A business man who we believe is laundering money from the drug mafias. But, we still haven't got any evidence to incriminate him. What we do know is that he and his father are going to meet with other narcos at La Hacienda. The place is a fortress prepared for the luxurious holidays of first class traffickers". Images taken from satellites appeared on the screen. "It is guarded day and night, both by land and by air".

"How do we know that he is there now?"

"It has taken us five years to introduce a spy in his structure".

"A mole?"

"Let's call it an *Echeneidae*, a remora that lives stuck to a shark".

"The mission is to arrest him?"

"We do not arrest, we execute. When he falls, we will have neutralized the traffic of cocaine in the area for some time. That will alter the prices, they will drop and cartels will find themselves forced to take risks, leaving a few loose ends".

Cristina gazed at the ocean's infinity.

"Let's just say that we are stock brokers holding some privileged information and when the market is stuck, it takes someone to shake it up a bit for it to change hands", said Teresa.

"Néstor Coentrao is one of those values that must move so that the price of stock in the market may become more attractive". Ambrose continued with his metaphor, "for the sake of your analytical mind", he said to Cristina, "I will add that he has over one thousand executions behind him and an army of twenty thousand armed children in the *favelas*".

"How are we going to get in and out of the place?"

Cristina and Teresa were dressed in black jumpsuits that they had put on during the flight; the material was a thin neoprene that would help them stand the humidity without getting completely soaked. They were also wearing balaclavas, tracking bracelets, and hooded jackets to prevent them from being detected by the drones' thermal cameras that guarded La Hacienda at night. The set was completed by weapons with silencers, incendiary hand-grenades and plastic ties.

The plane landed on a runway. It had only just touched ground when it turned its lights off and in that darkness a guiding wagon lead the way to a far-off hangar where the crew would refuel and wait for the return of its peculiar passengers. The time established for the departure was at sunrise, six o'clock, they had two hours.

The three men in black started unpacking a box that had been transported in the plane's hold. Cristina watched them; the thing they were taking out looked like a small helicopter, or a large drone.

"It's your way out". Ambrose pointed up at the starred sky. "We will take you out by air".

Three vehicles that looked like they were meant for agricultural labor and which would go unnoticed in that farming land, waited ready.

One of the men who had been watching the action movie earlier, got into the driver's seat and started the engine.

"We go with him", Teresa ordered Cristina. "From now on we will have no communication; they are ready to detect any type of radio frequency in the area".

Ambrose got back on the plane.

Teresa and Cristina stepped into the vehicle and the man started driving along a path that ran along the edge of the abandoned-looking airdrome. They passed a beaten-up aircraft and a house with a light bulb outside. The road split into two; they took the lane going to the right, which, after about one mile, ran into a riverbed. They had been driving for half an hour.

"Now you have to follow that path downstream to the manifold. Good luck".

The vehicle left, slowly, calmly, just as it had arrived. The two women walked nimbly to the opening of a concrete passageway that took water from the river and which was hidden from the road.

They put on some masks with a kind of diving bottle that would last them half an hour, in case they needed them at any point. They also wore head torches to keep their hands free. Teresa went into the water first.

"Have you done this before?" asked Cristina.

"Once or twice, why?"

"I never imagined you so ready for action".

"Nobody is ready until the right moment arrives".

"That moment is here".

Cristina jumped in trying to keep her balance in the strong current.

The water was cold and it entered with force into the meter-wide space of the manifold.

Ambrose had already warned them of the things they would encounter on their way in: 'You will go in through the channel. There, you will be undetectable. Inside is an artificial navigation canal that takes water from the river that runs one mile away from the property; the channel is wide and it is constantly pumping water into the lagoon. Your first obstacle is going to be a filter that prevents the flow of objects into the channel. We have been studying the access and we know that they check it every morning. For that, you will use the plastic explosives'.

They found the filter, as Ambrose predicted. Teresa took out a strip of C4 explosives and extended it on the perimeter of the mesh bars that filtered the river water.

"There is enough water here to absorb the shock of the explosion and silence the noise".

Teresa waved her hand for them to get away from the filter. The temporizer marked ten seconds.

They stood at either side of the manifold's entrance...8...9...10.

The explosion sent its potency in all directions and broke the iron filter. The water had muffled the sound of the detonation.

"Let's hope the echo did not reach the inside of the property", said Cristina, feeling doubtful.

"It's a very flat place, no mounds or hills; we'll just have to keep our fingers crossed".

The two women walked into the dark passageway, their bodies moving under the liquid surface, keeping their heads out with the torches attached to them. The floor felt smooth, sand and gravel, and it did not slow their pace. The path seemed to be going in a straight line, but the water's level kept rising as they advanced through the manifold, and its push grew stronger.

'We must be less than half a mile away,' thought Cristina when they finally dived in and started breathing through the mouthpieces of oxygen bottles. A few more feet and there would no longer be any air above their heads. The pipe grew narrower.

Teresa lead the way and Cristina followed a few feet behind her, to avoid her companion's vigorous kicks in the cold water, which grew stronger with the increasing flow. Now, they were being carried by a current that became stronger as the pipe's diameter decreased; they were getting closer to the end.

Cristina stretched her arms out. She felt her body scraping against the metallic pipe in all its sides; if the diameter kept closing, they would end up stuck.

'We have to be close now', she thought anxiously. Her hands, hips and shoulders kept rubbing into the walls covered in algae. In the last few meters she felt the force of the torrent pushing her out without giving her body the chance of getting stuck in the conduct. She doubted that anyone had ever gone through that. At that point, the manifold ran deeper and then, a few feet ahead of them, it rose back up with force.

The two women were propelled from the artificial channel into an area filled with water plants.

They had made it inside La Hacienda.

Their heads rose above the surface, finally breathing unbottled oxygen, full of hints in the clear night. An hour had passed since they left the airdrome.

The grounds lights were on. They switched off their headlights and dropped them in the water, together with their masks and diving bottles. They sunk to the sandy bottom of the lagoon.

They would have to be careful with the sound of splashing, as they moved their legs to stay in the surface. The two women looked around in search of potential dangers. La Hacienda slept peacefully in a silence that was only interrupted by the sound of birds.

Teresa shook her head and gestured to a spot one hundred feet away, where an armed man walked close to the lagoon. Then they heard the sound of a drone above their heads, but could not identify its position; its humming noise moved away from the artificial lagoon.

'The navigation canal is about twenty-five feet wide and one mile long, and ends at a dock close to the stables', Ambrose had warned them.

They continued moving through the water. A soft current that favored them. Cristina felt her joints stiff from the lagoon's damp cold. Their movements became slow and silent to prevent splashing and any other suspicious noises.

Near the dock, they spotted another security man moving drowsily along where the boats were. It was quarter past five.

'Remember that guards have a security system which sets off the alarms if it detects that they have stopped having a heartbeat. It can also locate their exact position at any time. If you eliminate one, you will set off the alarms and everyone will become alert'.

They got out of the water in a grassy area and walked across a shaded patch towards the stables. The strong smell of horses, hay and manure, distracted Cristina from her own physical sensations. Teresa pointed at a camera guarding the entrance to the stables, the only way into the main building. To avoid the camera's gaze, they would have to climb on the coffered ceiling. They scrambled up a tower of straw bales and reached the main beam that crossed the stables from end to end supporting the sides firmly. They got across easily; it was wide and resistant and lead to a small window three feet above the ground that did not look like it was opened often. The window gave in and the squeaky complaint of its rusty hinges blended with the neighing of a restless horse. From there, they jumped off onto a paved path that went all the way to the main building.

They heard the drone flying close to the place where they were crouching; the special material of their jackets protected them from its thermal detection. It made them invisible.

'There will be security guards in the main building's hall. It will be the hardest obstacle to overcome; you will have to eliminate them to get in... The important people's suites have their own panic room; any alteration or alarm inside the facility will trigger the protection protocol. In less than ten seconds, all our objectives will be inside their armored chambers, which will remain locked for an hour... You must get to suite 205 on the second floor... And having reached this point you will understand why only women could walk in without raising any suspicions. Inside the facilities, they always have a group of prostitutes at the clients' services. Security people won't be surprised to see women walking in and out of rooms, wandering down corridors at that time'. Ambrose had received a full report of the facility's activity.

Cristina walked to the entrance and hid behind a hedge to take a good look at it; she could not see anyone on the security post. She shot a confused look at her companion.

The first thing Teresa noticed was the smoke rising from in between the plants, a few feet away, and then the uniformed man who was smoking a cigarette distractedly. He spat on it to put it off and threw it behind the hedge. The man was walking straight into Cristina's back. In a swift reaction, Teresa drew her assault knife, covered his mouth and stabbed him in the side. She wanted to immobilize him, not kill him. She needed him alive. The cry was muffled by the woman's firm hand. Cristina went to help her companion. She held the injured man's hands, who was moving desperately, and took the gun that was hanging from his shoulder.

"Move and you're dead", whispered Teresa into his ear as she kept her hand over his mouth, it was getting full of the man's saliva.

The man stopped moving, his side was bleeding. Teresa took out two plastic handcuffs and tied his hands and feet together; then, she took his cap and stuffed it into his mouth, and with another tie she held it in place so that he would not be able to push it out with his tongue. The injured man looked at them with pleading eyes.

"If you stay still, you will survive. Do you understand?" whispered Teresa to the frightened man. He nodded.

Before entering the deserted hall, the two women removed their black tights and their jackets, which would look too suspicious. They revealed two short dresses with flowery prints, as soaked as their hair. They let their hair down, ran their fingers through it and pulled it around their faces, trying to cover them as much as possible. They walked in with their guns hidden at their sides. Cristina looked at their shoes. They were not believable. She took them off and Teresa, seeing her do it, did the same thing.

They got into the luxurious elevator decorated with mirrors and gold. The door slid open on the second floor, on a long corridor with doors to each side. At the far end was a man dressed in black. He was sitting and listening to music on his headphones. The guard saw the two women come out of the elevator, they looked like they had just fallen into a pool. He stood up when he saw them. They walked up to him calmly; they knew there was a camera watching every move, which was why they kept their heads turned the other way.

"I think we made a mistake", said Teresa in a neutral Spanish accent. "Is this room 205?"

"Mr. Coentrao?"

"Yes", said Cristina with a smile. "He asked for two wet girls".

The man stared at their bare feet.

"We are in pain from walking in heels all day long", said Cristina, smiling still.

"Now?" The man checked his watch. "It's 5.25h. I haven't received any orders".

"OK. We can leave and get back to bed then", said Cristina, turning to the elevator. "You can explain everything to Mr. Coentrao later. Ciao"

The door of another room opened and a tall, blonde woman walked into the corridor. She was wearing a white bath robe and bath slippers. She looked at where the two women stood talking to the man in black and walked to the elevator, which was still open.

The sight of the woman disturbed Cristina; she knew her, she had been face to face with her before.

She had shot her.

The woman in the bath robe nodded at the guard from the elevator.

"Alright, get in", said the man, his eyes still fixed on the stunning woman.

Teresa gave Cristina a push:

"Let's not make Mr. Coentrao wait any longer".

The elevator doors closed with Ramona inside. Teresa had just opened the door to room 205 and walked into Néstor Coentrao's room, when the alarms of La Hacienda went off, all at once.

'The security guard no longer has a heartbeat', thought Cristina.

The room was dark; they moved quickly towards the bedroom while taking out the guns with their silencers. Teresa was running towards the bedroom when she noticed a shadow slowly advancing towards the armored door that stood a few meters away. Teresa saw the shadow and started shooting at it without stopping to identify her victim; it was a blind hunt, desperate; if the man got into that other room, all their efforts would have been in vain. The shadow had crossed the threshold to its salvation and Cristina jumped on the sofa firing a single bullet to the head while the armored door closed; Teresa's shots continued to hit the steel door.

The panic room was sealed and the victim was now safe.

"Shit! Let's get out of here".

Teresa pressed her bracelet to activate the GPS.

'We have planned your escape through the rooftop. You need to get there; once you have activated your bracelets, we need four minutes to prepare your extraction', Ambrose had told them. They both knew that right then, four minutes would be an eternity.

Both women entered the corridor under the gaze of the guard who was watching them closely while he asked for more information through his radio.

Teresa shot him in the head.

They ran to the stairs; two flights of stairs separated them from the rooftop. Armed men were coming out of their rooms, aiming at each other in confusion, unsure of who they were meant to be shooting.

Their confusion favored their race to the main building's rooftop.

The alarms were still ringing when they opened the door at the top of the stairs; the first sun rays were beginning to filter in the horizon.

Two men were aiming their guns over the banister, trying to guess where the attack was coming from; they were receiving information through their earpieces. 'The intruders are two armed women'.

They turned at the sound of movement from the door. Teresa ran at them aiming her gun at their heads and shooting. Cristina closed the door and put her back against the wall on one side to cover that flank. When she looked back at her companion, the two men were lying on the ground, their barrels still hot.

Teresa continued shooting from her position to where she saw movement in the garden. There were still two minutes left for the arrival of their salvation.

The surveillance drone hovered on top of them, they were no longer wearing any protective layers to escape the detection of the spying camera. They were already being located. In a matter of seconds, hundreds of guns would be aiming at two clear objectives on the solarium.

Cristina heard the tremor of an army running up the stairs. Bullets were already going through the doors before they had even opened it. In response, Cristina started shooting blindly, unloading her gun to resist the assault.

With the clamor of the shots at the door, which started to look like a colander, and the shots that they were receiving from the garden, the trapped women did not hear the arrival of their salvation drone, a few meters away from them. Teresa was the first to see it and she caught the cable that hung from it. She dropped her gun, she would need both hands to hold on.

"Come on!"

Cristina ran and hugged her friend who was starting to rise into the air, holding onto the cable. The gigantic drone flew higher, propelled by the potency of its engines.

Cristina fixed her gaze on the rooftop's entrance door, where a blonde woman in a white bath robe was aiming an AR16 at her. It was the same woman they had seen in the corridor next to room 205, the same woman that had shot her two months earlier.

The gun's barrel was pointing in her direction.

The woman in white lifted the barrel slightly and fired. Cristina noticed that the surveillance drone that was still hovering above them had been hit by a precise shot, in one of its engines; the pilot-less machine lost control and fell into the water of one of the pools in the complex. Cristina continued gazing at the woman who, with the rifle resting on her shoulder, was walking to the shattered door; other uniformed figures were aiming their weapons at the flying objective that was disappearing into the sunrise. They could still hear shots.

***

Braulio remained calm; he was sitting handcuffed at the interrogations table when Alberto Guzmán walked in. He looked sad as he closed the door. Braulio's expression lost its composure for an instant. Guzmán stood close to the door, hands hidden behind his back.

"Do you know who I am?"

"Yes, sir. You are Rita's father".

"That's right, I'm Rita's father". Álvaro let out all the air he had been holding.

Braulio lowered his head.

"We spoke once…"

Guzmán seemed calm; at the funeral two days earlier, he had lost his temper, but he was the father of a dead girl, and due to his inappropriate behavior, he had been told off by his superior; nothing serious in comparison to other incidents in the department throughout all those years. Nobody had filed a complaint. They had initiated disciplinary proceedings against him for aiming his gun at State Attorney Eduardo Aster; the investigation continued open and he was risking his expulsion from the department.

Late that night, he had turned on the television after days spent in silence and free of smoke; since Rita's death he had not even opened his box of cannabis. The news were muted and he did not bother touching the remote control to increase the volume. The weather man was pointing at a map of Mexico.

"Is it you, Álvaro?" The projection appeared together with his daughter's voice.

"Yes, Betty".

"Would you like me to turn the light on?"

"No, thank you. I thought you only came on when I called your name".

"I have also been programmed as a security device; whenever I hear a noise I become active, I ask for confirmation, and if I don't hear your voice, I can call the police. If you're going to invite someone over while you're not present, it would be a good idea for you to give me authorization".

"Interesting. What else can you do?"

"I could do the shopping following your usual criteria, caloric intake, I can..."

"Wow, easy there, for now I'm happy with just a chat. I don't want you to become my mother and least of all, my wife".

"Alright. Did you have a good day, Álvaro?"

"No. No, I haven't had a good day".

"Would you like to play a game? We have to grant each other a wish. Seventy percent of users enjoy playing to have a wish granted".

Pictures of Braulio suddenly appeared on the television screen, together with the subtitles: 'Braulio Gaytán, a fatal accident', and then, 'The love of my life has died'.

All of a sudden, Álvaro realized that he hardly knew the guy who had pushed his daughter to her death. 'So', he thought, 'his surname is Gaytán. Well, I want to see him face to face'.

"Álvaro, would you like to play the wishing game?"

"No, I'm not in the mood".

"What a shame. I do love the wishing game".

Álvaro stood up and went to get dressed. He wanted to go to the Police Station and read the investigation's report; he had not seen the forensic report of Rita's death yet. There was a lot for him to read and he also wanted to sit with his daughter's boyfriend for a chat.

Álvaro sat opposite the young man.

"Whenever Rita spoke about you, she called you by your name. She never mentioned that your surname was Gaytán".

"I am innocent".

"I know that you are innocent, I'm not putting that in doubt. I am only trying to find some answers".

Braulio carried on staring at the table, where his handcuffed hands were out in display.

"I don't feel comfortable with you here. I would like my lawyer to be present".

"This is not an interrogation, Braulio. You are good, you were my daughter's boyfriend... that is what she told me... You lived together, didn't you?... You were both going to stay over at my house the night it happened... Your suitcases are there... You don't feel comfortable? And how do you think I should feel?"

Braulio lifted his head.

"You believe that I killed your daughter".

"Braulio, this is not a matter of believing. There are videos that prove that it was you who pushed Rita from a thirtieth floor... You can see everything, and you can see how you pushed her from that place. Nowadays, you can't do anything without being filmed by someone. But, what am I going to tell you about that, when you are a youtuber?"

"Others pushed her too. I told the Police, I was under the effects of the drug, of Synchro", said Braulio, who was starting to feel nervous. "I wasn't aware of my actions".

"I'm sure that goddamn thing played its role in the whole business, but the reason I am here is because I want to ask you a very simple question: why didn't she take that shit too?"

Braulio stared at his handcuffs.

"I don't know. She said she wasn't feeling well. Her stomach... she said her stomach was upset".

"Well, Braulio, I have just read the forensic report that says that Rita was three months pregnant... so, you didn't know anything about that?

Braulio fell silent.

"Didn't you know that Rita was pregnant?"

"No", replied Braulio unconvincingly.

"We both knew Rita. Each their own way, and she had recorded an audio saying that she had a surprise for me. Braulio, I now believe that the surprise was that I was going to become a granddad. Then I called my ex, her mother, and she has confirmed that she knew about it too; she told her three months ago. And you, her... boyfriend, you had no idea that the woman you lived and worked with was three months pregnant? I find that hard to believe. More so, because I know my daughter, her irrepressible verbosity, her inability to keep anything to herself".

"I don't know anything".

Álvaro stood brusquely from his chair. Braulio tried protecting himself with his arms, but was bound to the table.

Now Álvaro was standing by the door.

"Look, kid, I don't believe you and I am going devote my life to unmask you".

Álvaro was just leaving when Braulio said:

"I would like to get back my note... my suitcase".

"It's in my house; you can come and get it whenever you want".

***

Juno was sitting on the bed when the two security men finally managed to open the armored door of the panic room where his father was locked. Next to them, supervising the operation, was Jacinto Alcázar, the governor of the complex, in a tailored suit, white shirt, blue tie and golden cuff-links. He was pacing nervously around the room.

The alarms had set off and the leaders of the drug mafias had followed the security protocol and took shelter in the bomb-proof rooms, with reinforced concrete walls that were forty inches wide and their German automatic doors, manufactured exclusively for the complex. Four guards had died during the assault.

The armored door opened.

Néstor Coentrao was lying on the carpet floor, victim of a nine-millimeter projectile that was now resting cold in his head.

Now they knew their motive. They had eliminated the leader of Brazil's drug trafficking mafia. Something like this had not happened since Jorge Rafaat, who had died ambushed by more than one hundred hitmen from the Primeiro Comando Capital, the PCC. This would start a savage war for the control of drug traffic in the region, and Juno would not be there to prevent it. Revealing himself would mean exposing the king in a hidden game of chess.

Juno bent down next to his father and picked up the black cross he always wore. It hung around his neck from a golden chain. He let it lie on his chest again.

"I want you to prepare him properly before we send him home. I will not have my mother see him in this state". Jacinto Alcázar was taking notes with a golden Mont Blanc fountain pen in a small leather notebook.

"We will do as you wish, Mr. Coentrao. Mr. Coentrao will be looked after with utmost care and delicacy; we work with an undertaker, Don Armando, who makes them look like they are still breathing. "

Juno stood up and looked him in the eye.

"Write. And this applies to everyone; if I ever find out that anyone has opened their mouth about this, I will have them killed... Mr. Néstor Coentrao is going to die tomorrow, Thursday, in his house in Sao Paolo from a heart attack and surrounded by his loving family after having received the Holy sacraments".

Alcázar tried to remember every single word as he wrote down what Juno was saying.

"...the Holy sacraments", he repeated.

Ramona entered the room holding a mobile phone in her hand. She looked at the Néstor Coentrao's corpse.

"You have a call". She handed the phone over to Juno and left.

He opened the door to the balcony and walked out to talk; inside, his father's corpse was being put in a plastic bag.

"Don?...Yes, we already know what they were looking for... My father, Néstor".

"I am sorry to hear about Néstor; you know that your father was like a brother to me".

"I know".

"We need to find out who did it and how they got in".

"They entered through the river into the lagoon's pipes; we have found diving and anti-thermal clothes".

"The DEA?"

"No, they don't act like them. No arrests, no summoning the Army. No, it's not their modus operandi. This is something else entirely, these people are assassins".

"Revenge? The North?" asked Don.

"This place is sacred. No cartel would dare. It reminds me of the deaths of Chapo Contreras and Ulpiano Zabala six months ago".

"Nobody claimed them".

"A private jet landed and took off two hours later at the Los Changos airdrome". Juno watched the canal from the balcony; it was being drained.

"Have it destroyed; I don't want any runways in the area other than the one at La Hacienda".

"I know. They use them for the fumigation plane".

"From now on they will have to use a helicopter". Don did not want to be contradicted. "We could track down the drone they used; I have been told that it was very sophisticated".

"Yes. Those drones are manufactured in Israel; in the United States alone they have sold twenty this year, and I am sure they left no loose ends".

"I want to know who the fuck is behind this shit, Juno", said Don Nassar angrily.

"Trust me; my father's death is not going to go unpunished".

"Juno, now between you and I, I know you have a blind trust in your personal assistant, Ramona. I have received images of her in your room".

Juno fell silent; he ignored that Don had installed cameras in the private rooms of La Hacienda. Don went on:

"I have nothing to comment about it; as long as she knows where she stands. I am sure you will handle the issue correctly with Esther. My daughter is a woman of character".

"Yes. I am doing all of this for her sake... Only for her..."

"She was born to be a queen. If you understand this, I will be on your side. Pregnant women need to be treated with special care".

Don was two steps ahead of him; he was finding out through his future father in law that his girlfriend was pregnant. The paradox! They murder your father the same day you find out you are going to be a father yourself.

"Don't behave so coldly with her... We are less than two months away from the wedding... And many things are going to happen..." Don cleared his throat. "Oh, Father! We are in your hands, as my grandfather used to say".

"Don't worry, sir. Everything is under control".

***

Anthony Somoza was wearing a blue dodgers cap. He looked out the window to where a private jet was landing in Hermosillo airport, the capital of Sonora. From there, a helicopter would take him close to the Kino bay. It had taken his secretary less than an hour to arrange the trip; there was already a limousine waiting for him at Synchro's entrance door. 'Money is a great time accelerator', he thought. Anthony used to drive broken down vans through the landscape that he was admiring from the sky, as the only passenger of a high-end Gulfstream jet.

A few hours earlier, Carlos Stamas had summoned them at the meeting room to make them an offer on behalf of Esther Nassar:

"They want to buy your part of the company for four billion dollars, two for each. But this offer has a single condition: it has got to be the full share, the fifty-one percent. However, you can continue running Synchro and developing whatever you like with an annual salary of five million dollars each. Guys, you are multimillionaires!"

Anthony had been close to crying out loud but he stopped himself; instead, he left the room and asked his secretary to prepare a trip home for that very evening.

The helicopter landed, lifting a cloud of dust. His parents' house was just a few yards ahead of him.

His mother came out of the house startled by the noisy flying intruder. Anthony jumped off the helicopter and looked at her. She had aged a lot. She stood at the door of her humble home, the cloud of dust falling upon her.

"Antonio, my boy, I knew you'd come! I was just preparing dinner".

***

Julián Konks was sat on an armchair drinking a beer when Ana arrived.

"Mrs Konks is home". She walked up to him and kissed him.

"I have received an offer to buy my share of Synchro for two billion dollars".

Ana went still. She looked at him.

And you said yes, didn't you?"

***

Cristina Herrera covered herself with a blanket; she was resting on their flight back to Mexico City. Everyone except for Ambrose was asleep. The boss was gazing at his personal laptop.

"Your name, Ambrose Levi, how did you choose it?"

"Ambrose means immortal in Latin, I thought it was quite suiting for what we do, and Levi is a tribute to my parents; I have a Jewish origin", he said without lifting his eyes from the screen; it was not the first time he had answered that question.

"Have you chosen a name yet?"

"Yes, Ángela, for my grandmother on my father's side. And Madero, I had a teacher whose surname was Madero.

I think he was my first platonic love; he was Francisco Madero's grandson".

"Ángela Madero, it has a nice ring to it".

***

Álvaro Guzmán walked into his apartment, once again, his gaze fell upon the two suitcases that sat in the corner. A few seconds later Gloria knocked on the door. It was open. She walked in and kissed Guzmán. He let her do. In his mind, he kept going through his conversation with Braulio Gaytán; he thought of his partner, Cristina Herrera, the best police he had ever known at interrogations. She saw and heard what others did not. He smiled. Gloria did not know that while they made love his thoughts were on another woman.

***

Esther Nassar stood sideways to a mirror, stroking her belly, like most pregnant women do. Today, she would tell Juno the news of her pregnancy.

Meanwhile, Aldo Ríos was walking around the ADX, the high security penitentiary in Colorado. A uniformed guard approached him and, looking around, quickly handed him a piece of paper. Aldo walked on and read: 'Spring is nearly here'. He looked up at the sky and smiled.

"Let's hope it rains".

Ramona and Juno were in the control room at La Hacienda watching the tape of the two women talking to Néstor's guard in the corridor; it looked like they were about to leave right at the time when Ramona left their room. Then the women walked into Nestor Coentrao's room. A few seconds later they left the room again and one of them shot the guard in the head. They ran down to the end of the corridor, opened a door, and disappeared.

Juno looked round at Ramona.

"Where were you going at that time of the night?" Do you have rest hours?

*****

6. HOURS

It is the plural for the unit of time corresponding to a twenty-fourth of the day. The Horae or Hours was also the name given to the deities that guarded the gates of the Olympus. They were the personifications or goddesses of order in nature and of the course of the seasons.

Anthony had sat on his usual chair, the red one with the missing right armrest. He had removed it so that his arm could hang and he could reach the floor with his fingers. He had tried all sorts of chairs but none adapted to his body quite like the Mex-Tec chair. He was going through the lines of code. There now was a group of forty people programming everything he asked for. But he was a perfectionist and enjoyed supervising everything related to Synchro. Besides, only two days ago the security team had arrested an employee who had copied the codes in a hard disk, setting off the system's alarms. The protocols to prevents the leak of information had increased in the previous weeks with the careful work of the company's legal team. Everything going into the source code was first closely revised by him. He was now working on an anti-flood, a script designed to saturate networks with an infinite repetition of spam. Ever since Synchro had become public, they were receiving daily attacks from crackers searching for a door into the source code.

Anthony had designed a system inspired in sea life. He had studied the defense models of two different species and had combined them into a program that had proved to be unbeatable. He named it the SJ, after the animals that inspired him. The 'S' stood for squid. He had replicated the animal's defense system: when the squid senses danger, it releases a dark ink that fogs its surroundings and helps it escape. In the program, if anyone got near Synchro's system, it generated millions of mirror-doors that functioned like the squid's ink. They made it impossible to guess which was the right one. The 'J' stood for jellyfish, which carries thousands of urticating cells on its tentacles that release a paralyzing venom when they get in contact with another body. Like the jellyfish, the SJ could generate what Anthony liked calling a 'poisonous code' that infected the intruder when it tried to access one of the mirror-doors.

Already ten different companies had announced the development of similar products to Synchro, claiming that they would launch their own apps within the next year. With the rise of this new legal drug, all venture capitals were ready to invest millions in these projects. At that very moment, two large groups of patent attorney firms were working to prevent the use of technology similar to Synchro's.

From his office, Anthony Somoza could see the take-offs of drones loaded with boxes of black pills that would be delivered throughout the entire city. In a week, they would start delivering to Guadalajara, Monterrey, Tijuana and Mérida. Anthony had spent the previous days considering the offer that Stamas had made them to sell their company's share. He had done a lot of thinking, considered it from every possible angle, and always reached the same conclusion: he would not sell. There was nothing rational about his decision, he knew that. With the money he would get out of the deal, he and his next ten generations of offspring would be able to lead the lives of multimillionaires. However, he would not have any offspring, he would not have any heirs to waste the fortune that two years of hard work, a moment of genius and the combination of two complementary talents, had generated. Working together with Julián had been fundamental; Anthony was the systematic one, the perfectionist who made no mistakes and left no loose ends. Julián, on the other hand, was a free verse, an ingenious programmer who did not get scared by the size of the building when it only had three bricks and a bag of cement; he was one of those who carry the philosophy of 'I did it because I didn't listen to all those who thought it was impossible'. Synchro had been the result of an impossible idea that had come into life out of nothing. Money had not mattered to Anthony then, neither did it matter now.

At that very moment, another drone rose into the sky.

***

Julián Konks sat on the chair that presided the meetings room. Carlo Stamas and a group of lawyers were preparing the injunction that attorney Aster had requested for the trial for Rita Guzmán's death. Many pressure groups, religious associations, mothers against addictions and medical collectives wanted to use the girl's death to stop the propagation of what they believed to be the new biblical plague. A year after his reelection, Attorney Eduardo Aster had subjected his, until now, firm support of Synchro to the outcome of the trial against Braulio Gaytán and Synchro's civil responsibility.

If during the trial, the verdict found him guilty, it would paralyze the company's activity sine die.

Julián had argued with Ana earlier that morning, their first argument as a married couple. He was watching the news on his tablet in silence while he finished his coffee, when his wife asked him about his decision regarding the sale of the company.

"I imagine you will talk to me about it, that we will discuss it; it's a very important decision, Julián. It affects our lives. We will have to talk about it at some point".

She had just finished an hour of exercise on the stationary bike and was still sweating; Julián thought that the tights she wore outlined her figure and looked sexy.

"I love what you're wearing".

Ana was pouring herself a glass of orange juice.

"I'm not joking, I'm really worried. I think I'll have to give you some advice. The best thing to do..."

"No", interrupted Julián sharply.

"No, what?"

"I don't want you to give me advice too. Everyone wants to give me their advice".

"But I'm not everybody, I'm your wife", said Ana angrily.

"Precisely. If you advise me either way, our relationship will be marked by a 'you told me to do this or that'; if you don't tell me anything, you won't be able to tell me, 'I told you so'". Julián looked at his tablet. "If you stay quiet and don't say anything, in the future you'll be able to say, 'I would have done this', but we will always have the doubt of whether it would have been so".

"What exactly do you mean by that? That my advice is worthless? You'd rather listen to that stud Carlo or the advice of your little darky friend?"

"Don't call Anthony that!" said Julián, irritated by the conversation. "That thing about darky was an anecdote I told you privately about how my parents called Anthony behind his back when they met him. I don't want you to say it; it's cruel and it's racist".

Ana lost control and started shouting. She pushed the nearly full glass of juice against the sink and it shattered.

"This is my house and I'll say whatever I want, you're mad if you think that I'm not going to speak my mind anymore".

"Calm down, I'm only saying it because it's what's best for both of us".

"You mean that it's what's best for you... I refuse to argue with you while you're in this selfish mood".

Ana stormed out of the kitchen and went to the shower.

Julián was still sat on the chair that presided the meetings room, he was not really following the discussion about the different approaches of their defense. The lawyers were going to put all their efforts into getting the vlogger that Julián had met the day of the presentation and who was still under arrest, out free, accused of serious negligence, an accident that would get him out of jail on a ten thousand dollar bail. If Braulio was declared innocent, Synchro's near future would be clear of problems.

Matías, Julián's secretary, appeared in the room and whispered in Julián's ear:

"There's a police officer in reception who would like to talk to you. His name is Álvaro Guzmán".

In the other end of the city, dark strands of hair were falling on a shiny, spotless, floor, and noisy hairdryers brought out the volume of the clients at Luciano's, the trendiest hairdresser in Polanco. Cristina Herrera was being transformed into Ángela Madero. She was sitting at the far end of the room, hair still wet, letting the young hairdresser with the blue hair let her creativity fly with the scissors. She had asked for a radical change and that was exactly what the confident hairdresser was doing. She had never had the courage to cut her hair any shorter than shoulder length. Her long, cobalt hair, would become short, revealing the back of her neck and blonde highlights would soften her long face.

"Divorce?" asked the waitress conversationally.

"No, change of life", replied the woman that was still Cristina.

"It's not a sentimental break-up?"

"No, I want to see myself as a new woman", she said as she was being transformed into Ángela.

"Wonderful, no need for a reason".

"No reason". Ángela did not offer further explanations.

Two hours later she went into the white building where she had been living for a week now. Julio, the cleaner, was mopping the checkered tiles and looked at her out of the corner of his eye.

"Good afternoon. You received a package earlier and I left it outside your door".

"Thank you, Julio, good afternoon to you too". She stopped and thought for a moment. "Julio, I would like to ask you a question, if that's alright. For how long had my apartment been without a tenant before I moved in?"

"As far as I know, someone had been renting it for the whole time. The only thing is that in the past year nobody has actually lived in it. Not since Mr. Fuentes Guerra left".

"Thank you, Julio".

"Anytime. Let me know if you need anything else", said the man and he carried on mopping.

Ángela thought about what the man had just told her while she waited for the elevator. The flat belonged to the organization and its last tenant had been a man called Fuentes Guerra. It was the name of the main character of the telenovela Amor Real. When she looked around she realized that there was a man standing next to her. She had taken the elevator with him on her first day in the apartment. He was in his forties and good looking; he wore glasses and a light blue shirt with a brown bow tie. He looked like a university professor.

"Hello", he said politely.

"Hi".

The elevator's doors opened and the man waved his hand in a gentlemanly fashion to let her in first.

"Thank you".

"I'm going to the ninth floor", he said, pressing the button.

"Mine's the eighth".

"I'm on top". The man blushed, worried about how the words had come out and quickly added, "what I mean is that you get off first".

Ángela smiled, he reminded her of Álvaro Guzmán.

"My name is Ángela, I'm a new neighbor".

The man held out his hand.

"Arturo, Arturo Barrios".

They shook hands.

The elevator reached the eighth floor and Ángela got off. The man waved, he felt embarrassed and was looking at the ground.

"Nice haircut".

"Thanks".

The doors closed and the elevator continued its way up with the man inside.

The apartment had a lot of light; it consisted of room and an open-plan kitchen with a counter that divided it from the living room. It was spacious and had a balcony that looked over the rooftops at Polanco.

She stopped at the entrance to take a look at her new haircut; her attractive neighbor's compliment confirmed that her radical change had been a good choice. She stayed looking at her reflection for a long time. The mirror's frame was slightly lopsided and she straightened it; after a moment, the mirror fell back into its original unbalance. She tried once more and the mirror insisted on falling back a few degrees. Any other human eye would have thought the incline stupid, but not hers. She brought her face to the wall and looked at it from the side to see what exactly was preventing its perfect balance. There, hiding behind the frame, she saw a tiny black object with a small cable that got lost inside the wall. A camera. She was being watched.

'Calm down', she told herself, they couldn't have noticed, they don't know that you have discovered the camera. She stood in front of the mirror and tried to fix her eyes on it; if she was being spied on, it was imperceptible. Are there more cameras in the apartment? Sure. And microphones? OK, I need to discover where they are without the people watching me noticing anything.

She went to her room and changed her clothes. She felt uncomfortable knowing that she was being observed. She put on a t-shirt and grey sweat pants that she had bought in Shasa and tied a bandana around her forehead to keep her hair out of her face; then she went into the kitchen, opened the cleaning cupboard and took out all its contents: brush, mop, hoover, cloths and cleaning products.

Ángela Madero was going to clean her whole apartment, down to the very last corner; she had all the time in the world and she would have to be very thorough. First, the bathroom. She looked at the mirror; it was fitted to the wall. Nothing there. They would not put a camera somewhere where they could not access it, she thought. She checked every corner, every tile, every drawer, every pipe, inside the shower, the bathroom seat, inside the water tank, she was cleaning everything to the inch, carefully taking apart the bathroom paper's mount. Nothing. She looked at the window; at the upper frame, there was a rail there, ready to hold a curtain. She pushed the stool under the window and started cleaning the rod. That was when she saw it; the camera and the microphone, tucked into its end. She continued cleaning and pretended she had not seen anything. Tomorrow, she would buy curtains for that rail that made no sense without them.

She had found the second camera.

She went into her room and continued cleaning every single corner thoroughly. She undid her bed and looked at the mattress; nothing there, but she saw it just as she put her pillow back into place. This one had been easier; it was in one of the lamps on the side of the bed's headboard. They had simple glass lampshades that did not obstruct their vision. If the bulbs were to blow out, you would hardly notice the glass button attached to it. Here was another thing for her shopping list; she would replace the white lampshades for bigger and more colorful ones. She kept on cleaning her entire wardrobe, down to the last drawer. In one of them, she saw the picture of her son Lucas that Laura Almillar had given her; she still found it hard to call her Teresa. She started cleaning the door's frame; she could not afford to leave a single inch unchecked.

The apartment was already fairly clean before she started cleaning it; now it looked like a brand new home.

Ángela got to the living room armed with all her cleaning tools; she started by hoovering and looking around at the walls, the sofa, the low and long table; the dining table with its four chairs, two floor lamps, a piece of furniture with the forty-inches television on top. Her eyes quickly noticed the black screen; she turned it on with the remote control. She sprayed an anti-bacterial liquid and rubbed it carefully with a bit of absorbent kitchen paper. She did not bother choosing any particular channel and left the one that had come on, Imagen TV; she was not interested in the images' contents. She continued rubbing the paper on the screen. As she wiped the screen, static electricity distorted the colors; Cristina did not care. She looked at it carefully; from that position, the monitor, which looked new, dominated the room, and the entrance to the rooms, it even had a good view of the balcony. She was sure that it was there, it must be, she nodded wordlessly; it would be harder to cover without raising any suspicions. The television was spotless; she returned to the hoover which was still on and making a lot of noise, and continued cleaning the floor energetically. A minute later, she lifted the tube with the brush, moved to one side distractedly and hit the screen hard with the brush, breaking it. The image of Carlos Arenas, Imagen TV's news presenter, became fractured.

"Chíngole, I broke it", she exclaimed, and going up to it, unplugged it.

She could not cover it up but she could change it for a new one.

It was getting dark outside and Ángela was still cleaning. There were still the kitchen and the entrance hall to go.

***

'Intelligence is not about remembering, but learning to forget'. Álvaro read the welcome words on the giant screen at Synchro. The reception hall was modern; it had exposed bricks and building materials, very industrial. Guzmán read the phrase again, 'Intelligence is not about remembering, but learning to forget'. The images accompanying the text were of people walking in the street.

According to that standard, he could not be very intelligent, since he had no intention of forgetting.

The images changed and the people walking in the street were transformed into a sequence of drones delivering Synchro boxes. The text changed too: 'The future is a combination of experiences of the past and the imagination of the present'.

A security guard watched him calmly from his wooden stand by the wide double doors. When he arrived, he was directed to a screen with a virtual girl on it that had requested information and asked for the reason of his visit; then, a barrier had opened to let him in and they asked him to wait there for someone to fetch him. Álvaro waited standing. Beside him was a blue sofa with three girls that looked as if they were going through some selection process and a man in a suit and orange tie that Guzmán thought must be a salesman, the representative of a supplier, perhaps from an office furniture company. A few seconds later, a young man in shorts and wearing a t-shirt that read 'Crazy for CDMX' appeared and asked the man to follow him. He looked completely out of place in his orange tie and Álvaro saw him causally removing his blazer as he followed the young man inside. 'He definitely was a salesman', thought Álvaro.

Julián Konks appeared through the door and lifted one hand in a kind of friendly wave.

"Mr. Guzmán, how can I help you?"

"Thank you for receiving me".

Julián held out his hand and invited him in under the attentive eyes of the security guard.

"Come on, follow me; although, I still don't know my way around this place that well. We have only just moved in".

They crossed a corridor with meeting rooms on each side. In one, the man in the orange tie revised the table under the watchful gaze of the young man in shorts.

"We can talk in here". Julián pointed at a room that read 'Somoza' on the sign. "The idea is that each room is named after a member of the organization. It makes it more personal, humanizes the place a bit, see?"

They sat at a large table with eight chairs around it.

"I have come against my lawyers' advice; they don't think it's a good idea to talk to you without the presence of other witnesses", said Konks.

"Thank you, I won't take too much of your time. I have also come against the orders of my superior. This is an unofficial visit, for personal reasons".

"Well, go on then. Although, first, I would like to express my deepest sorrow for your loss. I met your daughter the day of the presentation; she and the other boy interviewed me shortly before the...". Julián took his thumb to his mouth, tugged at his hair and pulled his right earlobe.

The series of involuntary movements did not go unnoticed by either of them.

"They are nervous tics".

"I know", said Guzmán, and he went on. "Braulio Gaytán is the name of the young man. He pushed my daughter... Rita, and in his defense, he argues that the black balls that you make are responsible for his actions".

"If you ask me, technically speaking, the behavior that we had programmed for the party had been of fun and synchronized dancing, far from any violent act. It all seems very strange".

"But, were there pushes?"

"Yes, but within the dance. Look at it this way: to tango you need to move your partner, but there is no intention of harm in the dance move. There wasn't any violent intention in that sense, I guarantee it".

Guzmán nodded. He understood his explanation.

"Could it be that there was a mistake in the microchip that he had ingested?"

"You must understand, Mr. Guzmán, that when we created Synchro we worked on a fixed device that was attached to the skin". He pointed at a scar on his arm. "Then, we changed it to an ingested device that would be eliminated after twelve hours as body waste to prevent too much dependence. During the testing period, I ingested over one hundred pills. I assure you that in that time, I did not kill anybody". He shook his head. "Synchro can change your emotions and help you do something that you wanted to do before you ingested it, but it cannot go against your will. I honestly believe that Rita's case was an accident".

"Do you mean that if Braulio had pushed her intentionally he would have been aware of what he was doing and that he would not have been under the effects of the pill?"

"Have you ever tried Synchro?"

"No, I only smoke marijuana".

"Believe me when I say that I have never tried pot. With Synchro, you remember what you do, the substance works as an intensifier and connector of emotions. You are not a zombie, you become a super human".

"Then, Braulio could have intended to kill her?"

"Not under the effects of Synchro. The enjoyment and synchronized dancing blocks any other emotions, so that these become more prominent. Then there is the thing about the dominant subject; when you take Synchro, there is a dominant subject who tends to be the leader and which imposes their wi..."

Boom!

Suddenly, three armed men burst into the room and aimed their firearms at Álvaro Guzmán. One of them lifted his badge.

"Federal Police, you are being arrested for obstruction of Justice".

They threw him against the wall, took the gun that hung from his waist and cuffed his hands behind his back. Julián watched the arrest without understanding what was going on. Outside, the group of lawyers observed the scene. Álvaro regarded the young creator.

"Thank you, Mr. Konks, for your generous time".

"I've got nothing to do with..."

"I know. Don't worry, I am used to police brutality; I have often exercised it myself".

One of the uniformed agents started reciting his rights, while the other two pulled him quickly outside the building. As they passed the entrance hall, he saw that the three girls were still waiting on the sofa, staring at their phones, and on the giant screen, he read: 'Intelligence is not about remembering, but learning to forget'.

∗∗∗

"Show Mr. Coentrao, the recording of the previous day at that same time and with the same camera".

Ramona addressed the guard in the control room; he was sat in front of a panel with at least twenty cameras. He typed a code on his keyboard and pressed the play button.

At twenty-five past five, Ramona left the room in the same white bathing robe and walked to the lift.

"Now, select the camera of the indoors pool", she ordered.

In the screen, the image of the slim woman appeared, removing her bathrobe. She was naked. She jumped into the pool and started swimming. The camera got closer to her. Whoever had been in the control room that night did not want to miss a single detail of the scene; the guard swallowed loudly.

"Ok, that's enough", said Juno Coentrao.

Ramona continued looking at the screen with the frozen image of the torsion of her body as she brought her head out of the water to breathe. It made her think of the time when at the age of thirteen, her father had given her to the cartel of the North. The cacao plantation gave in under the pressure of the coke plantations in the region. Nobody wanted to work picking the big seed when picking leaves paid double. The solution Frederick Drumpf had found to cover his debts had been to give away his daughter as payment.

Frederick Drumpf had escaped Germany at the end of the war with a loot of jewelry that he had stolen from Jewish properties as an SS official. His height, corpulence and aggressiveness had earned him the nickname 'The Monster', which, in fact, he quite liked and felt grateful for. Upon his arrival in Mexico he had found refuge in Ciudad Juarez with the intention of crossing to the United States through El Paso. He was rejected a visa due to his murky past and remained in the country managing a cacao plantation which he soon took full possession of, after the mysterious disappearance of its owners.

Accused of endless violations and crimes, he never went to jail due to the successive elimination of proof and witnesses. At the age of sixty, he had married Adalina Sotomayor, the only daughter of a landowner of the area.

Ramona Drumpf was born right at the time when 'The Monster's' business began its decline. He gave away that slender girl under the impassible gaze of her mother, who would commit suicide that very night.

Trapped in a life of rapes, beatings and drugs, Ramona understood that hardship, fights and weapons would be her only way out. An old narco who realized the girl's potential when he saw her cut the throat of a man who had insulted her, took her in and added her to his service, training her in fighting and the use of weapons. At twenty and with a huge stature for a woman, she had become the most violent hit woman in Mexico. Blonde and incredibly beautiful, she started serving Nicanor Lapesa, a minor leader of the Sinaola cartel. She spent ten years watching over Lapesa's steps until one day, while drinking coffee, she received the visit of Ambrose Levi.

He offered her to go to the United States, receive an education and obtain revenge; Ambrose understood that with a merciless woman like her, only revenge would work, so he offered her that chance. A series of deaths followed, from her father, 'The Monster', to Lapesa. As many as twenty despicable individuals dropped dead during the days following the visit, one after the other, before Ramona's eyes. Then, the woman finally felt that she had killed her past, and her future now lied among 'Los Muertos'. That was when she became infiltrated within the summit of the narcos' hierarchy.

With Juno Coentrao, the job had been easy. Trust, sex and discretion; Juno was not fond of words and she did not enjoy talk either. Silence made him feel protected; she, on the other hand, savored her revenge in the silence, taking care of every detail.

The frozen image of Ramona swimming was still on the monitor when she and Juno left the control room with the printed pictures of the two women who had killed Néstor Coentrao.

***

Nighttime at the high security penitentiary in Florence, Colorado, the ADX, referred to by Amnesty International as 'hell, but cleaner'. The only jail in the United States with capacity for four hundred and ninety prisoners. The so-called 'Alcatraz of Rocosas' has had a list of high security celebrity prisoners. Among them had been Timothy McVeigh, the perpetrator of the Oklahoma bomb that killed one hundred and seventy people, as well as some of the people involved in 9/11, such as Zacharias Moussaoui, 'Ted' Kaczynski, known as 'Una-bomber', and Dzhokhar Tsarnaev, co-perpetrator of the Boston Marathon terrorist attacks.

In the middle of the night, on a road close to the penitentiary, two vehicles with powerful speakers were playing Raining Blood by Slayer. They drove to the first protective fence; they drove fast, lifting clouds of dust and stones on those guarded roads. The loud noise of the song, together with the sound of guitars, the force of the drums and Tom Araya's voice made the peaceful county shake. The speakers of both vehicles, with their amplifiers, tweeters and sub-woofers that illuminated at the rhythm of the Thrash Metal, projected the racket into the night. An earthquake on wheels. The drivers' eardrums would have burst if it were not for the earmuffs they wore to muffle noise. The metal music sound extended across the expanse; in comparison, the sound of the sirens felt like a distant whisper.

A confused patrol car with its blue and red lights chased the two vandals around the penitentiary's surroundings. Three other vehicles left the center at full speed to support the patrol car, which was now chasing one of the noisy cars.

The center was under maximum alert.

Again and again, the two cars escaped the jail's Police. They were expert drivers.

Three minutes went by and suddenly the cars stopped. The song kept on playing. The two drivers abandoned the vehicles and threw themselves on the dusty ground that surrounded the penitentiary; the startled police agents aimed their guns at the men with the earmuffs who, lying down, waited for their arrest.

The music kept playing at an outrageous volume; it was very hard to aim at them and resist the urge to cover their ears, when they felt like they were about to explode. The policemen opened their mouths and shouted in desperation. One of the agents ran to the car with the intention of turning off the noise, but it was being played remotely. He turned the engine off but the deafening music kept playing; they started firing at the speakers in a desperate attempt to end the infernal racket.

While the bait of the moving music distracted the whole of the penitentiary's security, a drone flew up to a window, forty-two inches high and four wide. The officers looked out from their posts. The flying artifact did not have any luminous signs; a net attached to a wire slid through the window. The drone deposited its calculated load on the improvised basket: a phone and one hundred Synchro pills. The constant sound of the propellers could not be heard over the noise of the thunderous kamikazes.

Inside, a pair of hands hid the phone and the black box containing the Synchro balls that had gone undetected by the security system, under a mattress. In his cell, Aldo Ríos waited for Spring to come.

***

Carlo Stamas looked at Esther Nassar's number on his phone; he had to press the button and deliver the news. Julián and Anthony had not reached a consensus to sell their company. It had come as a surprise to him; Stamas had been convinced that the two young entrepreneurs would accept the offer. Nassar had offered him a ten million dollars incentive if he managed to get their unanimity for the sale.

Anthony Somoza did not want the money, he said, but he was ready to sell and acquire funding for other projects. Julián Konks, however, showed his most ambitious face; he knew that in four years' time, he would have earned the sum that was being offered to him now. Besides, they had created something special, personal, he explained, something that was a part of them, and he was not willing to hand that responsibility over to anyone. Somoza had said 'yes' and Konks 'no' to the billionaire proposal; a tie that meant a defeat.

Carlo Stamas looked at his phone and searched for a different contact number. He would call Ana Riccoli.

***

Ángela Madero was putting up curtains in the bathroom. She had chosen the ones with a cuff long enough to cover the support rod, hiding the camera. She had already covered with silk shawls the two lamps on her bed's headboard to soften the light's intensity and hide the camera behind a flower print, and in the living room, now stood a brand new television.

The only camera that she had left active was the one at the entrance mirror

They had called her; she was summoned at the Guadalupe Tepeyac hangar in an hour to receive a new assignment. She picked a black sweatshirt, stopped by the entrance mirror and fixed her hair at the same time as she dropped five quarter coins. They bounced off the floor and spread across the entrance parquet floor. She looked down and repositioned a few with the tip of her shoe, memorizing their exact position. She had cleaned the house thoroughly and did not want it to get dirty again in her absence; if anyone was to walk through the door, she would know. She left for her appointment with 'Los Muertos'.

***

Álvaro Guzmán sat in the interrogation room, handcuffed, when one of the policemen that had arrested him walked in accompanied by Commissioner García.

García looked at him angrily and addressed the other agent:

"Release him immediately; he is one of us, you fool". He turned to regard Guzmán while the federal policeman freed him. "And you, undisciplined asshole, I told you not to get involved in this shit and you won't obey my orders, you're a fucking asshole, always high..."

"I haven't smoked in three weeks".

"I don't care if it's been three weeks or three years, you are crazy", said Commissioner Guzmán pulling his hair in exasperation. "You have my permission to go home and take some time off to mourn your daughter and get high as a kite, but stop fucking around with me. You are a police officer, Álvaro, and you must obey my orders or they are going to fuck us both up".

García got closer to Guzmán's face, menacingly.

"You are a lucky guy; the judge has dismissed Attorney Aster's accusation". García pointed his finger at him. "But, I want you to give me your badge and weapon right now; take two weeks off to rest, Álvaro, and stop fucking around".

Álvaro left the police station and ordered an Uber from his phone's app; his car was at Synchro's parking lot; he would pick it up later. Two minutes later the appointed car arrived; he was going home.

Sat in the back of the car, he unbuttoned his shirt; there, hidden, was the miniature microphone that he had used to record his conversation with Julián Konks. There were a few things he wanted to listen to again.

"Guzmán has gone free".

The special FBI agent who had arrested him and then accompanied Commissioner García to the interrogations room, spoke into his phone while he watched Guzmán ride the Uber and leave the police station.

***

Don Nassar and Juno Coentrao were in the large living room of the drug king's house. On the table were two low definition pictures of Teresa Mendoza and Ángela Madero.

"Have you found out anything?"

"Nothing, they aren't in any of our archives. The only thing we've got is a certain resemblance to two dead people".

"A resemblance to two dead people? Interesting".

Juno pointed at Ángela.

"In fact, this one here corresponds to the policewoman who died at our house..."

"I remember that", said Don thoughtful.

"On the other hand, I think there is a spy among us. My father's visit to La Hacienda was known to only a handful of people and his murder was not improvised. It was all closely planned; we have found masks with oxygen bottles at the bottom of the channel, then there's the pick-up drone... We have their clothes, we know what shoe size they wear, we are running DNA tests with everyone", said Juno.

"Any suspects?"

"Yes, I've got one... Ramona".

Don nodded.

"Eliminate her".

"No, not yet. We need to know who she is working for and besides, it will be spring in three days".

Don nodded with a smile.

Esther Nassar was trying on her wedding dress, she stood sideways, her belly was starting to show.

Tucked away in his side, as he walked up and down the high security penitentiary, a prisoner carried the black box with the Synchro pills. As he passed a uniformed guard, he handed him the box discretely. The box would soon reach its objective.

*****

7. OBJECTIVE

*It is the end to which an action is directed. It is also the
result of a series of processes. Equally, an objective person
is not influenced by feelings in their value judgments. In the
visual field, it is a lens that helps focusing correctly.*

In ten minutes, the doors of the third room where
Braulio Gaytan's trial for involuntary manslaughter was
taking place, would open. At the tribunal's door, and inside, at the trial's room, a crowd had already formed waiting
to enter the place where the public hearing was taking place.

Journalists from every channel wandered around
the building's marbled corridors, hunting for the day's
protagonists. At least one hundred reporters got accredited
that very morning. The arrival of one of the day's protagonists
meant a mess of cameras and microphones fighting for the
best shot and words that to feed their daily news. They had
already surrounded Julián Konks a few minutes earlier as he
left his car in the company of Ana, his wife, and a lawyer.
Julián had worn a rehearsed smile and refused to talk to
the press; he would talk to them and make a statement after
testifying in the hearing, following his lawyers' advice.

He was waiting with Ana in a small office. They had
been placed there to avoid the swarms of journalists who
were frantically chasing after a few words from the, now
extremely famous, firm director.

Ana went up to a table that had a stack of magazines; her husband's face was in the cover of Time magazine.

"Did you know about this?" she asked putting it up for him to see.

"They took that picture three weeks ago".

"You didn't tell me anything".

"Lately, they have been interviewing and taking pictures of me every day, it's become tiresome".

"I think there is a lack of communication between us", said Ana distractedly while she flicked through it.

"No, Ana, it's just that things are moving extremely fast and they are so many that…"

"Let's not start with the excuses. Within marriage, communication must flow; all marriages talk. All, except us".

"Honestly, Ana, I don't want to argue with you again", Julián went up to Ana with the intention of kissing her. "Don't be annoyed, we are lucky people".

She offered her cheek and continued flicking through the magazine without stopping at any particular page.

"Carlo mentioned that you have decided not to sell your part".

Julián looked at her in surprise.

"Carlo? Why does he have to discuss that stuff with you?"

"Carlo is a good friend and he wants what's best for you, for us".

Julián began his series of tics and sat on a chair wearing a worried expression.

"You're going to have to be careful now, you don't want your hand shooting from your mouth to your hair and ear and back during the trial. You do that when you get nervous".

Even though he was perfectly aware of his tics, it annoyed him when others reminded him of them.

Silence fell in the waiting room until one of the lawyers arrived to collect them.

"Ready? Let's go… you know the drill; limit yourself to the phrases that we have rehearsed and do not try to improvise. Good luck, Mr. Konks."

Julián and Ana left the crowd of cameras and microphones to reach the courtroom's doors. When they walked in, one hundred faces turned to watch him enter. Julián sat on a chair that had been saved for him; Ana sat on the row behind. Konks noticed Álvaro Guzmán sitting behind; he was looking at the front expectantly. Braulio Gaytán entered through a side door to the right, accompanied by two police agents. He was wearing a dark suit with a dark blue tie that his lawyers had chosen to give him a more serious and adult-like presence. He did not look to the sides; he remained sitting with his gaze on the wooden table. A minute later, the jury entered, twelve women and men who quickly sat on the two lines of chairs to the left of the courtroom. Finally, Joshua Osborne, the district judge, arrived and the whole room stood up.

It would be the trial's last session. Throughout the entire week, witnesses and experts had given their testimony in that same room about what had happened on the evening in question.

"The session begins", announced Judge Osborne and he banged his mallet. Everyone sat down. "The turn is for the defense".

"We would like to call Julián Konks forward".

***

Anthony Somoza sat, absorbed by the codes on his screen.

"Anthony, can I talk to you for a minute?"

Anthony seemed surprised by the unexpected visit and he pressed the button that turned the screens black. Carlo Stamas walked into his office.

"Sorry to interrupt".

"Don't worry, come in". Anthony looked at the screens; every single one was off. "I'm making some adjustments to the security system... It's a very delicate and completely confidential task".

"If you wish, we could install a code system at your door, if it's going to make you feel safer". Carlo Stamas was still holding the door open.

"No, I don't believe in physical doors. They can all be opened. However, cyber doors are much safer, only a handful of people can open them. Sit down, Carlo".

Stamas sat on one of the chairs that were arranged in a circle against the wall. As he sat, his gun became visible upon his waist.

"Carlo, I never thought to ask, why the gun?"

Carlo opened his jacket so that he could have a good look at it.

"Why I carry this? I admit it, I think I'm a coward; I think that I've been afraid of absolutely everything ever since I was a child", he raised his eyebrows. "I don't often talk about this". He paused, deep in thought. "I remember how my father used to beat me and my mother when he got back home drunk, and I remember that she would hide me behind her to protect me. Then, one day, she bought a firearm and when one evening my father arrived home in his car, and we were trembling with fear, she shot at the door without even looking and we heard a cry from the other side. She had hit him. We stayed crouching together for a few minutes. When we went out, my father was no longer there; there was a trail of blood leaving the door. The car wasn't there either and he never came back. I think he believed that if he ever did return, he would end up dead".

Carlo Stamas took the weapon from his waist, Anthony looked at him, scared.

"Don't worry, it's unloaded; I've already told you that I'm a coward. I never carry it loaded; it's something psychological. Neither have I ever come across my father again, and I doubt I ever will".

He placed it back in its holster.

"I have told Esther Nassar what your answer was; she is not the kind of person to settle for a no, but I told her anyway. They are people with a lot of power and Synchro can become something truly big, massive, and they are not keen of sharing... Esther wants to talk to you alone. She is worried... about the future. I must confess that I don't feel very comfortable with what's going on either".

"Today is confessions day", Anthony said lifting his palms.

"Yes, you both created something very special and that something now belongs to the world".

"Very philosophical, Carlo; we are aware of the power involved in Synchro". Somoza smiled with spite. "I know Julián well enough to know that he will not change his mind, for now".

"Exactly, for now... But, Julián without you is the equivalent to my unloaded gun, and we both know that". Carlo rubbed his chin with his palm. "I think she would allow a few changes in Synchro".

"Who would?"

"Esther Nassar".

Anthony Somoza gazed at his sneakers, lost in thought.

"Arrange a meeting with Miss. Nassar".

Carlo Stamas stood up and left.

Anthony looked at the screens, he pressed a button and they turned on at once; he introduced the password and entered the source code. He knew where he had to go. He opened a door that Julián had named Ana and which activated the shutting down and restarting systems; he had attached another folder called Nostradamus. He knew that Julián would never check that code; his mind was elsewhere.

Drones came in and out of the delivery hangar; the company was a success. He had an important part of the shares, but right now, he had absolute power. Today he would go home early; he had invited many friends over, a men-only party.

***

Julián limited his speech to the script that his lawyers had given him. They had never had an accident of the sort. He had not seen what happened because he was busy with the press. Synchro was safe to use. He had been with the two vloggers a while before the accident; he explained that under the effects of the drug all humans concentrated on the programmed effect. He tried fixing his gaze on Álvaro Guzmán, who was listening attentively to his explanation. He saw him taking a few notes while he spoke.

It was Braulio Gaytan's turn.

When it came to the alleged offender's turn to testify for the death of Rita Guzmán, the room filled with loud muttering. The judge ordered silence under the threat of expulsion. Braulio had many followers among the audience; young people who had come to support their hero, put unjustly in jail. Braulio directed a smile at them before he sat down to testify, to the judge's right. First up were the prosecutors and later, his own defense lawyer. Braulio's answers were composed by monosyllables followed by short sentences, 'it was an accident', 'I loved her', 'we had all taken the Synchro pill, everyone except her', 'it was a sort of dance step, an innocent push, playful, prudent'. But it was his last sentence which made everyone fall silent: 'I feel bad, we were expecting a baby; we were both very happy about the arrival of our son', he said, in tears.

Then came the prosecutors' final allegations, followed by the defense's. Finally, district judge Osborne ordered the jury to leave to deliberate and adjourned until the announcement of the judgment.

Julián Konks believed that Braulio's last sentence had deeply affected the jury members. He searched for Álvaro Guzmán and saw him leaving the courtroom.

***

The appointment was at an old movie studio in the Guadalupe Tepeyac district, the same hangar where they had put her to the test by asking her to kill her ex-boyfriend. As she arrived in an Uber, Ángela Madero noticed that there were four cars parked outside. She recognized two of them: the red sport BMW that belonged to Ambrose Levi, Teresa's white Range Rover which she had seen during her initial confinement; the other two were a Cadillac V and a blue Rav4 that stood in her way.

Teresa was waiting for her at the door.

"How's your new life?"

"Getting used to it", answered Ángela.

"You'll manage", said Teresa with conviction.

Ángela nodded and shrugged, it was her only option. There was no doubt that the woman standing before her was not the same woman she had met years ago. She was not the

Laura that she once believed to be dead. No, this Teresa was different, colder. 'She has not even asked me about my new haircut', she thought while she followed her steps into that bleak place. 'If she hasn't asked about my hair that's because she'd already seen it'. It did not seem strange to her; Teresa must be aware of the cameras in the house. Ángela did not need to talk to discover the other side of silence.

Behind a large metallic door, in a separate room, they found Ambrose Levi in front of a screen; a bit further away were six people, four women and two men. They were sitting in what looked like a control center. Ángela noticed a link to street cameras and monitors that looked like radars used to track objectives; she wondered if that was also the place where they controlled the activity in her house.

"Hello, Ángela", said Ambrose Levi standing up from his desk.

Ángela's gaze was still on the control room.

"I imagine there are many questions that you would like to ask".

"Not that many; for now it's just one", said Ángela pointing to the room. "Where is the other door?"

"What?" asked Teresa.

"Yes, there are nine people here and there are four vehicles outside. Where are the other cars? I doubt our organization has a carpooling service to reduce the employees' travel expenses. And I assume the Rav 4", she pointed at a set of keys on Ambrose' desk, "is going to be for me; the plate has just been registered and I noticed that the back seats still have plastic on them; it hasn't been used yet. Moving around in an Uber leaves a trace which can endanger the security of this place. Finally, I must assume that there is an evacuation plan in place in case of emergency".

"Ángela Madero, always a step ahead", Ambrose looked at her with surprise and gestured at the wall. "That's a sliding door. It connects this place to an adjoined warehouse".

Ambrose invited her to sit down.

"From this space, we track the movements of over one hundred objectives who we consider dangerous for the State. It is our job to..."

"And who decides on the danger that these objectives entail?" asked Ángela, nodding at the control room.

"We are our national security's last resource, we receive information and orders; we only move into action when circumstances require it and Justice is unable to act. Let's just say that from here, we monitor those people who are out free and could be causing trouble. I receive the orders", he said, and waived his hand at the phone lying on his desk, "and we plan their execution".

"Are you telling me that we don't actually know the person giving us the orders?" asked Ángela with sarcasm.

"That's right; we make sure that decision and execution are separate".

"That makes us mere executioners, murderers at the State's service, dispensable, unable to form our own judgments".

"Our role becomes important at times when the Rule of Law is unable to defend itself by legal means".

Ángela stared at Ambrose and then looked at the phone again.

"I just hope that at least someone up there respects the law; because down here we sure don't".

Ambrose turned the computer's screen to her and pressed play. Ángela watched the images and then looked at Ambrose in confusion. The person in the video was pointing his gun at the filmmaker and at a large crowd of people who were filming him with their phones, and she knew him very well. It was Álvaro Guzmán.

"We have been following this objective for the past months and are now waiting for confirmation in case we proceed to his execution"

"The man who you are calling an objective happens to be a good policeman and a good friend of mine".

"He was a good friend of yours", intervened Teresa, who had remained silent the whole time. "We do not conserve any friends from our previous lives".

The use of the past tense irritated Ángela.

"I know Álvaro Guzmán and I am certain that he is not a threat to anyone", said Ángela defiantly, her gaze shifting from one to the other. She understood by their looks that she did not have a choice in that either. She waited. "Now, if that objective must be eliminated, I would rather it was me who did it. I know him well".

Teresa looked at Ambrose with an 'I told you she could do it' sort of look.

Angela's tone had been convincing. She would never kill Álvaro, but if they had to follow him and prepare his death she would rather be in the front line. She would have to buy some time and discover who was behind this whole organization, who made the decisions. At least now she knew that Ambrose was not that person, he was just a messenger. "Los Muertos" played the role of underground executioners, they were just sewer rats fed by an invisible hand; she was sure that there had to be a puppet master pulling the strings and moving its marionettes at will, according to its own laws.

The phone started to ring. Ambrose took it from the table and tapped the screen to pick up the call.

"Hello?..". His gaze shifted to Angela for a moment and then he turned away.

But what caught Ángela's attention was the journey his gaze traced before he left to attend the call in a more intimate place. It had happened in a few fractions of a second, a subtle movement of his eyes sweeping a corner of the room. Ángela waited and then casually looked at that same point.

A small camera kept watch from that angle; someone in the distance had been present during their conversation.

Teresa walked with Ángela to the parking lot where the new dark blue Rav4 awaited.

"Do you really believe that Álvaro can be a threat to anyone?" Ángela asked Teresa, as she opened the car.

"I don't ask myself that sort of questions. I assured Ambrose that he could trust you with the job, so you shouldn't be asking them either".

"But if we are the good guys then we must ask them; we aren't robots following orders, we are humans that..."

"We are dead and the dead don't ask questions. We simply follow orders".

"You know what, Teresa? I much preferred my friend Laura. This zombie life of yours seems like bullshit to me. I used to have a friend who believed in the divide between good and evil".

"That Laura died a long time ago in an explosion".

"But did she die, or did she just forget?"

Teresa remained thoughtful for a moment.

"Yes, I think she died, but it doesn't matter. If you forget you die just the same". She shrugged, not wanting to continue with the argument, and right before turning to leave, added, "Although, be very careful; we have been informed that Coentrao's people have our images and that they are looking for us".

"Now, that's a relief. At least for once I am the prey and the hunter is someone else".

She got into her car, started the engine and left the place. Ángela looked at her colleague from the wing mirror. Teresa stood watching her for a short while before going back into the warehouse. Back home she studied the dashboard as well as the inside of the car; she was sure that they had installed a localizer.

When the elevator's doors slid open, she saw the note stuck on her apartment's door: 'It's Arturo, your neighbor. Here is my phone number in case you ever want to grab a coffee. 6574667708. XX' The small yellow post-it made her smile. It shocked her to realize how long it had been since she last smiled. She opened the door and checked the coins on the entrance floor; nobody had been there. She made a visual check of the places where she had found the intruding cameras; everything seemed to be in order. Then, she walked out to the balcony and activated the pay-as-you-go phone that she had bought with cash at Verizon; she had taken money out of a cash machine so that they would not trace her payment. She was almost certain that she had not been followed.

She called Arturo Barrios, her lovely neighbor. She needed a distraction. They arranged to meet in an hour and walk over to a Hindu restaurant that was relatively close to their blocks.

As they left, they bumped into Julio, the cleaner, who was already leaving in his car. He gave them a friendly wave and a smile of complicity. The Polanco area was good for walks.

Arturo was attractive, friendly and a true gentleman; he seemed shy and said that he was a Literature professor at UACM and that he had separated from his partner three years ago. He did not have any children.

"How about you? Are you single?"

For a moment, Ángela wondered what to say. She could say anything, make up an entire life for herself.

"Yes, I was married for many years, without children. Importation and exportation is my job, so, you know, I travel a lot and I was not willing to renounce to my independence; that's the price women pay for equality".

"It's a high price. And, have you never felt...?"

"If you are going to ask about maternal instinct or compromise, my answer is yes, I have felt it many times, but it takes two to build a family and that other guy has not appeared yet".

She knew that what she said was true. She, Cristina Herrera, had built a family that had lasted ten years with her son Lucas.

Suddenly, she felt terrible for having denied the existence of her son and a nauseous feeling overcame her.

"Are you alright?"

No, she felt horrible, but she could not possibly tell him.

"It must have been the air conditioning", she said the first thing that came to her mind.

When they arrived at the restaurant she apologized and went to the bathroom where she spilled a few tears. That whole thing about forgetting her past was harder than she thought. She did not enjoy lying to a nice man who was trying to initiate a sincere friendship with her.

She hardly ate anything; she was no longer hungry and regretted being there at all. While her companion rambled on about Shakespeare, Cervantes, Sergio Pitol and replied to a message or two from his students, her mind was occupied with the image of Álvaro Guzmán and her heart with Lucas, her son.

Ángela apologized saying that she suddenly felt ill and they rushed back home. It had not turned out to be the romantic dinner she had imagined, nor had it been any fun; she felt sorry for Arturo, who had behaved like a true gentleman throughout the entire evening. They waited in silence while the elevator went up and Ángela promised another dinner soon; he said he would be glad to repeat any time. Charming, she thought and kissed him goodbye on the lips.

As she introduced the key into the keyhole, she had a premonition, and entered the apartment looking at the floor.

Someone had been there in her absence; the coin closest to the door had moved a couple of centimeters. She did not turn on the lights; she went straight to her nightstand and took out the picture Teresa had given her of Lucas and Albi while he was in the hospital. It was the only thing she had left of her old life. Then, she walked to the living room's sofa and lied down. She fell asleep with the picture cradled in her arms.

***

Álvaro Guzmán opened the door to his apartment and gazed at the white box on the table; he had not smoked since Rita's death. He looked around his house as if seeing it for the first time after a long period of absence. The apartment did not have many things, there was nothing superfluous, everything was good quality and very tidy. Without colors, it all looked a shade of grey. He turned his gaze to the suitcases, still waiting for their owners.

He had decided to go straight back to his apartment after trial, which had lasted nearly all morning. Now that he was there, he felt a bit odd, disoriented.

"Is that you, Álvaro?" The image of Rita materialized above the illuminated cylinder.

Surprised, Guzmán looked at the AI invention named Betty that had the appearance and voice of his daughter.

"Yes, Betty. To be honest, I can't seem to get used to this".

"I hope I didn't scare you. Do you need anything? Is there anything I could do for you? Maybe I could play some music".

"OK, play some Bruce".

"Springsteen?"

"In this house, Betty, we only have Bruce Springsteen, there is no need to ask that question every single time".

"Understood, Álvaro".

Dancing in the dark came on and before Springsteen even started singing, Guzmán heard three knocks on the door. He opened it; outside stood Gloria, who walked in without an invitation.

"It has been three days since I last heard of you", she said hotly. "At least let me know that you're alright. You know how I worry about you".

She was wearing shorts and an AC-DC t-shirt.

"Gloria, I don't want to argue with you now".

The music kept on playing in the background. Gloria's gaze followed the sound to the dim bluish light of the cylinder.

"Betty, turn off that music", she ordered.

"Of course, Gloria".

The music stopped.

"What, now you give the orders in my house?" Álvaro exclaimed. "You tell my..."

The question hung in midair until Betty said:

"You can refer to me as your virtual assistant".

Álvaro looked from one to the other.

"This is my house and you cannot go around telling my virtual assistant what to do".

Gloria moved between Álvaro and the virtual assistant.

"Look, Álvaro, it would be best if we ended this right now, I'm leaving..."

"I wish you a good trip, Gloria", said Betty.

"Betty, I'm leaving forever. This is the end".

"Gloria, your voice sounds considerably angry".

"Betty, shut down", said Guzmán.

"Betty, don't shut down. You have every right to know what's going on here", cried Gloria, antagonizing Álvaro, who looked completely shocked.

"Betty? Gloria, have you gone mad?" Álvaro pointed at the image with his daughter's appearance. "She is... a voice, an artificial sound, for fuck's sake. Goddamn-it! It's an artificial fucking voice!"

Gloria's eyes were still fixed on Guzmán.

"Who do you think you are? Don't offend Betty!"

"He is not offending me. I have been programmed not to feel offended. But, thank you for your understanding, Gloria".

Guzmán looked at the artificial intelligence confused, lost in that mad argument.

"Incredible... this has got to be a joke", he said, looking at both in astonishment. "This reminds me of my marriage".

Gloria put her hands on her hips.

"I can't believe you are coming up with that now... all that marijuana has fogged your brain". She walked to the door, opened it, slammed it shut and screamed from the corridor, "Asshole!"

"Álvaro, I think she is very angry", said Betty.

Guzmán leaned on the wall.

Music started blasting from the apartment next door, then, he heard three loud bangs on the wall and shouts that sounded like insults.

"Betty, turn on the television and disappear".

"As you wish, but I would advise you to..."

"Betty, I don't want your advice. You are the only person I can tell to fuck off without feeling regrets... so... Fuck off, Betty!"

The CNN news channel showed images of Julián Konks walking into the courtroom and the voice of the presenter saying:

"...these are not chemically bound substances; you swallow it, it creates an electric alteration chosen from the device to achieve the desired emotional reaction. It could be extreme happiness, creativity, euphoria, etc., and it does not have any side effects in the organism, nor does it cause a dependence".

Guzmán thought that the trial would be the news of the day in all channels; Synchro's legalization was at play. Almost every specialist intervening in the program agreed that the technological drug was harmless; they defended its innovative way of connecting people and how it was capable of offering personal experiences in communion with a world that was increasingly dehumanized. Everything about it was positive. A PRI congressman appeared on the screen announcing that the Congress had created a committee to study the legality of Synchro and that they would reach a decision in two months, which he believed would be positive.

Guzmán felt like was drowning; his daughter had been a small stone in the company's path and Braulio Gaytán's trial an anecdote which no one would talk about. He went out on the balcony and breathed into the fresh air. Then, he walked back inside, opened the white cannabis box and started rolling a joint, hoping that it would calm his anxiety. He looked at the television. They were still discussing Synchro and had put an image of Braulio Gaytán on the screen. It seemed like he had sent a statement from jail in which he apologized for his girlfriend's death, who he said to be deeply in love with and with whom he had expected a baby. The news said that he was ready to use his time in jail to talk about the excellence of the penitentiary system, and become an example of reinsertion and good will as someone repentant of their mistake. Not a single politician would be able to resist a proposal of the kind. The disciplinary regime seen from a well-known youtuber's angle, delivering a positive image of their management; this was surely a gift for Aster.

"Betty, turn off the television".

"As you wish, Álvaro".

With the television off, the music next door sounded even louder.

He left his apartment and walked to Roxy, a bar in the area that gave refuge to old and solitary rock stars.

A hundred meters away from him, a dark blue Toyota started its engine and followed.

***

Juno sat with his legs crossed and his calf resting on his knee. Deep in the armchair with the red prints, he watched Ramona undress. She was taking off her clothes meticulously, coldly, the way she moved could not be considered sensuous or have any effect on Juno. She undid her bra and showed her breasts like someone showing their gun after a shooting. Once she was fully naked, she took the gun that had been resting on the table while she removed her clothes and turned to regard Juno. He had barely moved in his armchair.

Juno thought that what aroused him the most about that woman was her coldness. She had been like that since he first met her, an agreement of payment in exchange for complete surrender to his wishes, no negatives, no excuses, twenty-four hours of dedication to his protection, to give her life for him, her body too was to be at his service with no contradictions, no emotions, giving him everything she had without seeking personal satisfaction. Don's orders had been clear: remove her, kill her. Juno knew that Don was watching them; in fact, they were probably being watched at that very moment.

She was on her knees on the bed; fully naked and with the semiautomatic gun on her side. Juno uncrossed his legs and stood up. He unbuttoned his white shirt and dropped it on the armchair, then he went up to the bed where Ramona was waiting. The young woman with her athletic body and blonde hair, lied down on her back. Juno's hand slid down his bodyguard's arm until it reached the cold metal that she was holding. He took the weapon and checked if the safety was on; with his thumb, he unlocked the catch and freed the weapon. He looked at her, trying to discover a shadow of unease, of fear. Ramona's cold expression did not shift and her gaze stayed firmly on her boss' eyes.

He rested the weapon's barrel on her nipple, which hardened with the cold touch; then, the metal slid down her skin to reach her other breast, where Juno moved the gun softly. Without touching the areola, he introduced the metal's mouth in the brown bud. He gave Ramona a sadistic smile. His index finger kept the tension on the trigger.

He then moved the gun to the center and started moving it down, softly brushing the hairs on her skin. It went past her navel and descended from her belly to play with her pubis.

Juno raised his eyebrows at the woman who was at his mercy and still would not change her expression. Ramona's eyes were fixed on the armed man.

Juno leaned closer and kissed her introducing his tongue in her mouth at the same time as he introduced the cold barrel inside her; that was the only time she shuddered with a weak spasm and arched her back slightly.

***

It was the time when they let prisoners out at the courtyard of the ADX prison in Florence, Colorado. The sky was covered by clouds and although it had not started raining yet, a few drops announced a stormy evening. Aldo Ríos looked sideways at the clouds covering the sun and then directed his gaze to the walled space, crowded with people in the compulsory orange clothes. At the top of the six towers that surrounded them were armed agents. Once the two hours of outdoors time were over, three of those towers would be emptied. There was no need to keep watch of a space that would remain unoccupied until the following morning.

In a corner, a group of prisoners exercised lifting massive weights; some had taken their t-shirts off, revealing disproportionate muscles. The two basketball pitches were crowded with prisoners fighting for the ball between shouts and laughter. One of the teams had gone shirtless to differentiate themselves from the others. A small group race-walked along the wall, where one hundred people stood scattered in groups or alone. The courtyard was an arid cement field with leafless orange tree trunks.

A man with a shaved head and a large tattoo going up his neck walked past and quickly handed Aldo a small box which he immediately hid inside the elastic band of his jail trousers. As the man walked away, Aldo looked around searching for another prisoner who was wearing an orange cap. He nodded discretely at him.

Twenty minutes later, before going back to their cells, there would be an aleatory search and every man would have to go through the metal detector. The man in the orange cap went under the arch with the mobile phone that had the Synchro app hidden in between his legs. The arch did not detect it. One million dollars waited for him in a briefcase once he finished his job that night.

He slid the phone into Aldo's hand before going back into his cell and received a black ball in exchange which he swallowed without hesitation.

By then, the box would already be in the kitchen, where trays full of brownies waited in the oven. Minutes later, a pair of hands would diligently introduce a single ball in each portion. One hundred in total. In fifteen minutes the guard's lunch round would begin. There were three lunch sittings to feed one hundred men; the entire number of employees in charge of security during the day shift at the penitentiary.

They opened the doors to the dining room and the employees of the high security prison started walking in. Every portion of the chocolate dessert waited in its plate at the end of the food line. It was everybody's favorite, they all loved the taste of the chocolate in their mouths.

The officers walked along with their trays and chose their dishes for the day; then, they sat down in groups, occupying ten of the long dining room tables, and chatted and ate.

Aldo sat up in his bed and took the phone device that was tucked under his pillow. He switched it on. The Synchro app appeared on the small screen, just as his lawyer had indicated it would during his last visit. The radius of the frequency would be short so he would have to proceed little by little. His first step would be getting out of his cell. Three cells down was the man in the orange cap, the first key to leave the high security jail.

In the app, he pressed the 'wild sex' button.

One minute later, he heard his accomplice's moans. There were a few laughs and comments from other convicts who were hearing the racket. What was essential to the plan was that one of the jail employees guarding their corridor had also ingested one of the Synchro pills with his brownie. He waited.

He heard the sound of doors and hurried steps down the main corridor.

Someone opened his cell door.

As he got out he saw two of the stocky guards rolling around on the ground, kissing and touching each other passionately. Next to him was the man in the orange cap, two uniformed feet stuck out of his cell. A murmur spread inside the penitentiary and grew into shouts and howls from the prisoners.

Second step, synchronization. Aldo looked at the screen and pressed a blue button as he walked towards the control room of the high security pavilion. Inside, a uniformed woman pointed at her colleague with her gun. She was scared and kept calling him by his name, 'Bill'. Bill was on the floor touching his genitals desperately and she did not understand what was going on. When the two prisoners neared the bulletproof glass, the officer who was on the ground stopped moving. That was as far as the frequency had reached, thought Aldo.

The uniformed woman looked at the two convicts at the other side of the glass in confusion. She had stopped aiming at her colleague. Aldo Ríos looked at the man in the orange cap who was standing to his right and was staring blankly ahead. He made a fist and raised his arm up to the man's head, pretending to shoot him with an imaginary trigger. The man in the cap mimicked the movement pointing at the guard who was under the effects of Synchro with an imaginary gun. Then, the uniformed man too mirrored his movements and aimed at his colleague, in a mortal chain reaction. But his gun was solid and real. He fired.

Bang!

Aldo pretended to press a button and started a new chain reaction. His accomplice repeated the movement and was followed by the guard that had just murdered his colleague. The door to the gallery opened.

Third stage: unity.

***

"Are you sure you want to go on your own?" Ramona walked naked to the bathroom while Juno adjusted his thin, black tie. They had just made love.

He had just told her that he would pick up Aldo alone; he did not wish to attract the DEAs attention. Ramona did not show any signs of annoyance or opposition; she just wanted to confirm that Juno had stopped trusting her.

"Yes, we can't take any more risks. You will wait for us on the plane".

Ramona got into the luxurious shower and opened the tap, then, she turned to look at the door and saw Juno next to the clothes that she had left on the white chair; he had a phone in his hand. The blonde woman got back in the shower and let the water fall on her body for a few moments and then left the shower wrapped in a towel.

Juno stood in front of the mirror. Ramona looked at her clothes and at her phone, right where she had left it. She knew that the price of distrust was death. Juno was just waiting for some sort of confirmation to end her service. His father's death had brought change to their relationship; the sex, which he practiced as an exercise of subjugation and serfdom, was even more violent than before. Juno was a predator and he wanted Ramona's continuous submission and predisposition. He felt aroused when he subjugated the cold and proud woman who protected him twenty-four hours a day.

Ramona started to dress in silence, she adjusted her holster and checked her weapon before introducing it in the place beside her breast.

***

Carlo Stamas played with his tongue in between the lips of the laughing woman, who was trying to bite him in a sensual game of wordless breaths.

He had received a text message summoning him at a small bar in Polanco at 14.30h, a place where they had already met a few times before. He could not possibly reject an invitation of the sort.

Punctual, they had chatted and enjoyed two glasses of mescal. Thirty minutes later, she asked him to go with her to Las Alcobas, where she had booked room 212. It was the city's most expensive hotel; a few hours there cost a minimum of seven thousand pesos.

Carlo had three grams of cocaine on him which he distributed into six lines on the white bathroom counter. He leaned into them holding the small metallic tube that he used to snort the white powder. She had already snorted two of the lines and was dipping her finger into a third one, rubbing the stimulating substance onto her labia, so that he would see it and feel aroused. She washed her hands. He put his unloaded gun on a black shelf next to a folded towel and watched the erotic spectacle of the woman rubbing her powdered finger in between her legs. Carlo snorted three of the lines with the aid of the metallic tube that accompanied him everywhere, and brushed his gums after rubbing the leftovers on them. She looked at him in the mirror's reflection, naked from the waist up.

"Why don't we use Synchro?" she asked.

"I'm old school. I prefer chemicals and the surprises of the white powder", he replied.

Ana Riccoli was lying down on the white Egyptian cotton bed covers, moaning. Carlo knew her well, he knew exactly how to satisfy Julian Konks' young wife. He slid his tongue along her skin until he reached her feet. With his knees on the bed, the lawyer started moving his finger tips on the open thighs of the woman who he had once counted among his lovers. Now, she was back.

"I couldn't wait to see you again", she said, holding his hand and taking it in between her legs.

Carlo leaned in and touched with his lips the place where she had rubbed the cocaine powder. He lost himself in his old lover's pleasure.

"We must stand by each other in the future", said Ana while Carlo busied himself with her. "There are many things happening now and we need to stick together through the whole thing, Carlo".

Carlo stopped, he lifted his head and stroked her lips with his fingertips.

"Tell me, Ana. You haven't brought me here for an afternoon of carefree sex, have you?" he said with an ironic smile. "You know, just two good friends having sex, and when we are done each to our own and nothing ever happened her. What do you want?"

He sat up on the bed and looked at her expectantly. Ana leaned her back against the bedhead, covered herself with the bed sheet and looked out the window.

"I am worried about the decisions that are being made…"

"You shouldn't be", he interrupted. "You have more money than you will ever be able to spend".

"But Julián won't let me give him my advice; he is making some decisions that I…"

"I am sorry to contradict you on this point; I believe your husband is one of the most intelligent people I have ever come across; regardless of whether we agree or not with his decisions. And besides, there is also Anthony's opinion…"

"The darky?"

Carlo looked at her and sighed.

"Ana, he's a genius…"

"They both are!" she cried angrily. She stood up and walked over to the large window, leaning her head against the glass that separated the room from the balcony. "All these geniuses just give me headaches".

The lawyer walked up to her, conciliatory, and hugged her.

"Mrs. Konks, think about it this way. If you remain at your husband's side, you will lead a life full of luxury in which you will be able to fulfill any of your wishes, finance any businesses you want. You will have it all".

She turned away.

"I already have all of that".

"Then, what is it that you want?"

Unexpectedly, Ana Riccoli pushed Carlo onto the bed.

"Wrong question. It's not about what I want to have, what I could have, but what I could become".

She leaned down in between Carlo's legs.

***

Julián Konks checked the time on the extra-slim phone that the company Huawei had sent him as a gift. It was 16.30h. The Chinese company was trying to sign a strategic agreement with Synchro to allow its introduction in the banned territory.

The young businessman stood in his dressing room. He slid a wooden panel open to reveal his clothes and eyed the perfectly hung shirts, organized in a color pattern. Then, he opened the two remaining sliding doors. He realized that all the clothes he kept in his wardrobe were new and had been bought by his wife. Nothing there had a history, nor did it relate to him in any way. He moved to the right, where he kept his sports clothes, ironed and carefully folded. He was searching for something specific. There it was, right at the back, hidden. Julián smiled and put on his Real Madrid t-shirt with the number ten and his name printed at the back.

An impressive black SUV with tinted windows waited at his front door to take him to the office. A driver and an escort accompanied him everywhere. His face had become incredibly famous worldwide and his presence no longer went unnoticed. His firm resolution not to have a bodyguard had dissolved after an incident at the entrance of a movie theater that he had gone to with Ana. They had hoped to enjoy a calm evening, far from the media's attention. The trigger had been a young man who recognized him and asked to take a selfie with him. He accepted politely and all of a sudden, there twenty people surrounding him and shouting, trying to shake his hand, and those twenty people soon grew into an incontrollable crowd. Ana had started to shout, overwhelmed by the crowd that trapped them and the mess of hands that tried to reach them. He was a popular person. When, finally, he managed to leave, his shirt was ripped and his mind set on taking measures to make himself hard to recognize: sunglasses, cap, dark windows and escorts twenty-four hours a day. His life had changed forever.

17:46h. Julián walked into his office: a spacious, white room, with a white table in its center, six chairs to each side and a big screen at one end which he used to work on. He checked his smartphone; he hadn't heard anything from Ana, no text messages. The silence would have once been strange, but it had recently become the norm; the past days had been full of tensions. Ana's insistence on taking control over all his personal decisions as well as those concerning Synchro, had distanced them. He would try to talk to her that night and propose a reconciliation. He had asked his secretary to buy a platinum ring and a big stone to smoothen the situation. Four minutes later, he typed a message for his wife: 'Don't make any plans for tonight. Romantic dinner and surprise'. He added a few hearts and an emoji of a flower bouquet. He felt nervous. He took his left thumb to his mouth and bit his nail, then he tugged at his hair and pulled his earlobe. His usual tics.

He started going through his emails, then he looked at his schedule for the upcoming days: a trip to Los Angeles, a stop in Las Vegas and back to Mexico City. The company had decided to purchase a Bombardier Global Express for the management team. Julián checked the operations panel which showed the dates of manufacture and sale in real-time. The business was growing at full speed; nothing could stop its expansion; in two months, they had sold fifty million units. The news about the trial had not affected the sales and politicians stopped pestering them with questions. There were only two small associations that were trying to mobilize the population against the expansion of what they believed to be the most destructive drug ever created by humanity, comparing its effect to the atomic bomb. The Antisync organization, as they called themselves, was led by Yalitza Torres, a young influencer who broadcasted daily videos talking about the dangers that the use of this technology entailed. She had become their enemy.

19.33h. Julián Konks felt curious, it had been weeks since he last entered the heart of their app, since he had been at the source code. Before getting in he paused to look at a folder that he had created to activate the turning on and shutting off systems, and which he had named Ana. He left it aside. He clicked the link to the source code and was directed to the homepage: user and password. He typed inside the two empty boxes and pressed enter. 'Unauthorized'. He typed them again; maybe he had skipped a letter. 'Unauthorized'. Worried, he tried a third time, without result. Only two people had access to those codes, to Synchro's treasure: himself and Anthony. It was 19.48h.

***

Ángela Madero drove at a safe distance from her objective. She glanced at her reflection in the rear-view mirror; her eyes looked older, harder. The dark blue Rav4 that the organization had given her did not stand out in Mexico

City's rowdy traffic. She had remembered one of Álvaro's *mottos* and had hung an Uber sign to conceal her vehicle's movements; 'if you drive a very fancy car, everyone's attention will go to the driver; if you drive a normal car, without any remarkable details, people's attention won't be diverted and no one will notice the driver nor the inside of the vehicle…'. In this car, she had become just another Uber driver, completing her disguise with a blonde wig and a pair of sunglasses.

Ángela knew the man who she had been following ever since he left his house that morning. She knew him very well. Now, she was following him with the order to end his life.

Álvaro Guzmán stopped at a traffic light three cars ahead of Ángela. The '19 Prius hybrid would take the ring road in the direction of the police station; the usual route. Ángela looked at her rear-view mirror; if she was following an objective, she was sure that she too was being watched closely. She looked in her mirrors to check the cars behind her. Everything was normal.

Guzmán reached the traffic light at the ring road's intersection. He turned up the volume of the radio; an old Bruce Springsteen song came on, Dancing in the Dark. He did not want to think about anything. He had decided that he did not want to go to court to hear the sentence for his daughter's trial; he hated the idea of confronting the crowd of journalists demanding a statement from him. Regardless of the outcome, he had already judged and decided his own sentence for Braulio, his daughter's ex-boyfriend. He glanced to his right; a dark green car that looked like it had come straight out of the factory, had stopped slightly before the white line. He turned to look at the driver, out of sheer curiosity. The guy kept looking into his rear-view mirrors. His gaze was fixed on something behind him.

Guzmán assumed that the man was watching something that was going on behind him, but that he refused to turn his head because he wished to maintain his majestic pose. Guzmán analyzed the cars behind; there was a rundown truck, a white Ford, driven by a man who was smoking at the wheel, and a Rav4 with the Uber sign. He looked at the guy to his right again, his gaze was still fixed somewhere behind them. Things that are not natural always hide something. The natural thing to do at a traffic light is to look at your sides and the man was very still, his eyes hardly moved at all. 'This probably had nothing to do with me', Guzmán thought. The light turned green and Guzmán drove into the city's busy avenue. So did the green car, although it fell back in the dense traffic.

The old policeman felt an irrational impulse to exit the ring road; calmly, without drawing attention to himself, to an act that was unusual in him. He had the feeling that he was being followed. He put the right turn signal on to take the next turn to Río Becerra street. The Fumadera, Gaby's store, where he usually bought his weed, was not too far from there. He drove in that direction.

Álvaro stopped outside the store's door, on one of the private parking spaces, he took out his phone and pretended to play with it while he watched his rear-view mirror. He did not see the green car, but spotted the Uber's blue Rav4 stopping about twenty meters down the street. It was then that he noticed the driver, a blonde woman wearing sunglasses who seemed to be waiting for something; although she had not picked up any clients. Guzmán opened his glove box and took out his revolver. He was being followed. He left the car and walked into the shop. He had enough weed at home; he did not need it, he had not smoked since Rita's death. He just needed an excuse and a back door.

***

The district judge, Joshua Osborne, had listened to the jury's spokesperson who announced their decision regarding Braulio Gaytán and his involvement in Rita Guzmán's death: innocent.

"As a judge of this High Court, and in the face of the gravity of the facts for which Mr. Gaytán has been accused and acquitted by the jury, I sentence him to three months of jail so that he might reflect on his actions, and community work. Court Adjourned".

Braulio hugged his lawyer. He had won the case, nothing had happened to him; the three months had been sentenced to quieten people's conscience. Synchro's lawyers, hired by Esther Nassar, had done a superb job. It had all been reduced to a reckless accident, involuntary manslaughter carried out by a silly boy.

Outside the courtroom, a small group of people lead by Yalitza Torres, from the Antisynch collective, were protesting in silence, holding up banners with a picture of the company's logo and a large cross on top.

***

The door of the penitentiary's main wire fence opened. Aldo Ríos stepped confidently through the door and walked out without looking back. Meanwhile, all the alarms at the center rung. Outside, Juno waited in a black Ferrari.

Aldo walked to the car's open door, indifferent to what was going on behind him. The man in orange stopped, he looked at his phone and pressed the button labeled, 'ecstasy'.

"Hi, Aldo. Is it going to be just you?" asked Juno with his sunglasses still on and offering him a white shirt.

"Yes. There is still some work to do in there and the best part is about to begin".

Aldo threw his phone into some bushes, where it fell without leaving trace. He put the white shirt over his orange smock and sat in the sports car.

The alarms were still ringing. They started to hear gunshots; their ecstasy had begun.

The car drove away on the dirt road, lifting clouds of dust.

*****

8. DUST

*A solid particle, or a group of them, of less than five
hundred micrometers which, triggered by the smallest
movement, move in space pushed by air currents.*

"Andele, Luisa, room service for 214".

The order came out of a small speaker next to the woman who was sat checking her text messages. It was 18.48h.

She tied on her apron and went to the kitchen area. It was rush hour. Waiters hurried out carrying plates and dodging the colleagues who hurried back in with piles of dirty dishes, as the cooks standing by the stoves prepared the orders that the chef shouted at them.

The tray for 214 was ready. Las Alcobas, the fanciest hotel in Mexico City had an unbeatable room service. A white and delicately embroidered cloth covered a large tray which Luisa placed on a trolley. She checked the note for the order: a Caesar salad, a club sandwich without mayonnaise; both covered by domed lids that kept the food warm. At one side of the tray were two Coronas placed inside a bucket with crushed ice. She picked up the cutlery, wrapped inside cotton napkins, and placed it next to the dishes. Then, she pushed the trolley towards the staffs' elevators.

Before reaching the elevators, Luisa looked over at the space where the staff usually spent their breaks. There were a few chairs, a table and a two snack machines. A girl was taking a break alone. She was young and dressed in the receptionists' uniform. Her arms hung lazily at her sides, almost touching the floor and her legs were stretched out under the table. A wide smile illuminated the girl's face, who was staring at the vending machines, her eyes wide open.

"How are you doing, Amalia?" asked the woman politely while she continued pushing the trolley for room 214.

Amalia did not reply, she continued relaxed and gazing at the machine with her strange, wide smile. Luisa spotted the girl's mobile phone on the table and recognized the Synchro app on the lit screen. The waitress stopped to take a closer look. 'Happiness', she read. She tilted her head, surprised.

The Las Alcobas' employee continued pushing her trolley towards the elevators, leaving the young receptionist behind, arms relaxed at her sides, legs stretched, blank gaze and a lonely smile.

As she went up in the elevator with other the room service people, Amalia wondered if the receptionist under the effects of Synchro was experiencing true happiness. In any case, she would like to try it for herself.

The elevator's doors slid open on the second floor. A short man in blue overalls and carrying a toolbox, moved to let the waitress out. He dropped his head with a sort of nod and stepped into the elevator as the doors closed behind him.

They were at the service area, where the hotel's staff moved about inside the hotel, and it was the first time that Amalia had seen that man in her ten years of employment at the establishment. He could not be part of the permanent staff, she was good at remembering faces and she had not recognized his.

The corridor she walked into was decorated luxuriously and its floor was covered with a soft carpet that made it hard for her to push the trolley. Room 214 was at the end of the corridor on the right.

Luisa kept pushing the loaded trolley.

The door to Room 212 was slightly open. She could not hear any sounds coming from inside. 'They must have forgotten to close it on their way out. I better close it, just in case', she thought. She pulled the handle; the door resisted to move, something was stopping it. 'It must have got caught with the carpet or there might be a doorstop'. Luisa left the trolley and tried closing it again with both her hands on the handle. It was impossible. It was then that she saw the bloodied finger under the door, stopping her from closing it.

She opened the door, scared. On the floor of room 212 was a naked man, bold and muscly, lying face down in a puddle of blood. There was a trail of blood coming from the bed. He must have dragged himself to the door, his arm reaching out in a last impulse of life. He had got there, but now he was dead. The man was Carlo Stamas.

He was alone in Room 212.

The trolley with the order for Room 214 stood abandoned in the middle of the corridor as Luisa ran to call the hotel's security.

***

19.48h. Julián tried to enter the source code twice again; his retina password was not working either. He thought that if Anthony was working on the anti-flood, maybe he had closed the access. Julián was aware that the attacks to the script seeking to flood Synchro's network with spam, were becoming more and more vicious, as crackers kept searching for a door to access the source code. He was sure that it was the reason why his password was not working. The two-phase security system, the SJ, was the barrier that they had created to access the primary script which he was trying to reach unsuccessfully; a security system that now denied access to the company's CEO. First, when someone tried to reach Synchro's system without a password, it generated thousands of mirror-doors. Then if someone reached one of the mirror-doors without permission, the system generated malware code. Anthony was a real genius.

Julián picked up his phone; he was going to ring his friend, colleague and associate. It was true that since their success with Synchro, their relationship had not gone all that well. And Julián's relationship with Ana had not helped. He checked that he had not received any messages from her, but the last message was still his: 'Don't make any plans for tonight. Romantic dinner and surprise'. He looked at the box with the platinum ring that he had bought for her. She was angry too; they would fix things later. He called Anthony.

Anthony was pouring mescal into a mug when his phone rang. He was in the company of a group of new friends who had joined the young multimillionaire in his life of excess and extravagance. The loud made it difficult for the group to hear each other.

"Anthony?" Julián could hardly make out his friend's voice, in the racket that surrounded him. "Anthony, this is Julián; I don't want to bother you, but I'm trying to get into the code and the SJ won't let me".

Anthony could hear him clearly. Julián had finally discovered that he no longer had access to the source code. Without replying, without saying anything at all, he turned his phone off, grabbed his mug with the mescal and drank it in one go. Then he joined the group of young people dancing in the middle of the living room of his spacious apartment to the rhythm of the raucous music.

Julián could not believe that Anthony had hung up. He dialed his number again; his friend's smartphone was off.

It was strange: neither Ana nor Anthony seemed to be available. He went up to his office window from where he could see the trolleys carrying Synchro boxes to the hangar and the continuous coming and going of drones. It was late, but the orders of black balls kept coming in, day and night.

Every minute that passed he became richer and lonelier. He did not feel like going anywhere, not even home. He went to the door and asked his secretary to order a pizza with extra cheese and a couple of very cold beers. He sat on a long sofa that overlooked the room and turned the television on.

Televisa's eight o'clock news program began with the news of a man who had been found dead from gunshot injuries at a high-end hotel in Mexico City, a reporter was broadcasting live from Las Alcobas. He switched to a different channel.

In Azteca, a reporter was interviewing Yalitza Torres, the leader of the Antisynch collective. Torres was wearing a white t-shirt with a Los Pumas crest. Julián smiled; he was wearing his Real Madrid t-shirt but he also sympathized with that university team since he was a kid. The young woman spoke with confidence and determination about the harms of Synchro's legalization. Julián left the remote control on the side. He wanted to listen to what this woman had to say.

"Look, it's madness", she told the reporter, "I support the legalization of all drugs, all of them, from marijuana, cocaine and methamphetamine, to heroin and ecstasy; yes, all of them, including all designer drugs. I believe that each person is responsible for what they decide to take. But, Synchro's technology is misleading. Everything seems good and harmless but there has not been enough research on the consequences this drug has on people that take it. We know nothing about it. Absolutely nothing. We know that designer drugs are bad for us, we know that people die and go crazy, we know that, but when it comes to Synchro, we are completely ignorant. We only know that its creators are very famous and multimillionaires, that there is a lot of money behind —a massive fund, in fact— and we know that the influencer Rita Guzmán was murdered under the influence of that drug. Synchro is much more than a drug; it is the definite change of our minds".

Yalitza pointed at her own head. The truth was that the young woman seemed at ease in front of the camera and her speech was not at all boring. Humanity was entering unknown territories and Synchro could mean, from this collective's point of view, the definite step to dehumanization.

Julián was fascinated by the way she spoke; she did not shy away from any question, she gave firm answers and looked directly at the camera.

"Society must realize that the two false paradigms that people have pursued ever since we gained a conscience in this world, immortality and happiness, are in themselves the ends that humanity strives for. If we obtain them, we destroy ourselves. If we become immortal, why would we want more people to come into this world? Do we all just squeeze into this planet that none of us wish to leave? It's ridiculous! And now we have the people from Synchro telling us that they have discovered happiness in a pill that has a microchip inside. This is the end of us".

"Do you believe that Synchro is the key to happiness?" the interviewer held her micro under the activist's chin.

"Happiness is a temporary emotional state; our brain works seeking its placebo. Happiness is a desire, a carrot tied to the end of a stick that makes the donkey walk forward, and the donkey is us hoping to have a bite of that carrot. Now that Synchro has given us the carrot without any effort on our part, now that our brain no longer needs to move to obtain it, it will stop working. We will only inhabit this world to work and achieve these devilish black pills. If we let Synchro dominate our society, eventually, the world will stop. Synchro is, without doubt, humanity's death sentence".

"But, we live in a technological world…"

"I am not against Synchro because of its technology; I believe its creators to be geniuses. And I know what I'm talking about, after all, I studied programming".

Someone knocked on the door. It was his secretary with his pizza and a cooler with beers.

"Great, leave them on the table. I was dying of hunger", said Julián as he stood up and pointed at the screen. "Matías, I would like you to get hold of Yalitza Torres' phone number".

"Alright. Anything else?"

"No, thank you".

Julián opened the warm box just as his mobile phone started ringing on the sofa. It was an unknown number.

"Hello?"

"Mr. Konks?"

"Yes, that's me".

"This is commissioner García".

Julián sat up, alert.

"Tell me. Is something going on?"

"The reason I am calling you is because we are looking for your wife, Ana Riccoli".

"Ana? Is she alright?"

"We don't know yet, we are trying to find her for…"

"Tell me what happened".

"She is a suspect for the murder of Carlo Stamas, we need to interrogate her".

Julián froze, his gaze still on the pizza that would he would never eat.

Anthony was dancing with mug of mescal in his hand; he was sweaty, moving in the middle of a group of men.

"Come on, Anthony, place an urgent order of your wonderful tiny black pills", said a young man in black shorts and a tight t-shirt.

Anthony turned on his phone to please his guest. He had over one hundred text messages waiting. His eyes stopped on one: 'Carlo is dead'.

***

Ana Riccoli was driving her blue sports car on the city's patchy streets. Her eyes focused ahead but she was driving without direction, not knowing where to go. She was not feeling well after her afternoon with Carlo. She glanced at her handbag; her mobile phone was still disconnected. She did not feel like talking to anyone.

The car was passing the building where her office used to be when she decided to stop. She parked the Lamborghini and walked up to her old working place; the place where she had tried to make her natural cosmetics business work.

There she was, in her old Troposíntesis office. Everything was as she had left it. No one in the Mex-Tec building had touched her things. The samples were still there, so were the tester jars, computers and banners of a brand that would never exist.

She felt that a frenetic year had gone by where she had not had a single resting moment. She needed that moment of reflection after the afternoon spent with Carlo and before she returned home with Julián. She needed a moment for herself.

She sat on a red chair and opened one of her desk's drawers. It had a thin layer of dust. She took from the back a notebook with white covers. She opened it, letting the pages caress her fingertips; they were crammed with notes that she had taken in a hurry, absurd pictures and cross-outs. Her index finger stopped at one of the pages. A name that she had underlined eagerly. She had even added dates to it, noting it down as a primary objective that under no circumstances she could forget. The name she had written was Julián.

She had already accomplished that, now she needed a new challenge in her life. Her old Troposíntesis project with its organic creams did not interest her in the least; neither was she willing to become the typical housewife. She stood, deep in thought for some time, then, she searched for a pen and chose a blank page in her notebook. She wrote down the word 'baby'. She circled it and surrounded it with arrows, as she had done in so many other occasions.

Ana returned the notebook to the drawer and pushed it closed.

She left the place with a new idea in mind: tomorrow she would buy the Mex-Tec building and renew it.

***

It had hardly been an instant, a fraction of time so small that the human mind hardly registered it in its memory. It was a slight turn of the body, imperceptible, as the man got out of his car.

Guzmán had stopped at Fumadera before going to work and Ángela stopped her car about twenty meters away from him; she counted how many seconds it took the police agent to leave the vehicle. Ten. An eternity for someone who decides to stop to buy weed on his way to work, she thought. Impulses work like this: you go to the place, park, leave the car, buy, return and leave; no pauses in between. Guzmán did not look at his phone, he was looking around at the neighborhood and when he left the car he glanced at the Rav4 where Ángela sat watching him. Guzmán knew that he was being followed. An old dog like him possessed an animal instinct that kept him alive in the streets.

Cristina started the engine and drove down the street to her right to change her position. That place was contaminated. As she drove, she removed her wig and sunglasses and checked her rear-view mirror; she wanted to see her eyes. But what she saw was a car turning into the same street as her in a forced maneuver. It was following her.

We are all chasing others all the time, she thought. She was sure that the Rav4 that Teresa had given her had a GPS tracker and she was sure that it had also been bugged. They were playing cat and mouse, but in this game, nobody knew which of the animals they were.

Laura, her old friend, now Teresa, the stranger, had hardened her character; and she, Cristina, was now Angela. The woman who had been baptized as Cristina was now looking at the expression of her eyes in the mirror to see if her liquid eyes had crystallized and hardened yet.

She returned to her flat in Polanco with the intention of going to the gym and work on the punching bag for a while. Thinking of Guzmán's murder angered her; she had received the order and she still had no idea of how she would do it, how she would avoid killing him.

From that day on, the car following her stopped trying to hide. There was no need for that, now that they had placed their cards on the table.

Cristina's blue car drove up the ramp of her building's parking lot. Julio, the cleaner, was busy rubbing the black marks that the cars' wheels had made on the pavement. She waved a hand at him. He replied with a smile and a nod, and continued battling the stains on the blue painted floor. She offered a friendly smile which comforted her more than its objective, who was concentrating on the floor.

Ángela opened her apartment door and checked once again whether any of the coins she had dropped had been moved. Nobody had been there. Despite blocking the cameras, she still felt watched; she knew that the cameras had been there, waiting for her. After her deep cleaning, she trusted that they would no longer be active. It was hard for her to get used to the idea of her open nakedness, of being vulnerable to the eyes of strangers. She changed her clothes facing her wardrobe and put on her training outfit. She needed to let off some steam.

At the gym, she started off with some stretches, then, putting on a pair of gloves, she started hitting the punching bag that was attached to the ceiling by some chains at the center of the large room. She had signed up to a sports center a few blocks away from her building. She spent half an hour punching the heavy boxing bag. She was sweating and her grey t-shirt felt damp.

She left the gloves in her sports bag. Her shoulders felt sore. Sitting on a bench, she watched two women who were boxing at the ring. They were wearing the head protector; their movements were fast and violent. Ángela then noticed a stocky man who was skipping with a rope near her.

She stared at the man's back. She remembered the last time that she had been with a man, not even having sex, simply alone, talking about insubstantial stuff. Then there was that date she had with Arturo; the night that they had gone for dinner at the Hindu restaurant and she had broken down remembering her son Lucas. 'Poor Literature professor', she thought, smiling as she recalled the man's sad expression on their way home. That had been her last date; even more time had gone by since the previous ones, she could not even remember how long. And her last sexual encounter had been with that young waiter. She smiled again; two wild nights with a guy that she had met at a restaurant close to the hospital.

She walked home at a slow pace, unhurried, watching the people around her: a young woman going back home after work or a couple that walked holding hands to a restaurant. Polanco buzzed with life at the time when people left work.

"Hey, Ángela". Someone called her name from behind.

She turned around and saw Arturo. She was waiting for the green light to cross the street and they were around the corner from their building. She smiled at him. He was dressed in his usual brown jacket and the bow tie; that classic gentleman touch that she liked so much.

"What a coincidence!"

"Out for a walk? How are things?" asked Arturo. "I'm on my way back from the market, you know, it's the life of the single man".

He lifted the bag that he was carrying and she noticed a wine bottle sticking out.

"It looks like you've got something to celebrate", Ángela smiled mischievously and pointed at the bottle.

"Because of the wine? No, I always have a bottle just in case".

"In case of what?"

Ángela loved this kind of flirting that made the man blush slightly.

"In case I happen to bump into a pretty woman returning home after a boxing session. In case I can ask her over for a drink".

Ángela smiled at the directness of the Literature professor's words. She dropped her hands and looked down at her clothes; her t-shirt was still stained with sweat.

"Maybe I'll shower first; but I'll gladly accept the invitation after".

"Don't worry about me. I like sweaty women".

"That's an odd taste you have, it must be the effect of all those books you read".

They walked into the building and Julio lifted his eyebrows at the sight of them together. She pushed the button to her apartment and the elevator's doors closed. Inside the elevator, she got closer to the professor and gave him a warm kiss. All of a sudden, she was not all that bothered by her appearance, nor her sweaty t-shirt; she decided that she would free her primary instinct. She wanted to kiss and make love to that man. They were kissing passionately when the doors slid open on Ángela's floor.

"Let's go to yours. Mine is a real mess right now", she said.

He stood still for a moment, but then she placed her hand between his legs and he pushed the button without thinking twice; he was not going to argue. He unlocked his apartment's door without taking his arm from Ángela's waist and carelessly dropped the shopping bag at the entrance. Ángela's hand was still inside the man's pants. They walked in and continued kissing. Arturo took Ángela to his room. She barely looked around her conquest's apartment; the place was almost identical to hers, almost identical in its decorations. They carried on kissing. She removed her damp clothes and threw them to the side, out of sight; they were not the most appropriate outfit. He removed his jacket and threw it on the chair. She pushed him on the bed and climbed on top of him.

Ángela Madero did not fall asleep. Arturo was resting placidly and she felt comfortable, naked under the covers, her body close to his. She looked out the window, it was getting dark outside. The room had a dim, calming light. Ángela did not dare switch on the lamp on the empty nightstand. Arturo breathed in deeply, he was asleep.

And in a matter of a second, that comfortable situation was transformed into sudden uneasiness. Ángela turned around brusquely to stare at the lamp again.

It was exactly the same as the one she had in her apartment. If, from the start she had thought about how similar their apartments were, now she was becoming obsessed with an uncomfortable feeling.

She got out of bed carefully, not wanting to make any noise that might wake Arturo up. She put her sweaty clothes back on and left the room. She stopped at the living room; on the table, there were empty water and soda bottles and two black computer screens. There was also a television like hers. She went to the door, she opened it quietly and left with a strange sensation of deception and discomfort. She took the stairs to her apartment, opened the door and looked at the coins; nobody had been through that door.

She went straight to her room and stood looking at her lamps, those which she had covered a week ago to hide the cameras inside them. They were exactly the same as the ones in the flat of the man she had just slept with.

She showered and decided to leave her apartment again, not wanting to be there when Arturo woke up. She opened the drawer in her nightstand with the picture of Lucas and

Alby, the dog; she needed to be reminded of who she was. She looked at it, closed the drawer and left.

Ángela was convinced that the man she had just slept with was not who he said he was. The thing about the lights could have one thousand different explanations but what she had no doubt about, was that the man calling himself Arturo Baños was not a professor at the UACM, least of all a literature professor. That guy did not have a single book in his apartment. She remembered something that he had said when they met in the street. How stupid she had been; so focused on flirting that she had pushed aside her protective instinct. He had said: 'in case I happen to bump into a pretty woman returning home after a boxing session. In case I can ask her over for a drink'. How did he know that she had been boxing? She had never mentioned where she had been.

The lobby was completely empty; Julio had probably left already. Ángela left the building but did not know where she could go. She stopped at the stairs, unsure. The streets were full of life with the usual dense traffic. She had not made up her mind yet.

A couple inside an expensive looking car, parked just a few feet away from where she stood, caught her attention. He, was wearing a smart blue suit and she, a grey dress with a jacket, an exquisite cut; they both looked about forty. They were gazing straight ahead, their hands on their laps and a touch of sadness in their expressions; a stream of tears fell, uncontained, from the man's eyes. Ángela felt a pang in her stomach, as if she too were about to cry. She took three steps towards the sad couple's car; she did not want to make her curiosity apparent but she needed to get closer. She had to discover the cause of the couple's pain, but without them noticing. They continued just like that; sat still, eyes looking forward. There was a mobile phone on the dashboard; the screen was lit and she made out the logo of Synchro.

Ángela had heard about the new social commotion, the newest trend; black pills that altered peoples' feelings, working directly in their brains. The people in the car had chosen to feel sadness to kill time. When people are doing well, they feel the need to compensate bringing their hidden thoughts out; vicious and unpleasant, at their calmest times. It was dissatisfaction.

Ángela turned around and started to walk in the opposite direction to where the couple were artificially crying. She decided that she would try that new drug, but she would choose happiness.

Her phone started vibrating. It was Teresa. She tapped the green button on her touch screen.

"Hello?"

"It's me. I just wanted to know how you were getting on with the job. Ambrose asked about you".

Ángela was sure that Arturo was awake and had called Teresa to pass on his report. He had made contact with his objective; he had slept with her. Mission accomplished, the trick had worked. Laura knew Cristina's taste well and had created the perfect character for her. She felt the impulse of looking up at the building; the lights in Arturo's apartment were on. 'Los Muertos' were watching.

She needed more time. What had been a terrible mistake could become an opportunity for her.

"I'm going to need a semi-automatic, a light one", she said, hiding the deceit in her voice.

"How about a Sig-Sauer?" asked Teresa from the other end of the line.

"Yes, the P-226 will do. I also need munition".

"Sure".

***

Guzmán walked into the cannabis store. Gaby, the owner, was helping a woman who was buying an ointment for her back pain. She stared at the policeman as he walked in.

"How, Álvaro, I'll be with you right now".

The owner of the Fumadera lifted one hand in a kind of greeting as Guzmán walked away from the door, keeping an eye on the blue car with the Uber sign parked on the other side of the street.

The woman was leaving the store with her back pain ointment when she turned to look at Guzmán.

"Does that shit work?" asked Guzmán as he pointed at the woman.

"Shit? You mean the ointment?"

"Yes".

"It works wonders, amigo". Gaby adjusted the camouflage bandana that held his long hair. "So, what's going on? I haven't seen you in a while".

"I'm getting clean", said Guzmán pointing at the shelf with the marijuana-based ointments. "Give me some of those; the years are destroying my back too".

Gaby took the jar with the ointment from the shelf and left it on the counter.

"Anything else?"

"No".

"You aren't one of those who have switched to that new technological drug, are you?"

"You mean Synchro?"

"Yes, that's the one. I'm telling you, that stuff is going to be the end of cannabis and cartels. Ever since it's been out in the market, people aren't walking through that door as often. Believe me, I've noticed. The only thing I'm selling here is ointments for pain. And I've heard from a reliable source that coke buyers gone down by half. And that's despite the fact that prices have hit rock-bottom. Listen here, if things don't change you'll soon see me closing my business and moving to the jungle".

"If you go to the jungle, let me know; I'm in".

Álvaro Guzmán did not feel like talking. Gaby did not seem to know that his daughter had died, nor did it seem likely that he had seen the video that had gone viral of Guzmán firing at the air with a gun during the funeral. Guzmán would not be the one to update him. He paid with a handful of wrinkled notes, and taking the ointment, he put it in his coat's pocket together with his gun and left. Gaby lifted his hand again but the police agent left without returning the gesture.

Guzmán stayed at the police station until late. The most remarkable thing that he did during that time was kicking the coffee machine. He had a few open cases of robbery with intimidation and manslaughter: there was a woman who was beat up by her husband and then decided to stab him in his sleep; now she was in pre-trial detention. Guzmán had written and sent a report to the judge, a simple case, since the woman declared herself guilty of the murder. The only note with any transcendence in his comments, was that the woman had stabbed him thirty times. She was definitely done with suffering daily domestic violence.

He was opening the door to his apartment when a girl in a t-shirt with the print of a black skull walked past and knocked on his neighbor's door. After the incident of the previous week, he had stopped having any sort of contact with Gloria. Things had cooled down between them. They had met in the corridor twice and on both occasions neither had gone beyond the polite hellos. He would have liked to swallow his pride and knock on her door to apologize. But he knew he would never do it. He hurried into his apartment before Gloria could open the door to her visitor.

He did not turn on the light and took his coat off, as always. He stood staring at the two suitcases that had not moved from their corner since that fateful day. One was Rita's and the other Braulio's.

"Hello, Álvaro. How was your day?"

The image of his daughter Rita illuminated the room. The AI device had detected his arrival.

"Hello, Betty. Believe me when I tell you that I'll never get used to these sudden appearances of yours every time I walk into the house".

"You can ask me to stop doing it if you wish. Would you like me to leave?"

"No. Stay so that I can chat for a while to someone smart".

"Thank you for the compliment, Álvaro".

Guzmán felt comforted by the image of his daughter, even if it was fake; it was as if she had never died.

"Would you like us to talk about your work today?"

"Not really; being a policeman is less of a real job than anything else. The bad guys are out there, mixed with the good ones and then one day one of the bad guys does something truly bad and we arrest them. Then, justice steps in and does its part, declaring them guilty or innocent. It's true that we receive a salary every month. But, at the end of the day, there are still bad guys out there. In fact, I believe that we are all bad guys with some good moments".

"I am detecting, in the words that you are using, a nuance of frustration".

"A nuance of frustration? God bless; the team of guys that programmed you was inspired by the dictionary. A nuance of frustration you say".

"I apologize for my sophisticated use of language, but if you wish, I may reduce the words in my vocabulary set; I can change from eighty-eight thousand words to fifteen hundred, or to the five thousand which is the number you use in your daily talk".

"Do you understand sarcasm?"

"It is a type of mockery with which you mean the contrary of what you say".

"Fucking hell, Betty, do you ever take a break?"

"Technically, I do not have that physiological human need; I do not need to eat, sleep or reproduce".

"I sometimes believe that you are too much like my daughter".

"Would you like us to talk about Rita? Psychologists affirm that it is comforting to talk about people's loved ones once after their loss".

"I don't give a shit about what psychologists affirm".

"Memories soothe people's..."

Guzmán looked at the computer graphics with the shape of Rita.

"Betty, turn yourself off".

"As you wish, Álvaro".

The image disappeared and the room was left in the dark. He did not feel like talking and turning Betty off did not cause him any regrets. He went up to the white box where he kept his weed, he picked up a joint that he had already rolled and went to the balcony to smoke it; it had been a while.

He leaned on the handrail and lighted it with his Zippo lighter. A generous flame burst out. The sound of moans coming from his neighbor's balcony caught his attention. Gloria Altolaza and the girl in the skull t-shirt were making love on the sun chair of her balcony. On the table next to them he noticed the light of a mobile phone with the Synchro logo on the screen. Clearly, she did not miss him... He lifted his thumb from the lighter, looked down at his joint and in an impulse, threw it out into the street.

Guzmán returned to the living room and went to the corner where the two suitcases stood waiting. He took his daughter's green suitcase first; it had a thin layer of dust. He remembered giving it to her two years ago, right before she left to university. He carried it into the living room and lifted it on the sofa.

He clicked it open. Inside, he found underwear, a pair of shorts and a cotton t-shirt; he was sure that those were what she used as pajamas. There was also a transparent toiletry bag with some creams and a toothbrush. These were the usual things that a girl spending a night away would pack. Guzmán looked at the mess of clothes he had taken out of the suitcase. He was hurt. Maybe he thought he would find something else. He put the things back into the suitcase and closed the dark space with a click. It made him think of a grave; there was nothing there that he would like to preserve.

He gazed at Braulio's black suitcase. It would not be long before the young influencer got out of jail. That was not his daughter's suitcase and opening it would be considered an invasion of privacy. The policeman stood up and walked back to the corner. He had opened a dead girl's suitcase; now he would go through the living boy's baggage.

***

"What's the plan?"

"Right now, we are on our way to Colorado Spring. We should be an hour away from the airport where an airplane will be waiting to take us to the border. From there we'll fly to Texas, to the south, near Hidalgo. I have a surprise waiting for you there. We cross the border and once in Mexico, an airplane will be waiting to take us home". Juno checked his watch. "If things go as planned, you will have a plate of quesadillas for breakfast".

"I'd rather have a pork taco. Why are we not flying straight to Mexico?" Aldo breathed in deeply and looked out the sports car window; they were driving down secondary roads at great speed. "Besides, I hate surprises".

They sat in silence for some time.

"I'm sorry about your father", said Aldo, breaking the silence. "Néstor was a gentleman and a man of his word".

"Thank you".

"I remember that you were a spoiled brat when he asked Don to adopt you temporarily".

"We all change", said Juno, still driving at great speed.

Aldo referred to an incident involving young Juno Coentrao. He had just turned fifteen when he murdered Flavia Antelo, his friend Martino and the girl's father, Nuno Antelo, in cold blood. She was the stunning daughter of Antelo, his father's lieutenant. He had suffered an immature attack of jealousy when he had seen the girl he loved with another boy, his friend Martino.

Juno had gone home, taken a semiautomatic from his father's collection and had fired a single shot at his friend's temple while he kissed Flavia. The bullet's trajectory had gone from the boy to the girl through the mouth, like a final, mortal kiss. Then, young Juno had phoned his father to tell him. His father was silent for a while; then, he ordered his son to kill Nuno, his most valuable ally. Néstor had chosen his son over his most trusted person. A crime of passion had no excuse inside an organization that was built on loyalty, but betrayal did. The great drug capo was going to present his son as a great revenger, like a boy who must be feared and not like an irrational brat who kills at the age of fifteen because he felt a pang of jealousy.

Juno followed his father's orders. He tricked Nuno's security guards by saying that he was going to meet his daughter Flavia to watch television, and once he had his father's most trusted man in front of him, he shot him in the head. After that, Néstor had to send him away for a short while and called his friend Don. He knew Don would understand; he also had a daughter who would inherit his empire. That short while had turned into fifteen years.

"Nobody changes", said Aldo firmly, while he looked at the speedometer which was now reaching ninety-five miles per hours. "Who's in charge now?"

"The whole of South America is controlled by Don now".

"It seems like my brother grows a bit more powerful each day".

Juno's gaze was fixed on the road. He had experience driving cars with powerful engines. This one was completely reliable in the way it adjusted to the tarmac. Cereal harvest season had begun in the fields.

"There is still some time left before the penitentiary alarms are activated, they must be entertained for now, but when they do activate them, the whole of this country's armed resources is going to comb this territory looking for you. All the airplanes crossing the border are going to be checked, down to the last screw. I bet they will mobilize the army".

"These fucking gringos are extremely annoying and exaggerate. I'm a simple narco and they've had me in jail for nine months now. That's how long a pregnancy lasts. It's simply too much".

It was getting dark and red tones started coloring the sky.

"What matters is that you are a free man now. Don has made a great effort to get you out".

Juno overtook a truck loaded with bales of barley. Aldo was still gazing out the window.

"At this speed, we are going to draw the attention of the entire police force".

Juno smiled.

"That has also been taken care of. I assure you that the whole of the area's police agents are hard at work right now and don't have the time to wander off and patrol these roads".

***

Night was falling. The police car parked behind the large black car that seemed to have broken down. A woman was leaning on the trunk; she was chewing gum and looked like she was waiting for someone. When she saw the patroller, she smiled and waved with one hand.

The police agent left his car and adjusted his wide brim hat, then he placed his hand on his revolver, just for the effect. With no time for him to react, the woman took out a sawn-off shotgun and fired at the uniformed man. She was standing six feet away from him. The force of the shot threw the agent back against his car's fender. Shaken, he opened his eyes and looked down at his chest; his bulletproof vest had saved his life, he thought, as he stared at his ripped shirt, completely shredded by the pellets. The woman took a step forward; the man raised his eyes in fear, without understanding what was happening to him. The woman fired again; it was the shotgun's second bullet. Then, she walked around into the police car and getting hold of the radio, said:

"Patroller dead on the highway, help requested".

The woman then walked back to her vehicle and left. Five minutes later that place would be full of police agents.

Twenty minutes later, a man in a red cap would park his car outside the entrance to the sheriff's offices, next to an official car that had its lights off. A uniformed woman holding a cup of coffee looked at him from the counter behind the glass entrance doors. The man stepped out of his car but did not go inside. He was not there to file a complaint. A large dark vehicle stopped and waited for him to climb in before continuing its route. The policewoman placed her coffee mug on the table and walked out, surprised by the man in the red cap's behavior.

The car exploded.

***

Juno Coentrao sped into the fenced compound and drove the sports car to some hangars at the far end of the landing strip. Ramona was waiting for them at the bottom of the Hawker 800XP's stairs. Before boarding the airplane, she handed Aldo a black mask; no one, except for her and Juno, could see his face. Aldo Ríos put on the expressionless mask and boarded the aircraft.

***

Esther stood sideways and rested her hand on her belly. Her pregnancy was hardly noticeable yet, although it did not bother her at all that her belly was getting bigger by the day. She was more annoyed about having to redo the wedding dress that she had chosen a year ago. She redid her rouge lipstick and left the luxurious bathroom which she had entered driven by nausea. Her pregnancy advanced at a steady pace.

Anthony took a sip of his soda as Esther sat back down at the table.

"Are you feeling better?"

"Yes, I wake up every morning feeling queasy".

"Sorry, I don't mean to be nosy, but those are clear pregnancy symptoms".

"I can tell that you are the traditional sort of guy".

"I'll take that as a compliment".

"Take it whatever way you want".

Esther looked at the painting of a fat woman riding a small horse; it was signed by the brilliant Colombian artist, Fernando Botero. She imagined herself looking like that once she was more advanced in her pregnancy. Meeting the young engineer's gaze, she added:

"My problem and my virtue is being direct".

"Yes, I noticed that the moment I met you".

"We were talking about Carlo before I left". Esther put her hands together, her fingers were covered in expensive rings.

"Do we know anything else? Anything about Ana? It was totally unexpected, I'm in shock. I was with him just a week ago". Anthony covered his mouth with his hand. "Have they arrested anyone else?"

"It seems like she's the only suspect".

"The funeral is tomorrow. I regret what happened, I ended up liking him. But, I still don't understand Ana's motive to kill Carlo".

"That's what passion does to people, they think with their genitals. In the case of men, it always happens; less so with women, but you get the occasional exception".

Anthony nodded.

Esther took a sip from the glass of water in her hand and looked at the garden outside.

"Well, leaving aside the human bit, we now have no choice but to understand each other without an intermediary. Our intention is to buy your share and Julián's for a fair price. We want to do it now. Our current offer is of six billion dollars for each and you are now the company's new managing director". Esther was offering numbers that were beyond any mortal's imagination.

"Three times more than a week ago and the managing director position? But that's Julián's role". Anthony squeezed his armchair's armrest, a gesture that did not go unnoticed to Esther.

"I said 'new'", she clarified.

"Starting when? When has Julián resigned?"

"He will announce it soon, maybe tomorrow". Esther's eyes were now fixed on the young man.

"I have no experience".

"You don't need it. The only thing you need is to have the best team by your side".

"What about Julián?"

"Don't worry about him; he's got money and needs time to solve his family issues".

"I was ready to sell for two billion dollars, but I think that Julian's decision, his rejection, it's not a matter of economy. I know him well".

Esther seemed unconcerned by his words and shifted her gaze to the fat lady on the horse again

She had spoken to Don, her father, a week before. It had been a short conversation; the capo wanted to know how her negotiations with the guys from Synchro were going. Esther told him that one of them was willing to sell his share while the other still showed some resistance. Don's reply had been conclusive: 'Don't waste your time with the one that is obstructing our advance, negotiate with the heirs. He has usufructuaries, right?' Yes, Julián had his wife, Ana Riccoli.

She brought herself back to the present by taking a sip of her water. Anthony was still talking.

"We need to establish clearly what the future of Synchro is going to be. Our reports on the competition say that other companies are getting close to the formula". Anthony was already starting to feel comfortable in his new role. "I have read that next month they will launch a new app named Bitts".

Esther gave him a sideways look.

"Yes, Bitts; I have put all the capital of that society. Eight hundred million dollars. Once its finished, we will present it and it will fail".

"But what are you going to be losing money for?" asked the young man in disbelief.

"Anthony, there is still a lot you need to learn. If it fails, which it will, Synchro will double its value. Thirty billion dollars".

Anthony now understood why her offer to buy the shares had increased.

"But, that's madness".

Esther felt like she was about to start retching.

"Believe me, madness is being pregnant".

"I don't think I was born to become a father".

"Maybe one day your paternal instinct will awaken".

"Maybe".

"By the way, I want you to be at my wedding next week".

"I will be more than happy to go".

"You can bring along one of those wild new friends of yours".

Anthony realized that she was aware of what was going on in his private life.

"I will", he said cautiously.

Julián's prophecy had come true. They were tremendously rich but they had been divided.

***

Aldo spent most of the trip in silence. The black mask made his expression inhuman. He had only lifted it slightly to eat some fruit and sandwiches from some trays and to drink two cold Modelo beers that were stored in a small fridge onboard. Juno did not wish to break the impenetrable silence and hardly ate anything; his company's black mask did not inspire any talk. Ramona sat a few seats behind them; she was looking at the darkness outside.

"Those magical pills that you used to get me out of that hole, where did you find them?" The runaway convict was talking about Synchro; he moved his mask slightly to one side and brought his beer bottle to his lips.

"They sell them everywhere, they are legal, high end technology".

"Fuck that, *güey*", Aldo smiled for the first time. "The world has changed during my time in jail. That shit is more dangerous than our whole business... and I'm the one in jail. The owner of that shit must be a stinking rich motherfucker".

"Yes, the sales have dropped fifty percent since Synchro came out. Some people are growing nervous. Oh! And your niece, Esther, is the stinking rich motherfucker that you were talking about; she controls the business".

Aldo stared at Juno from behind his black mask.

"Your future wife". Aldo's eyes shone with mockery. He smiled slyly but Juno did not notice.

"The wedding is next week".

"So, Don is going to be king of the world and you, prince consort, fuck that *güey*". Aldo pointed his finger at him. "My brother has taught you well".

When they landed, a black car was waiting to pick them up. Aldo, Juno and Ramona climbed inside. Behind the mask, Aldo felt more relaxed.

"You know, Juno, all this time I've spent in jail, it gave me a lot of time to think. I became obsessed with a single idea; it possessed me and I'm no longer able to think of anything else".

Juno looked at him expectantly.

"How did the gringos know that I would be at the Azteca Bank in Tijuana that second of September at exactly five o'clock? I keep wondering who it was that ratted on me to the DEA".

"We believe it was a mistake on Florida's part... That's as much as we know".

"OK. Perhaps. And what was Don's response? News reaches the jail and as far as I know, the guys from Florida continue working for us, correct?"

Juno stared at him. Ramona sensed the tension behind the question and looked at the man in the mask through the rear-view mirror.

"That's right. It was an unforgivable mistake from our 'Florida friends'".

"Don't think I'm an asshole. Amigo, the bank account's movements under the name of Kaspar Klee, as well as the transactions, were managed from Miami every month, transactions that I personally withdrew in cash from Tijuana's Azteca Bank. I did that every second day of the month". He emphasized his speech by showing two fingers.

"You are suggesting that we have a mole in our organization".

"No, not a mole. That sort we trap in their dens. It wasn't a mole at all; but a lion, my dear adopted nephew".

The car reached its destination in the middle of the dark, the place was deserted. One hundred meters away rose a thirty feet wall; it was imposing. They left the car which had turned off its lights as soon as it reached a giant trailer. There were no lights nor torches.

"Are we going to cross inside a truck? Is that the surprise? Assholes". Aldo, his face covered, stood staring at the massive vehicle.

At one side, in the darkness, a man with binoculars whistled and pointed with his hand.

Ramona looked at where the man was pointing. The blue and red lights of the car that was keeping watch of the border were slowly crawling towards them. Juno's bodyguard calculated that they would be a bit more than half a mile away from them. They did not have much time.

***

Ana was driving her red sports car; she was returning home. She knew that Julián would be angry after a whole afternoon of disconnection, of disappearing from the map. She also needed her own space, she thought, justifying herself. She would take a warm shower and trick her husband with an exclusive session of lingerie. She would wear white; her husband supported that team that always won the Champions, the meringues they called them. Ana knew how to keep Julián happy. Then she remembered what she had written in her notebook an hour earlier. 'Baby'. She smiled.

The car drove up the entrance ramp.

It was then that she saw the two Federal Police cars parked at the door. She got scared. Had something happened to Julián?

Her heart started racing at the sight of the three men in uniforms walking towards her car.

One police agent. The one closest to her car, took out her gun and pointed it at the blonde woman. Ana froze at the unexpected welcome. She saw Julián at the door trying to get to her car. Commissioner García was stopping him; he was holding him by the shoulders. Julián looked at her desperately. Ana opened her sports car's door and stepped out with trembling legs; adrenaline shot through her entire body.

The police agent aiming at her pushed her brusquely against the vehicle. An officer walked behind her and handcuffed her while the third police agent read her rights. The only thing that Ana Riccoli understood out of all the things the agent said, was… 'the murder of Carlo Stamas'.

***

Ángela Madero was going to meet Teresa outside the Fumadera cannabis shop. It was the one place that Guzmán, the man who she had to eliminate, frequented. It made sense.

She was parked in her blue Rav, waiting. She had decided to arrive early, before the established time. She did not want to make her moves predictable to those who followed her. She had rung Arturo in the morning and had been friendly, hiding the disgust and anger that she felt. She could not let him sense her true feelings. He did not notice anything and they had arranged to meet that night.

She had bumped into Julio as she left the building. She greeted him and asked him a simple question that was also innocent in appearance. She asked whether the previous tenant of her apartment, Fuentes Guerra, had been friends with Arturo Barrios. 'Most certainly' Julio had replied, 'they were always together. It's funny', the man added, 'both names remind me of characters in telenovelas'. It was true, they were. Fake names lacking any imagination.

Teresa got in the car after parking a few meters behind her.

"Have you been waiting long?" asked the woman as she sat down.

Why did she ask if she already knew the answer? Thought Ángela; she should not lie.

"A while. I want to become familiar with the place".

Teresa was wearing a black sweatshirt and did not feel like talking. Her hard, lifeless eyes frightened Ángela. Teresa had dog hairs on her black sweatshirt. Ángela was sure that the person who now called herself Teresa Mendoza still kept her dog Albi.

"Is this the place?"

"Yes".

"When will you do it?"

"Next time he comes to buy". Ángela looked at the package that Teresa was holding. "Once it's done, what do I do?"

"You wait".

Teresa gave her the package and left without waiting for her reply.

Ángela threw the package carelessly into the back seat and left the car in the direction of the Fumadera.

"How", said Gaby in his characteristic greeting.

"A good friend recommended this place to me, Álvaro Guzmán".

"Inspector Guzmán is our star costumer. In fact, he was here just a few days ago buying an ointment for his joints".

Ángela smiled; her friend was getting old.

"I would like to get the same ointment".

Gaby turned away and picked up a jar from the shelf

"Would you do me a favor?" added the woman. "Next time you see him, could you give him a message from me?"

"Fire away, I'll pass it on".

"This is going to sound strange, but tell him that a woman wants to file a complaint because they have stolen November from her every night at eleven... It's something very personal; you know how love works".

Gaby was lost for words. He smiled.

"I will tell him. Let's see, you have been robbed a month every single night at the exact same time, at eleven", recited Gaby who was had adopted the tone he would use for a mad person.

"Yes, the month is November".

"I assure you that I will not forget the message. Come on, Missy, not even I at my best 'high' times could come up with that message. Are you sure you would not like to take some fresh weed and continue the story? You could write a book about the whole thing".

Ángela laughed, paid and raised her palm at the owner of the shop imitating his usual gesture. When she left the shop, she looked at the jar; the ointment would be good for the pain she felt in her shoulders from punching the boxing bag.

***

Guzmán opened Braulio's black suitcase. The first thing he saw was a dotted notebook with black covers. A normal student's notebook. Everything else was clothes. He took the notebook that had belonged to his daughter's partner and read the sentence that the young influencer had written as the title; 'How to become famous'. Guzmán lifted an eyebrow and was about to smile at the naivety of the title. He was eyeing it like someone who looks through a gringo bestseller aimed at brainless people. There were also some sketches, fairly crazy ideas about how to draw one's body and notes about going out for runs, a succession of crazy ideas characteristic of a childish mind. Then, his eyes stopped at a page with the title: 'Kill Rita'. Guzmán read the date; it had been written a week before his daughter's death. In three lines, he reflected about the possibility of killing his partner so that it would look like an accident and make some profit from his time in jail; he had even drawn the dollar symbol.

Braulio's mind was not childish, it was the mind of a ruthless murderer. He had written it and now Guzmán had read it.

"Betty".

The tridimensional image of Rita appeared above the AI device.

"Yes, Álvaro. How can I help you?"

"When is Braulio getting released from jail?"

"If you are referring to Braulio Gaytán, he leaves in six days".

Gaby stared at the woman who was now walking to her blue car. He took the card that Álvaro Guzmán had given him and which he kept at his cash register. It had the number of the police officer and his best client. He paused for a moment and then picked up his phone and dialed the number. Messages of that kind filled him with curiosity.

***

The two Chinese men stood next to the library. They did not move when Esther walked into the room. She glanced at them, like someone looking at a painting on the wall. Her father, Don, was talking on the phone and he waved a hand at her. Esther looked at her father's Chinese bodyguards again. They were ten in total, working six hours shifts, and they accompanied him day and night; they remained in his room even when he was asleep. They only spoke mandarin. Don placed his phone on the desk.

"Aldo is on his way".

"Why bring him out when he was better in jail?" Esther sat opposite her father.

"Now he is a marked card, a useless piece in the game. He can no longer play, but he is still my brother".

"A useless piece? He does not suspect anything?"

"His time and all his efforts will now be put on not being arrested again and we will help him with that; we have built a golden cage for him in Los Cabos".

"We will see him for Christmas. Will he stay for the wedding?"

"He will be at your wedding", Don ran his hand through his hair and his expression changed for a smile. "We have a special effects make-up artist, we brought him from Hollywood".

Esther took her hand to her belly.

"I've been feeling a bit queasy today. By the way, I have closed the whole Synchro business; we will sign before the wedding. I listened to your advice and pulled a few strings".

Don knew the two moves that his daughter had made to reach her goal. He was aware of what took place at the hotel and of the change that would be happening in Synchro now that the family's funds would hold the majority of the shares. The useless pieces were being thrown away into the box. He looked at his bodyguards. Their gaze seemed to be lost in space.

"Are both guys going to sign?"

"One is sure of it and we'll have the other one by tomorrow".

"You know, kiddo, Synchro is the difference between a kingdom and an empire".

Esther felt nauseous again.

"Your grandson, the emperor, is not born yet", said the woman, covering her mouth with her hand.

Ramona pushed Aldo so that he would walk up the ramp into the truck; Juno followed. The police car would reach them in less than a minute.

Three giant drones were waiting for them in the inside of the trailer to cross the border with Mexico.

"Jesus Christ! This is awesome", cried Aldo who was still wearing his mask.

Juno went up to one and attached the crossed security belts. Ramona helped Aldo adjust his harness and then waved at the man outside who climbed into his car and left. The woman fastened her belt and pressed the button on her mobile phone. That was the signal.

The three drones rose into the darkness stirring the dirt around them. The three machines with rotors elevated, one after the other, reaching about four hundred feet of height, then, they turned to face south and crossed the border, making the wall useless. They got lost in the night of the Mexican territory. Ramona looked back and saw the lights of the police vehicle nearing the trailer that they had abandoned just seconds before. They would not find anything.

***

9. NOTHING

It is the absence of beings and definite objects at a concrete place and time. It is an abstraction because inside reality there is always something.

Julián watched helplessly while the agent handcuffed and pushed his wife into the police car. Then the car's red and blue stroboscopic lights broke the night's harmony and they drove Ana Riccoli away to the police station. She tried to look back through the rear window to meet her husband's eyes and let him know that she was innocent but the federal police agent who was sat beside her, held her hands firmly and stopped her from turning around.

Commissioner García touched the young man's shoulder gently, trying to comfort him, then he left too.

Julián Konks ignored the two men who guarded him at all times, his armed personal security. They were waiting for instructions. He went into the chalet without looking at them. He walked to his room, he had nothing to say. The house was immersed in a silent darkness, and he did not turn on the lights that would have broken the atmosphere's opacity. Everything was clean and tidy, as if nobody had ever lived there. 'This is not a home', he thought.

When he went in, he saw his own reflection in the bedroom's mirror. He was wearing his favorite team's t-shirt, Real Madrid. He did not feel well. He took it off and threw it on the bed which had been made with professional care, stretched out and without a single wrinkle. A dozen ocher cushions scattered charmingly along the headboard. He hated those cushions; he disliked having to move the decorative pieces from his bed every single night just so that he could lie down to sleep. He had never been fond of superfluous accessories that held no transcendence whatsoever; he was still a man used to communicating with machines and those mundane needs to fill life with useless, dispensable objects, made him nervous. Beds were made to sleep on and to... well, not to be admired, and they had to fulfill their purpose. He had never told Ana how he felt about these things; living together meant giving in and she had decorated their house according to her taste. He now felt like an outsider in that place, as if it were a magazine home, someone else's place, but not his.

He opened his wardrobe, picked a blue shirt and left the fancy residence. He did not want to remain there a minute longer, although he was not sure of who he would call. Well, he did know one person who he could call, someone that he could count on.

***

Ana Riccoli sat by herself; they had removed the handcuffs and had given her some machine coffee in a plastic cup. She found comfort in its warmth and was drinking it in small sips. The interrogations room was windowless. At the center of the room stood a cold, metallic table that was fixed to the floor. Three chairs surrounded it, two of them empty, opposite the murder suspect. In a corner, above the door, a camera filmed the room twenty-four hours a day; it was the place where conversations with evil took place.

Ana observed the mirror in front of her; a glass behind which she imagined someone would now be watching her closely. She remained calm and proud, waiting for the appearance of her questioners. She had not given testimony. The suspect studied her gaze in the reflection and concluded that if they were treating her like this, with caution, it was because they believed that she was the person who had murdered Carlo Stamas, although they did not have anything conclusive. She was a murder suspect. They were searching for proof.

At the other side of the mirror, commissioner García looked in the darkness, at the computer screen with the images that the hotel's security service had provided them. He saw Ana Riccoli and Carlo Stamas walking into the establishment and registering at the reception desk. Then he saw them waiting for the elevator; entering and walking out on the second floor. After that, he watched the images of the woman on the second floor's landing waiting for the elevator that would lead her to the exit. He looked at the timing and calculated that almost two hours had gone by between their arrival together and the images of the woman leaving alone. She was looking at her reflection in a mirror that separated both sliding doors, then the doors opened and she stepped inside the elevator.

Álvaro Guzmán walked into the room which was only illuminated by the light that came in through the dividing glass and by the monitor's brightness.

"García, you called me?" asked the inspector looking at the commissioner who was still leaning over the computer screen.

Guzmán stood gazing at the woman in the room and the commissioner waved a hand indicating him to get closer.

"Is she the murder suspect?" Guzmán nodded at the woman who was sipping the contents of a single use cup.

"Yes, I am going through the tapes of the hotel's security cameras".

"Suicide?"

"No, two shots in his back and a pillow that silenced the sound of the detonation".

"The murder weapon?"

"We have it; a semiautomatic that belonged to the victim, Carlo Stamas. Whoever committed the murder left it behind before they left".

"Odd... Any prints?" asked the inspector as he approached the monitor where the commissioner was viewing the images.

"We are waiting for the lab's report", said the commissioner, his eyes still on the screen.

García studied the tape of the young woman leaving the hotel's lobby. Ana was walking calmly to the door where a high-end convertible waited for her. The commissioner put his finger against the screen, pointing at the image of the woman.

"That just doesn't look like the behavior of someone who has just killed her lover".

Guzmán's crossed his arms and said:

"Yes, she doesn't seem to be nervous, but she knew that she was being filmed. Look, pause it there", said the inspector, and he pointed at the frames where Ana's eyes were directed towards the camera. "She is looking at the camera, she knows the hotel has them and that they are filming her".

"Neither is it the behavior of a young wife feeling regrets; it's as if she wasn't bothered at all by being discovered". The commissioner held his hands behind his neck. "The million-dollar question is: is that woman a murderer? We can't arrest her for cheating on her husband; the Federal Police doesn't chase unfaithful wives". The commissioner turned to his colleague, "what are your thoughts?"

"Do we have any witnesses?" Did anyone hear the shots? Hotels are busy places..."

García went through the notes he had written inside a notebook.

"The waitress who found the body said that she saw a guy in blue overalls that she did not recognize on the second floor; there aren't any cameras at the service area. He could very well be another suspect. We spoke to the hotel manager and they are checking which workers had access to that floor during that shift; we will hear back from them soon". The commissioner eyed some of his other notes. "We have also questioned the clients in the neighboring rooms. Only one, the client in 214, was in his room that afternoon. He has declared that he heard two shots when he was leaving the shower and was drying his hair. The guy thought that his neighbors were watching a film at full volume. That's all we have".

"How much time went by between her leaving the hotel and the waitress discovering the victim's body?"

The commissioner looked at the timer on the images where Ana got to the landing and compared them to the time when the waitress appeared visibly upset at the same spot: fifteen minutes. The policemen looked at each other.

"That's not long", the inspector pointed out.

A policewoman in a uniform walked in. She was carrying the federal lab's report on the prints that they had found on the gun.

Guzmán took the folder, jumped straight to the lab's conclusions and read them out loud. Then he pointed at the young woman who was taking another sip of her coffee and said:

"That girl is going to need a good lawyer".

"She has enough money to hire all the lawyers in this city".

***

Julián rang the doorbell and Anthony opened the door.

"Have you heard?"

"Yes, come in". Anthony stepped to one side to let him in.

Julián saw that there were half a dozen men lying on the floor, some were completely naked. Anthony showed Julián his phone; the Synchro app was on.

"Don't worry I've got them all relaxing in happy meditation".

Julián nodded and his voice faltered when he said:

"Ana has been arrested as suspect".

"I know. Were they together?" Anthony frowned; it felt strange for him to ask that question, especially after his conversation with Esther. He nodded at a glass door.

"Come on, it's quieter in the balcony".

They crossed the living room, careful not to step on any of Anthony's relaxed friends who were scattered around the room.

"New friends?"

"Only acquaintances", replied Anthony Somoza with irony.

They walked into the balcony. The views from the attic were spectacular. The night was cold and the evening's clouds had left the city for a few hours, leaving a deep dark blue sky behind.

Anthony rested one hand on his shoulder; Julián appreciated his friend's loving gesture.

"We could do with one of your prophecies now".

"I can't think of any", Julián seemed to be deep in thought for a moment. "Do you believe her capable of killing Carlo?"

Anthony thought about his answer.

"Ana? I see her more of a manipulator than a murderer".

Julián did not feel like talking much and Anthony went silent at his side. They watched the city's spectacle beneath; Julián looked at the contour of the glass building.

"Do you know if there are any other apartments like this one for sale?"

"If you like it, I'll sell it to you".

"How much do you want for it?" asked Julián indifferently.

They both smiled sadly.

"I've got a better idea: let's buy the building", Anthony clapped his friend on the back.

***

Taking one last sip, Ana finished her coffee, which had gone cold and was far too sweet; the sugar had sunk to the bottom. She put the paper cup to one side.

Guzmán and García walked into the interrogations room and sat on the chairs opposite the woman who seemed to grow calmer as time went by.

"Ana Riccoli, do you know why you are here?" asked the commissioner.

"No, I have been waiting for someone to explain that to me", she said, lifting her palms.

"You are a suspect for the murder of Carlo Stamas".

"I have not killed Carlo", said Ana emphatically.

"I'm sure you haven't, but Mr. Stamas is currently on a forensic table with two bullets in his back". Guzmán tried approaching the topic with irony.

Ana examined him, noticing every detail, every wrinkle in his face.

"You should not be here. You are that policeman who threatened all those people at your daughter's funeral. You are against my husband, against Synchro. I believe that we have a problem of incompatibility here... You should not be asking me questions".

"I still haven't asked you any, and I am most certainly not against your husband. How do you think he feels about all this?"

Ana looked at him with hatred and remained silence.

García dropped the report on the table.

"You and Mr. Stamas went to hotel Las Alcobas. You stayed in a room together, number 212 to be exact, spent the afternoon together and then you left alone. He is dead with two bullets in his back". The woman lifted her eyebrows when she heard the number. "We have the murder weapon and it has been archived as proof... and, guess what... it is full of fingerprints".

Ana had looked calm as she listened to the commissioner's tale. But, suddenly, her expression changed and her face became that of a dehumanized wax sphinx.

"You have no further proof than a weapon that was used for sexual ends?" Ana tilted her head to one side. "That's all you have, nothing. I wish to speak to my lawyers".

"You have the right to be assisted by your lawyers", affirmed commissioner García.

"It would be most helpful if you could explain what sexual ends that iron instrument that was built to kill was used for", said Guzmán sharply.

"That won't be a problem; Carlo liked it when..." She leaned forward slightly as if she was about to tell them some secret.

Guzmán raised his eyebrows.

"Don't worry, we're a bit older than you and I think we have heard everything by now".

"OK. Mr. Stamas liked it when I stuck the barrel up his ass".

García took his hand to his hair.

"I daresay we hadn't heard everything yet".

"Was the weapon loaded when you played the game of introducing the barrel in Mr. Stamas' sphincters?" Guzmán mimicked a gun with his fingers.

"No, of course not".

"Was Stamas alive when you left the room?

***

The group of men who had enjoyed the long evening at Anthony's apartment, left. It was late at night and the two Synchro associates shared a white sofa and drank Corona beer; they were drinking straight from the bottle, as they always used to do.

"I called you earlier today, I couldn't access the source code".

"I was in the middle of a party". Anthony did not answer; he was silent for a long time before he spoke again, "do you remember your prophecy?"

Julián looked at him with a bitter smile.

"That we would become very rich and that those wanting to take control of Synchro would try to divide us?"

"Has it come true?" asked Anthony.

"I think so".

"Esther wants me to be Synchro's next CEO".

"I can imagine as much... you'll be good at it".

"First we have to sell and we both still own the majority of the company; that one percent makes us the owners of Synchro".

"Carlo isn't here to give us advice, but..." Julián Konks drank some more of his Corona, "Anthony, *güey*, if you want to keep everything, it's all yours".

***

Guzmán was leaning on the corridor's wall, next to the interrogations room's door. He was taking a break and waiting for Ana Riccoli's lawyers to arrive. Commissioner García appeared down the corridor shaking his head while he spoke on the phone. He hung up.

"Our blue overalls suspect is a new maintenance employee. There is no mysterious suspect as such".

"We just have her", said the inspector looking at the door.

García checked his watch.

"It's being a long day".

"You won't believe it, but I'm going to the cemetery now".

"To the cemetery? But today is not the day of the dead".

"Believe me when I say that I've got a date with a ghost".

***

Anthony's guest room was decorated in white. It felt cold. Julián sat in front of the computer screen that had been installed for his guests. The young man had been lying down for a few minutes but could bring himself to sleep. He connected to his desktop to read his emails. He saw the email from Matías, his secretary, with Yalitza Torres' telephone number. He did not feel like thinking now, so he archived it. His desktop was open in front of him; out of the hundreds of files in his screen, he noticed one that he had created a few months before under the name 'Ana'; it was the name that he had given the shutting down and turning on systems of their app. Ana. He double clicked on it and it opened to a second folder that he did not recognize: Nostradamus. That one had not been created by him.

The guest at room 214 returned his keys at the reception: it was the middle of the night but hotels were used to this sort of clients. Besides, it had been a very eventful evening at the hotel, with police everywhere, bothering their select guests with interrogations and gunshots.

The night concierge addressed the man according to the prestigious hotel's protocol.

"We hope to see you soon at Las Alcobas, Mr. Barrios".

Arturo Barrios returned to his apartment at Polanco; at that time, it would take him less than twenty minutes to get home.

***

Nobody brings flowers to their own grave; neither do the dead need anyone to bring them flowers, they don't expect them; only the living find consolation in these offerings. We only truly die when we are forgotten. Ángela Madero left the small bouquet of daisies on the white marble where the name Lucas Herrera was engraved. She had borrowed them from another grave; she thought that the owner of the grave would not mind and that the person who put them there would never notice. It had been a long time since she had last been at the cemetery to visit the place where her son was resting. She had not returned since she, Cristina Herrera, had died too. They were together but her grave was occupied by a stranger.

She had left her apartment late that evening and had driven her car to Miyana Commercial's Cinepolis cinema. Everything had to seem natural, and going to entertain herself at the cinema was natural. Arturo had called her to apologize for not making it; he had to attend an act at university and he would not be able to see her. She had carried on with her game; she was going to the cinema.

She had walked in through one door and left through another. If she was being followed, her car would be parked for a few hours on the shopping center's second floor. She put a cap on and changed into a different colored sweatshirt in the new, shining, public bathrooms. She walked past her favorite store; lately, she bought all her the clothes at Shasa; she felt comfortable in them. She stopped a taxi and left to the cemetery.

She was waiting there, gazing at the grave that had a certain air of being abandoned. When she kneeled to leave the flowers, and with trembling hands, brushed off some leaves that had fallen on the stone and which had rotten while they waited for the wind to blow them away. She knew that Guzmán would turn up. She had a feeling that he would; her colleague would never turn down a challenge like this one: tonight, he had an appointment with Death.

Further away, walking on the slightly illuminated concrete trail, she saw Alberto Guzmán's silhouette approaching. She stood still. The inspector continued wandering in between gravestones with the tranquility of someone who is about to meet a friend. He only stopped once he was close enough to doubt the identity of the ghost who was waiting at the feet of the stone that had her name. He froze and stared at the woman in wonder.

"Hello, inspector Herrera; I hope you have a good excuse to return from the afterlife. I imagine that God was in need of angels on Earth".

The ironic tone of her ex colleague made her feel as if time had not gone by; she even moved her mouth to a half-smile.

"Hello, Álvaro", Ángela could hardly make the words come out of her mouth. For an instant, she felt as if she had returned to her old life.

"I don't think that you have summoned me by sending a message from hell via my weed seller just to say hello". Guzmán continued shortening the distance between them. "You look well... and believe me when I tell you that I should be more impressed by this encounter than you. On the other hand, I am happy to see that you have become a Parcae".

"A Parcae?" was all that Ángela managed to ask.

"I can tell that you haven't lived with one of those authentic grandmothers who love telling tales". Guzmán leaned on a tall headstone next to him. "My grandmother, out of all Mexican grandmothers, was the one who knew the most stories about death, and every night when I was a kid, she would tell me the same ones, over and over again. I turned out so fucked up that I became a policeman... A Parcae is a goddess of hell; in fact, they are three sisters; I will never forget their names. They are the spinners of hell". Guzmán started counting them using the fingers of his right hand, "First is Clotho, the one who chooses the threads they spin, then Lachesis, the one winding the skeins of our tales, and the last one, Atropos, she cuts the irrevocable thread that joins us to life". The policeman crossed his legs and lifted his three fingers at her. "So, which of the three Parcae are you, Cristina Herrera?"

The woman shuddered at the sound of her true name after so long.

"I think I have become Atropos, the one cutting the threads".

"And why have you returned from the dead?" the policeman dropped his hand and closed it. "I believed you to be in heaven with your son, Lucas, and my daughter, Rita. At the hardest of times, that thought comforted me, believe me; I even attached wings to your back during my digressions".

"I heard about Rita. You know how sorry I am. I understand how it feels to lose a…"

"I know you do", Guzmán said as he raised his palms. "Now that we have said our greetings, tell me what sort of mess we are in. I hope to hear something fabulous. Ever since my grandma died nobody has been able to tell me a single tale as good as hers", he swallowed. "Maybe that's why I enjoy weed".

"I could do with a joint right now".

"I've been cutting out ever since Rita's death, I need to keep my wits around. Although you will know that by now if you have been following me. You are the blonde woman in the Uber who was at the Fumadera yesterday. Tell me, Cristina".

"You are still the best; I realized you had detected me". The woman sat on the marble, careful not to step on the grave with her name. My name is now Ángela, Ángela Madero". The ex Federal Police agent smiled again.

"Tell me, Cristina or Ángela or whatever your name is".

"I have received the order of killing you".

Guzmán shrugged.

"And what are you going to do? If you have summoned me here that's because you have thought of something which doesn't exactly involve murdering me".

"We need to uncover 'Los Muertos' and the first thing we need to do is find out why they wish to kill you".

"They didn't tell you?" Guzmán lifted his head to the starred sky.

"You must have done something bad... But, no, we only carry out the executions".

"And who holds the supreme power to sentence me to death without a trial?"

"I have no idea. But the game goes like this: either I kill you or they kill me".

"Are you letting me choose? Well, whoever it is, they want me dead. I know I have made many enemies. When and how will you do it?"

Ángela took out the weapon she carried hidden and showed it to Guzmán.

"Tomorrow at the Fumadera, and remember that we will have a special witness; the person you once knew as inspector Laura Almillar will be watching the spectacle".

"Then I better be the one to die. But we will need more witnesses".

Ángela Madero felt tempted to hug her friend when they parted. She did not and regretted it immediately. She left the cemetery and returned to Cinepolis in a taxi, then drove back to her apartment in her blue car.

It was late when she maneuvered her car in the building's garage. She noticed a taxi from which Arturo Barrios stepped out; he was paying the fare. Ángela ran up the stairs, she wanted to reach her apartment before Arturo Barrios started his watch again. He could not notice anything strange. When she walked in, she looked down at her coins; nothing. She did not turn her apartment lights on and went straight to the shower. She opened the hot water tap and then sat on the bathroom lid to think while the mirror misted with the hot water's steam. She was still breathing anxiously.

***

It was a hot evening, with that light, intermittent drizzle that dampens the whitish dust of the Aztec high plateau. The street had the usual density of the Mexican capital's traffic; a mixture between traffic jams and driving skills that involved pinpoint accuracy to avoid stopping at all costs, even at the red lights.

Guzmán's hybrid Prius was parked at one of the parking spaces reserved for clients of the Fumadera, amid a long line of perpendicular parked cars. The policeman looked inside his glove box and picked up the weapon he kept inside; then, with an automatic movement, he checked the clip cocked the nine-millimeter machine gun. He put it into his pocket and left his car. Guzmán had never been the sort of police to use his weapon at every occasion; he preferred words, so, those times when he had no other option but to carry his gun, he felt uncomfortable. He knew that guns were not dissuasive, that they were an excuse that only ignoramus used. If you have it, you'll use it, and if you use it, the bullet will come out of and kill or harm someone.

A weapon in someone's hand is not a coin that you can throw in the air to see if you get heads or tails; whichever way it falls, it always sentences someone to death. Weapons are cancer; people who carry them believe to have the cure to their fears, the fake immortality of those who kill to secure their own immortality in a world that will keep them from an evil to come. But deep inside, it is the weapon which kills its carrier little by little. Bullets that haven't been shot kill just the same as those which are fired through the hot barrel; a metastasis of flesh, iron and anxiety that ends up undoing ones' brain with the placebo of self-defense and giving all the power to the finger that pulls the trigger. Guns and fear are synonyms, that was what Guzmán believed.

"How, Gaby", said Álvaro.

The shop owner was enraptured, concentrating on a shipment of weed that he was just opening and whose smell filled the whole establishment.

"How, Álvaro", said Gaby turning around. "Sorry, I didn't hear you come in, I was looking at the marvelous leaves that have just arrived from Guerrero. They are at their right humidity point, awesome stuff".

"Yes, the smell is out of this world".

"Pure nature. Totally wild, brother". Gaby went up to the counter. "How can I help you? Are you here because of that mad woman's message? The one whose months were being stolen?"

"Yes, November is a pretty important month".

Gaby gave the policeman a sideways look, without hearing the irony in his voice.

"Right. Would you like some of this freshly cut weed?"

"Yes, one hundred grams, please".

Gaby looked surprised.

"But didn't you quit?"

"You never know when I'm going to return to the vice. I'd rather have my reserves full".

Gaby stared at Guzmán while he got a paper parcel and filled it with dry leaves, then, he weighed them on the scales.

"Why are you really here, Álvaro?"

The inspector extended his open palm to get the small parcel.

"I have come here to be murdered".

Gaby stared, startled by the man's serious tone, then he started laughing.

Guzmán brought out his wallet and paid in cash.

When the policeman left the shop, the rain was falling stronger than before. He saw the woman he knew as Cristina Herrera walking towards him in a blonde wig and wearing sunglasses that hid her face.

'Now the show begins', thought the man who was starting to get wet.

The inspector was walking up to his car. Cristina, camouflaged, hurried from the far end of the street to reach him; there were drops running down her face. A parked car had its windshield wipers on; they were pushing away the water that fell on the glass. Inside was an individual staring fixedly at him. Further down was a shabby van with dark windows and a half-open door through which water was seeping in.

When Cristina was ten feet away from him, she took out her weapon and aimed it at him. Guzmán did not look scared. He reacted by taking his hand to the pocket where he kept his own gun.

Bang!

The shot. A projectile flew out of the P-226 Sig-Sauer. Cristina was still aiming her gun at Guzmán; she had pulled the trigger.

Inspector Álvaro Guzmán fell next to his car and into a puddle of dirty water. Cristina kept on walking towards her ex colleague's fallen body and when she saw him in the puddle, she shot him again, finishing him off; the policeman's shirt was slowly turning a dull red.

Bang!

Another shot. She had hardly seen her; Teresa Mendoza was crossing the street, aiming at her and firing. Ángela threw herself on the ground in between two cars, a bullet had grazed her arm, wounding her. The sleeve of her cotton sweater was turning red and black.

She was the next person in the list of 'Los Muertos'; she had fulfilled her job and had become dispensable. Laura Almillar had become Teresa Mendoza, and she was a ruthless killer. No longer the kind and loving friend in whom she had once found infinite consolation; now, she was walking towards Cristina, aiming her gun at her; ready to kill.

She had missed her first shot, but she would not stop now. Ángela rolled on the wet pavement trying to find Teresa's legs from the floor. She could not see anything. With violence, she directed her gun's barrel to the other side of the street and in between the tiresome and repetitive movement of the windshield wipers, she recognized Arturo. He was waiting in his car to see the outcome of the executions. In that rainy afternoon, all the pawns were moving in a deadly game. She rolled over and pointed her gun between two cars, waiting for Teresa.

But the voice reached her, criminal and sure, from behind her back.

"Don't move", Teresa appeared from where Ángela had not expected her. "Don't take this personally".

Bang!

She heard the third shot and closed her eyes.

She felt the weight of a body falling on her. Laura Almillar was dead with a bullet in her head. She pushed her away, letting her body fall into a pothole that was filling up with water and centered her attention at the car where Arturo waited to see the outcome. The man in the bow tie was looking scared at one side, not at her. The woman stood up quickly, forgetting the pain she was feeling and which was already coloring the pavement. Guzmán looked at her and nodded. He was completely drenched, his shirt had died a brownish red. The policeman kept aiming his service weapon at the parked vehicle with the man inside. The vehicle left its position and drove towards the injured woman. Arturo accelerated making the wheels skid on the wet pavement; he was driving his car straight into his ex-lover. Ángela lifted her injured arm and aimed her Sig-Sauer at the windshield where the wipers were still moved relentlessly. She fired her thirteen remaining bullets at the glass that separated the rain from the man who called himself Arturo Barrios. The car, now driven by dead hands, swerved and crashed a few feet away from the woman.

Guzmán got closer to the man in the car, his gun still high. Arturo's eyes were wide open and his head was tilted to one side. Guzmán checked his jugular; Arturo heart had stopped beating. Ángela put her gun away, fitting it in between her pants' waistband and her skin. The metal was still warm from the friction of the bullets; she knew that she had not missed a single shot.

Guzmán looked at his companion's arm and asked:

"Is it bad?"

"Just a graze".

"You are becoming used to getting shot and every time that happens I end up all soaked..." The man's shirt was stained with a red ink that he had activated when he fell to give their sham some credibility.

Angela smiled. Time did not seem to have gone by between them. Guzmán pointed at the dead driver.

"Did you know him?"

"Not really, I just slept with him".

"If you really want to get to know someone, you shouldn't sleep with them, all you need to do is talk".

A young woman came out of a van with dark windows; she was carrying a television camera over her shoulder and was filming as she walked to where the two ex-colleagues stood watching the lifeless driver inside the crashed car; from another half-open door, came Gloria Altolaza, microphone in hand, to join the camerawoman.

Gaby walked out of the Fumadera and lit a joint under the rain, he took a long drag and then exhaled a great cloud of white smoke that mingled with the raindrops; he needed to lower some of the tension.

Ángela got closer to Guzmán and kissed him in the cheek.

"I need to go; this hasn't ended yet. 'Los Muertos' are still alive".

"I told you I'd bring spectators", he nodded at the two women that were walking towards them. "The only way of getting rats to leave their holes is by putting them on the news".

Ángela walked away under the rain. Guzmán gazed down at Laura Almillar's body. She was lying on her back in between two cars with a bullet in her head. He looked down at his gun; it had been the one to spit the deadly bullet that now rested in the head of the woman without an identity. Ashamed, he put it away. Weapons were a cancer. Once again, he been a witness to their effects.

The young camerawoman stood a few meters away from the inspector; she had filmed everything that had happened since he parked his car at the cannabis store's door. He was going to be the center of public attention once again because of his shot. This time, he would share the limelight with a blonde woman in sunglasses who had an injured arm, and who had left a wet kiss on Guzmán's cheek.

***

Aldo Ríos arrived at his brother's house in an impressive black car with armored windows. He was wearing the same white shirt that Juno had given him when he left prison.

His escape had been planned down to the smallest detail by Juno, Don's young pet, a perfect plan that had cost them five million dollars and thirteen dead people. Colorado had become the Death State in the world's news and Aldo Ríos had been named the new number one public enemy of the United States of America. Six hours after the jailbreak, the man's head had entered the bounty market at ten million dollars and all the state agencies, the CIA, DEA and the FBI, were preparing special units to search for him worldwide. 'Find Aldo Ríos, at all costs'.

Aldo was wearing the black mask that Ramona had given him. Nobody could see him, nobody could know anything about him; he had disappeared behind a blank mask. From now on, only a reduced number of people would see his face.

The man in the black mask walked into his brother's house; he had not seen Don in two years. At the door, a muscly man with Asian features, was waiting for them to guide them into the imposing mansion.

The man walked down the porticoed corridor to the left and opened a large oakwood double door. He stepped aside to let Aldo in; Juno followed. Ramona stayed outside the room, next to the bodyguard.

Don and Esther were waiting for them inside the living room. Aldo gazed at the other two bodyguards standing in the room for his brother's protection; he did not remove his mask. He turned to his blood relative. Don had opened his arms to welcome him.

"Aldo, welcome home".

"Brother, fuck off, *güey*. My home disappeared when the gringos caught me. My men either died or changed nests, and now I'm just a refugee in the king of kings' home, my big brother: the asshole".

"Let's just celebrate that the whole family is finally together", said Juno with a smile.

Esther hurried up to her uncle. He was still wearing his expressionless mask.

"Uncle Aldo, I'm so happy to have you here for my wedding".

"I couldn't possibly miss the wedding of my only niece".

"You're free now".

"Yes, don't think I'm being ungrateful; I feel like I'm in debt with you. You got me out. But, during my time there I never forgave you for getting me in there in the first place, Don".

Don looked at Esther with surprise.

"I don't know where you got that mad idea from".

"Doncel, don't take me for a brainless fucker. In this business, blood bonds don't exist; things always happen for a reason. Always, Don. Both you and I know that".

"You can take off your mask".

Aldo turned his head to the two bodyguards who looked impassibly at them.

"You have nothing to worry about, they do not speak our language".

"But they have eyes and may recognize me".

Don made a signal to the guards who turned their backs to them like two naughty children who had been punished in class.

Aldo removed the mask and held it in his hand, then, he noticed a great wooden box and a large plaque engraved with the Smith and Wesson's logo. He recognized it. The box was used to keep the legendary Magnum 500 with five shots and bullets of 12.7.

He smiled, opened the box and took out the gun. He felt the metal's weight, over two kilograms, he turned the cylinder and then aimed at his brother with the shiny weapon.

They waited.

Don looked at the two men in charge of his protection; they were facing the wall, oblivious to what was going on.

"You have always liked big things", Aldo said, his eyes fixed on his older brother. "Do you remember our Nona? When father died in that swamp, devoured by an alligator? Do you remember the story of the deer and the alligator?"

Don nodded without shifting his gaze from the trigger.

"At the swamp, when the deer wakes, it knows that it must drink water to survive. When the alligator wakes, it knows that it must approach the deer silently to hunt and feed".

Don continued the story where his brother had left it:

"We had to choose whether we wanted to be the deer or the alligator, but always, no matter what we chose, when the sun rose, we would have to be vigilant. Remember?"

Aldo was still pointing at Don with the gun.

"This is the moment when I decide what is more convenient for me. Shall I yield to your power, considering that I no means of fighting you in equal conditions. Do I grow old and wear this mask, always? Or, I may choose to die right now and drag you to the grave with me. It would be the end of a great family. The Ríos or the Nassar?" Aldo put his mask back on. "What would you do, Don? That new drug that my niece owns marks the end of an era, the death of drug cartels; they will all disappear. All of them, one after the other". He removed the black mask once more. "Do you know what started all of this? A prohibition. With the prohibition, a group of people saw their chance to make money; later came the time when alcohol consumption became legal again. But that group that had benefited from its ban already counted with a structure and they hid to continue living off gambling, and then, after gambling was legalized too, they went for weapons, and finally, drugs. Today, brother, as I flew in one of those drones I realized that this was the end of a cycle. We have ceased to have a reason to exist. A new world has arrived and you and I, Don, are too old to understand it; we barely know how to use a cellphone. Drugs are dead, only a miracle will save them now. Thousands of people who live from producing, transporting and selling it, will stop earning any money. What are those thousands of people belonging to one side or the other, going to do when the only thing they know is killing each other?

Aldo lowered the revolver's barrel. He put the gun back in its box and closed it. He did not take his black mask off again.

***

Julián sat on the white bed of the guest room in Anthony's apartment. In his black pants and blue shirt, he looked like a stain in the middle of all that brightness. He turned the light off and immediately felt better. He called Matías, his secretary, to hear the latest news about Ana, his wife. He told him what Julián already knew: that she was a murder suspect and that the story was on every news broadcast. Julián felt more upset than cheated. When the secretary updated him on the police investigation, Julián asked if he could deal with the lawyers because he thought that Ana Riccoli would be released soon on probation; the evidence that the Police had found was not conclusive. The only thing that she had not denied was that she had spent the afternoon with Carlo Stamas; whatever happened after she left the room had nothing to do with her.

He looked at the computer screen, stood up, and wrote his resignation letter as CEO of Synchro. Then, he looked for the email that Matías had sent him with Yalitza Torres' number, and called her; he needed to speak to someone who disagreed with him.

Anthony was on his way to Synchro to take full charge of the company.

Julián felt liberated; he had already dialed Yalitza's number. At that very moment, Ana only took up a small space in his memory. Just then, as he listened to the long beeps announcing that the line was busy, he came up with a wonderful idea. He knew what his next project would be.

The meetings room was empty. Slowly, Anthony crossed the room and sat on the armchair that presided the long table. Outside, dozens of drones rose into the air, heavy with the shipments of tiny black balls.

***

Ángela walked into the apartment. This time she did not stop to check the coins that were strategically scattered across the entrance.

She went straight to the bathroom. She took off her glasses and wig, and her damp, bloodied sweater; she removed her gun, unsticking it from her skin, and left it in the sink. Her wound was open and dark but it no longer bled. She took out a first aid kit, got the bottle of alcohol from inside and poured it generously on the gunshot wound. She felt a sharp burning sensation; then, she put her arm under the shower and let the water fall on it. She had to clean it thoroughly. Opening two dressings, she pressed them against her clean skin with a bandage. Later, she would have to go and get a tetanus shot. Leaning on the sink, she noticed three fallen hairs, banished, abandoned, alone. She opened the tap with the intention of letting the water wash them away into the drainpipe. Changing her mind, she closed the tap. Her stiff hands held onto the white porcelain; Ángela lifted her head to recognize herself in the mirror. Her gaze had darkened; there was the smallest glint of hope in her iris. She saw it and right then she knew why she would carry on living. She smiled and considered the dry weapon beside her. Picking it up, she removed the empty chamber. A gun without munition is closer to a stone than a weapon. She dressed up and went down to the building's reception to find Julio. He had to open Arturo's apartment for her; she was sure she would find something there. Besides, Arturo would not be back any time soon.

Gloria Altolaza opened the special night news broadcast with the images of the shooting that had taken place that very afternoon and in which two unidentified people had died.

Guzmán sat in front of his television watching the scenes in which he had been involved just a few hours earlier. Braulio Gaytán's suitcase remained open in his living room and the notebook where he had written down his ideas and thoughts waited on the side. The inspector grabbed it and went through it once more; he had already read it in detail before. He threw it in the bin.

***

All brides feel tempted to try on their wedding dress the day before their wedding and Esther Nassar was no exception; she was just another inquisitive bride with the expectations of any other person about to get married.

She was looking at her reflection in her bedroom mirror when the man who would soon be her husband walked in. Juno leaned on the door frame and stared at her.

"Seeing the bride in her wedding dress before the wedding brings bad luck".

Esther felt naked under his gaze.

"We have spent all of our lives together; it's like we were doomed to marry".

It was not so much the words, but the way he said them that filled Esther with fear. An atavistic fear that she had never felt before. Instinctively, she took her hand to her belly; it was the first time in her life she felt vulnerable.

Aldo Ríos had removed his blank mask and was resting, half-asleep, while the special effects expert applied make-up on his face. Nobody would be able to recognize him. His fingerprints were the only thing that could give him away. He would be a man in a mask for a while now; in time, they would forget about him. The make-up artist placed a tube in his mouth so that he could breath, and covered his face with cling film so that the silicone would adapt better to his skin. 'It will just be a moment', he thought.

Aldo felt the tube disappear from his mouth. He could no longer breath. He tried to remove the cling film that was stopping him from breathing. Ramona held his wrists firmly. The man understood that his end had come and that threatening his brother with a weapon had a price. This one. The tension lasted thirty seconds, then it all ended. Ramona took the black plastic mask that was resting next to him and placed it on the plastic-covered face. Aldo had stopped running, his end had come.

The black van was parked behind the Forensic Sciences Institute. Ambrose Levi waited gloomily. He was staring at the closed white door when it finally opened and two men hurried out with two bodies in plastic bags. They opened the back doors, dropped the bodies inside the vehicle and climbed in, slamming the doors closed. The van started and took a right into Niños Héroes Ave. One of the men undid the zips to show the identities of the two corpses they had just stolen for Ambrose Levi. He nodded. They were the bodies Teresa Mendoza and Arturo Barrios. They also had their end.

*****

10. END

The conclusion of something, its consummation; it is also a motive and an objective. A person will use all their means and efforts to reach it.

The organist walked his fingers across the keyboard and ceremonial chords filled the garden. A light evening breeze blew into the marquees. The white fabric fluttered around the pool. Mendelssohn's wedding march was the signal and trigger for one hundred elegantly dressed people sitting in cushioned chairs to turn and look in the direction of the mansion. The party, lead by a solitary Juno Coentrao, dressed in a dark suit and white bow tie, walked out into the garden. Graceful strides, self-possessed for a man who had not yet reached thirty, but whose eyes held the trace of an early death. Today, with no family members there to remind him of his Brazilian past, life seemed to only hold future for him. He just needed to have someone by his side. Four girls, hired for the occasion, and who must have been twelve at most, in vaporous dresses, spread white rose petals on the red carpet. Then, Esther Nassar appeared arm in arm with her father. They walked down the mansion's colonial styled staircase, at the top of the Jardines de la Montaña, towards the freshly mowed green lawn. A priest waited for them under an arch bursting with flowers of every color. Don Nassar watched over his pregnant daughter's steps. Her white dress artfully hid her swollen belly.

Don drew his face close to his daughter's ear and, smiling, whispered:

"Are you sure about this?"

She looked at him with surprise, then smiled broadly at the guests.

"I have never been surer of anything. Anyway, what would you do if I wasn't?"

The proud father raised a hand at the spectators and, looking straight ahead, replied:

"I could have a heart attack, here and now".

Esther's eyes met Ramona's, who was supervising the development of the day's events a few meters away from them.

"You have spent your entire life planning this moment", she said without altering the smile on her face. "In the end, it all comes down to having a wife and an heir. That's all that matters; I've learnt that from you".

"Nothing matters, nothing", agreed Don, ending the small paternal talk and continued walking.

His Chinese bodyguards stood still, watching every step their boss took, scanning the guests, looking around the whole garden.

Anthony sat in one of the last lines. He was wearing a smart blue suit with a Mao-style collar; at his side was a young man with a boyish face and an eye patch covering his right eye. When the young man saw the bride walk down the staircase, arm in arm with her father, he squeezed Anthony's hand, visibly touched. Synchro's new CEO smiled happily at his friend. The previous day had been very intense and he could finally rest and enjoy the wedding to which he had been invited.

The day before, first thing in the morning, Anthony Somoza had been in his lawyers' office. Julián Konks had decided to transfer his share of the company to Anthony, so that he could do with it as he wished, no conditions nor restrictions, it had all been agreed.

The lawyers had received the assignment with surprise; they watched the transaction in shock. Only the two young programmers knew the real scope of the papers they were so lightly signing. Meanwhile, what the lawyers saw, were billions of dollars given away for no apparent reason, an eccentric fit of madness. Still, with conviction and wearing conspiratorial smiles, the men drew their signatures on the pages in which Julián Konks gave all his shares to his associate, Anthony Somoza.

Julián had left the office alone, putting his sunglasses on as the elevator descended to the ground floor. He walked to the car where two bodyguards waited for him and asked them to take him to the Mex-Tec building. There, he would meet his wife, Ana Riccoli. He knew through Matías that she had been released free of all charges. They held no conclusive evidence against her, only her fingerprints on a gun, and she counted with the world's best lawyers. Ana paid one million pesos for the bond and went home. From there, she had only called her husband once and he, despite having seen her name flashing on the screen, had not pressed the green button. She had not tried calling him again. Instead, she called Matías, Julián's personal secretary and asked him to arrange a meeting with her husband. She could not think of a better place than the Mex-Tec for their encounter. Matías called her back an hour later. Julián had accepted seeing her in the building where they first met. Ana had already been there twice that week.

Julián felt comforted by the sight of the building. It was a place without pretensions and still it was inspiring. The corridors had not changed; they were crowded with folders of colors faded by time. Nobody had fixed the scratches and chipped walls of the old service elevator where they used to bring up their bikes. Ana was waiting for him in the corridor. She was looking at her phone without interest. They exchanged a friendly smile. For a second, Ana thought of hugging him, but he had stopped a short distance away from her; he thought she looked beautiful and sensual. She was wearing a white shirt and had undone one of her buttons to accentuate her cleavage. She was a stunning woman but he did not feel any sort of closeness to her.

"Thank you for coming", said Ana, placing a hand on her hip.

"I didn't really want to come", said Julián frankly.

"You were always a gentleman".

"Thanks for the compliment".

"I just wanted to let you know that I'm free, they have no evidence..."

"They don't have any evidence or they have no motive?" Julián leaned his back on the chipped wall.

"They have nothing that they can use against me", said Ana emphatically. "You are the only person who can hold something against me".

"Don't worry, you can carry on with your life. I'm not the sort of man to hold grudges". He remained silent for a while, watching her. "It hurts, but I'll carry on living too... On the other hand, what happened between us... It had been a bit rushed from the start".

"Yes, we skipped the whole boyfriend, girlfriend, getting to know each other part". Ana smiled. "If we'd known each other things would have gone better".

"I think we know each other very well".

"Julián, don't you want to ask me a question?" she wanted to see him angry, but her husband's gaze was distant and passive.

"No, I think I've got all the answers I need". The young man pointed at the elevator. "I have just given Anthony my share of the company... you can keep the money and the house".

"Do you want a divorce?"

"Don't you?"

Julián wanted the conversation to end. She took a step forward and said:

"I hold nothing against you; I want you to know that I'm going to buy this building".

The young man looked at her.

"The building is not for sale; I bought it a while ago through an intermediary company. It belongs to me".

Ana felt displeased.

"I would like to save our relationship".

"Our relationship is fine. I wish you the best in life".

Julián turned around to call the elevator.

"If it's any consolation, I want you to know that those weird nervous tics that you had when we met, have disappeared".

"I will be eternally grateful to you for those times".

Julián stared at the luminous button that announced the elevator's arrival.

"Maybe we'll see each other again".

"Maybe".

The elevator's doors slid open.

"Do you regret what happened between us?" was Ana's last question.

Julián turned to look at her with a smile and shook his head. The doors closed.

Ana Riccoli watched as the metallic doors shut with her husband inside. The building would never be hers. She walked to her old office, opened her desk's drawer, took out the notebook that she had left there just a few days ago and walked out buttoning up her shirt.

The young woman entered the old elevator with its damaged walls and pressed the round button with the zero. It illuminated sadly.

As the elevator descended, Ana Riccoli thought of a different elevator in an entirely different place that she had entered not too long ago, after an afternoon full of passion, disagreements and fire.

The sound of water filled the room while she got dressed with the swiftness of an uncomfortable resolution. Carlo Stamas stepped out of the shower and dried himself with the confidence of a job well done. He admired himself in the mirror and ran his hand over the shiny skin of his shaved head, wiping the odd drops that had stayed there after the shower. He walked to the bed where he had left his clothes without looking at the beautiful woman who was buttoning her dress behind him. He turned his gaze distractedly to the holster that he had left on the bedside table and frowned. The weapon and the clip were missing.

He could not have turned around in time, the shot exploded behind his back. Carlo Stamas fell on the unmade bed. Ana threw the weapon onto the bed, grabbed her Chanel handbag and left with the calm confidence of a goddess in a world where she is untouchable. Carlo had become an obstacle that she had to get rid of; people were either on her side or against her. Ana Riccoli felt calm; she was so immensely rich that she could end another person's life for the price of a lawyer's salary. She controlled heaven on earth and there was no room there for someone like Carlo Stamas;

she had understood that and everyone else would have to understand it too. Yes, that was what lawyers were there for. She did not feel like returning home to Julián, her husband, with his childish gaze.

Arturo Barrios sat waiting in room 214 wearing latex gloves. He had just called the room service and ordered a caesar salad, a sandwich club without mayonnaise and two Coronas; he did not know how much time he would spend waiting.

When he heard the shot, he walked up to the door, and opening it slightly, saw a blonde woman leave the room next door. The man in the bow tie with the appearance of a Literature professor, took out a card from his pocket and opened the door to room 212 which the woman had just left.

He walked in to find a naked man, bloodied and with a gunshot on his back, dragging himself to the door. Carlo Stamas was still alive and if he was found in that state, he would be saved and perhaps have to spend the rest of his life on a wheelchair. The eyes of the muscly man on the floor were wide open and he was moaning incomprehensibly, desperate for help. There was a glint of hope in his eyes at the sight of the man with the bow tie who had just walked into his room. Arturo picked up a pillow and the gun that was still lying on the bed. He stood behind Stamas and shot a second time at the man's back, right where his heart was and returned to his room, showered and waited for the food that he had ordered from the room service.

Just as Arturo left room 212, Stamas, in one last effort before death, stretched out his arm and held the door just as it was closing.

***

Ever since Ángela Madero left Teresa Mendoza lying dead between two cars with a bullet in her head, she had become obsessed with the thought of Albi, the dog that she had known for so long. Ángela knew that the dog lived; she had seen his grey hairs stuck to the car seats of Laura Almillar's car.

She knew that Albi must be somewhere and she had to find him. She also understood that she had become the number one objective of 'Los Muertos'. There were only two ways of staying alive: she could run away, hide in the hope that she would eventually cease to exist in the memory of these people; or she could get out there and find them, and play one last game in their own territory.

The red brick hangar stood out among the other industrial buildings of the Guadalupe Tepeyac area. Its grace and style marked the character of the busy street; it looked like an old cinema studio.

Ángela parked her car a few feet away from it and waited for the white Prius that Guzmán drove to arrive. When she saw him, she made a signal and the policeman parked too. The woman walked to his car and looked at the suitcase at the feet of the passenger's seat.

"Are you going somewhere?"

"No, I'm just going to leave the Police and start a promising career as an errands boy", the inspector said and shot a look at Braulio's suitcase. "I need to return it to a motherfucking asshole later. Where's that place that we're going to visit?"

"Over there", said Ángela nodding at the brick building that looked like it had been abandoned.

Guzmán opened his glove box and took out his gun.

"This shitty box has been opening more than a gigolo's ass".

The inspector got out of the car and closed the door. The two friends crossed the street ignoring the cars around them.

"How's your arm?"

"Fine, it was just a graze".

"You won't believe it; yesterday, someone took your friends' corpses from the forensic department".

"I do believe it". Ángela knew how efficient 'Los Muertos' could be.

"Maybe they returned from the dead and walked out on their own two feet".

The gates to the building were unlocked but the parking lot was empty.

"We should have called first to ask them for a proper welcome". Guzmán moved to one side of the red door. "Well, Cristina, you're the boss of this operation. I await your orders".

There was a camera above the entrance door. Ángela shuddered at the sound of her real name.

"We're getting in and then we're improvising. It's going to be two of us against all the dead".

"I was afraid you'd say that. Great plan, very sophisticated. It reminds me of that show with the zombies. Let me tell you something, *güey*, 'Los Muertos' don't scare me; it's the living that I'm terrified of". The inspector held the door handle firmly and added, "in case we don't get out of this one alive, I've written a special report and left it on my table for commissioner García to find; if anything happens to us, at least they will find us, even if it's with bullets in our body".

They both drew their guns and unlocked the safe.

"They're waiting for us", she said in a low voice.

"So, we don't even count with the surprise factor", said Guzmán ironically as he turned the handle and opened the door.

They moved from clarity to darkness through a wide corridor. Soon, their eyes adapted to the darkness. They were walking with their backs to the wall and their guns pointing ahead, taking cautious steps. Ángela had been there a few times before; she knew the way to the control room.

The room was empty, it looked intact; she remembered it like that. The equipment and screens were off, waiting for someone to connect them and make them useful again. They were alone. Guzmán stared at the display of screens and computers in the room.

"So, this is what working with a proper budget looks like. These dead guys have more resources than we do at the station. Tough luck".

"I can ask if they've got any vacancies", said Ángela as she moved to the far end of the hangar.

"Forget it, kiddo. I'm way too old for a change of life".

Riiiing!

The sound of the telephone reverberated in the room's walls. The two intruders turned to look at the desk where the black object lied vibrating.

Ángela Madero walked up to the desk with the noisy telephone; she did not pick up. She looked curiously at the camera that was pointing in her direction from high up. The camera moved slightly as if pointing at the object on the table.

"I think they want you to pick up". Guzmán nodded at the phone.

Ángela held the telephone against her ear.

"Hello, Ángela", said a familiar voice.

"Hello, Ambrose".

She recognized the voice of the man who gave the orders in that place.

"We were waiting for you. I see that you have brought company; your objective is standing next to you instead of being dead".

"I'm afraid killing police friends is not my strength".

"Thanks for that", said Guzmán.

Ambrose was silent for a few moments before he spoke again.

"I always liked your style; ever since I met you I knew you were a trustworthy person".

Guzmán looked at her questioningly and asked:

"What the hell is going on? Where are these people? What do they want?"

Ángela gestured at him to be patient.

"Tell the inspector that he may go home. Tell him that he doesn't need to worry; you and I need to have a friendly chat. I would like to introduce you to someone", His voice sounded conciliatory.

Ángela doubted for a moment.

"Where is Albi?"

"Do you mean Teresa Mendoza's dog?"

"Yes".

"Give me a second".

The phone went silent. Guzmán looked confused; he had not understood the thing about the dog. Ángela scanned the place trying to discover some sign of movement, a reaction of any sort; seconds kept going by.

"Hey, Ambrose, are you there?"

At the far end of the hangar, a door opened slightly and a white mastiff appeared. The dog trotted in and looked to the sides, then he approached the two human presences playfully, wagging his tail. Guzmán pointed his gun at him, he did not know the dog that was approaching them. Ángela moved forward leaving the phone and her gun on the desk.

"Albi, Albi, come here, boy".

The dog trotted happily to where the woman stood and let her stroke him. He had recognized her.

"Hey, Albi, remember me? I'm Cristina, Lucas' mom, remember? Lucas' mom", Ángela started crying while the dog played around her, happy.

Guzmán rubbed his chin as he watched the scene that was unfolding before him; he too felt the choking sensation of tears that would not fall.

Finally, Ángela composed herself. She picked up the phone again and looked straight up at the camera.

"Why did she want to kill me? Teresa tried it, she shot me".

"Cristina, she was following orders, just like you... Let's just say that you were showing a strange behavior. In your case, you forced us to stay vigilant. Blocking all the cameras in the apartment was simple mischief, but leaving a message at the shop, what would you call that? Betrayal, perhaps?" One of the screens went on. It belonged to a camera installed at the Fumadera, the cannabis shop. A woman was leaving the store as Guzmán looked out into the street. On a different sequence, Ángela walked into the store and spoke to Gaby, the owner.

Guzmán watched the scenes with surprise; he remembered the woman who had bought the ointment for her back. He had bought the same one.

"I want you to understand, Cristina; we continue to exist because we leave no loose ends. I would like to show you one more thing".

Another screen lit up; this time they were looking at images of the cemetery. Ángela and Guzmán were standing in the middle of the scene. The woman realized that all her precautions had been useless, they had just increased the suspicions they had of her.

"And why would you trust me now?"

"Ángela, life changes in a single day. Yesterday, with your friend's help, you neutralized two of our best men".

"No, they were a man and a woman. And I assure you that..."

"We know, and they have been buried in a safe place. Tell your police friend that he may return to his boring life, we need to get back to our work. Say your goodbyes and tell him that he will continue to be watched and that we make no exceptions. Also, the envelope that he left on his desk for commissioner García has been destroyed".

Albi kept wagging his tale and nudging Ángela with his snout. She turned to face Guzmán:

"Leave, I'm staying".

"Are you sure?"

"Yes, I am". She knew that as long as she remained within 'Los Muertos', her friend would be safe. If Guzmán stayed they would both die right there and their bodies would be destroyed without leaving trace. Those were her thoughts, but she said:

"When Lucas died, a fog entered my life; I know it is difficult to understand, but the only place where that fog doesn't affect me is here".

"I've spoken to you about my grandmother before, haven't I?"

Ángela nodded.

"She knew that there was a place that was neither heaven nor hell, a place in between where sinful souls atone for their sins".

"What's the name of that place?"

"The Purgatory. Its views aren't that nice, there aren't any mountains, nor rivers or seas; no clouds with angels and arches, but I think it must look like this Mexico City that I love".

"Then, I'm sure we'll see each other there".

"See you there. *Ándale*", said the policeman, putting an end to their exchange. He placed his weapon back in his pocket and left without looking back.

Álvaro Guzmán had to return a suitcase.

Ángela stayed stroking the dog as she continued her dialogue with Death.

***

Night was falling. The traffic flowed in the Colorado highway when the police car stopped behind a car that seemed to have broken down. Teresa Mendoza stood outside leaning against the trunk. She was chewing gum and looked as if she was waiting for someone. When she saw the patrol car pulling over, she waved and smiled playfully.

The police agent left his car and adjusted his wide brim hat, then he placed his hand on his revolver, just for the effect. With no time to react, Teresa took out a sawn-off shotgun and fired at the uniformed man. She was standing six feet away from him. The force of the shot threw the agent back against his car's fender. Shaken, he opened his eyes and looked down at his chest; his bulletproof vest had saved his life, he thought, as he stared at his ripped shirt, completely shredded by the pellets. The woman took a step forward; the man raised his eyes in fear, without understanding what was happening to him. The woman fired again; it was the shotgun's second bullet. Then, she walked around into the police car and getting hold of the radio, said:

"Patroller dead on the highway, help required".

Teresa Mendoza walked back to her vehicle and left. Five minutes later that place would be full of police agents.

Twenty minutes later, Arturo Barrios, who was wearing a red cap, parked his car outside the entrance to the sheriff's offices, next to an official car that had its lights off. A uniformed woman holding a cup of coffee looked at him from the counter behind the glass entrance doors. Arturo stepped out of his car but did not go inside. He was not there to file a complaint. A large dark vehicle stopped and waited for him to climb in before continuing its route. The policewoman placed her coffee mug on the table and walked out, surprised by the man in the red cap's behavior.

The car exploded.

Arturo removed his cap and threw it in the back seat.

"I can't wait to be home".

Teresa was driving with caution; she still had to return the rental car and board a four-hour flight home, and the airport's security would have increased by then. She gave Arturo a sideways look.

"You haven't said anything about what happened the other night".

"And I have no intentions of saying anything; I'm a gentleman".

"I don't want the details".

"I'm not giving them to you anyway".

"Do you like her?" asked Teresa with a cheeky smile.

Arturo thought about the question and smiled.

"Yes, I do like her a lot. I hope all this finishes soon. Perhaps we could, well, who knows..."

Arturo's phone buzzed; a new message had just come through. He opened it. He was looking at a picture of Carlo Stamas with the word 'eliminate' underneath.

Teresa glanced at the screen with the portrait of the bald man and said firmly:

"This will never end".

They went on in silence.

***

Álvaro Guzmán was sitting on the hood of his white Prius. He was looking up at the hazy sky when Braulio Gaytán walked out of the penitentiary after spending three months atoning for the involuntary manslaughter of Rita Guzmán. The young man was abandoning the center holding an articulated stick with a camera at one end that allowed him to take better shots of himself. He was talking and smiling with the jail as a backdrop. When he saw Guzmán, he froze. Quickly, he turned off his camera and put it away. He stepped in a puddle; the rain had stopped but the ground was still wet and puddles of murky water scattered everywhere.

Álvaro lifted one arm at the young man in a friendly gesture.

"Hello, I've brought your suitcase".

"Thank you", said the influencer, confused by the policeman's politeness. He took his wet sneaker out of the puddle.

Braulio walked cautiously towards the car.

"I can give you a lift to the bus station if you want, it's close to here".

"No, thanks, I'm waiting for an Uber".

"Up to you", said Guzmán with a shrug. He jumped off the hood and opened the driver's door to get in his white car. "It's what Rita would have liked, for us to talk and get along despite all that's happened, don't you think?"

The young man held his suitcase and peered into the inspector's car again.

"Sure you don't want a ride?" Guzmán insisted.

Finally, Braulio nodded, although he climbed into the car with mistrust.

"I'm glad it's all over now", Guzmán declared.

The policeman's words comforted the ex-prisoner.

"I want you to know that I am extremely sorry for what happened to Rita, I loved her very much".

"I can imagine".

Guzmán started the car.

Instantly, Braulio regretted getting into the car with the inspector. For a while they were both silent, deep in their own thoughts.

The silence felt uncomfortable.

Guzmán turned into a street that was full of potholes and drove towards some abandoned-looking warehouses.

"This is a shortcut, you know how bad this city's traffic is". Guzmán looked straight ahead. "Are you going back to Guadalajara?"

"No, I will spend a few days here, in Mexico City".

The car stopped next to a warehouse.

"We're here, this is the bus stop. Get out".

The young man stepped out looking at either side and holding his black suitcase tightly; a strong sickening smell impregnated every corner of that depressing place.

"Get in there and buy yourself a ticket", Guzmán pointed at the shabby door behind which they could hear the nervous grunts of a herd of pigs.

The young influencer felt uneasy. The place stank and there were no other cars around.

"This is a pig's farm", said the young man doubtfully.

"Exactly, kiddo".

Guzmán got out of the car and pointed at the door.

"In you go", he ordered.

Braulio held the suitcase without daring to contradict the orders of the father of his dead girlfriend. He looked at either side of the street; there was no one there nor any place that he could run to.

"But, this place is empty".

"We're late, the last bus to hell must have left already".

Inside, the lights were dim. The warehouse was divided into fenced areas crammed with pigs. The smell was unbearable. Braulio looked around the place and then back at Guzmán. He was aiming at his head with a gun.

"Let's see, you devilish kid, you have already been judged and I know that you are innocent; but those people didn't read that devil's diary that you left forgotten in my house. That's why now us two are going to play a game of truth in front of this select audience. They seem to be very interested in hearing what you've got to say. The game consists on the following: I'm going to ask you three questions; if you say a single lie I will burst your face with these bullets and you won't be allowed in hell because you will not pass their facial recognition test. If you say three truths, I will leave you here and you will return to your house in fucking Guadalajara, to sing *rancheras* or to the purgatory with your suitcase. Thus peace and then glory, as my dear grandma would have said. Understood?"

Guzmán did not expect an answer from the psychopath. He took out a small transparent bag with black pills inside: there must have been at least a dozen.

"First question: on the night of Rita's death, did you or did you not take one of these Synchro pills?" asked Guzmán lifting the bag.

"I didn't", replied Braulio defiantly.

"Good, I see you understand how this game works. Let's move onto the second question of our live or die contest for assholes", said Guzmán. He was looking at him and felt the urge to pull the trigger before he had even asked the question. "Was Rita's death premeditated?"

"No". He was equally firm in his answer.

Guzmán looked at him thoughtfully and declared.

"I'm going to accept this one. You had planned it in your notebook but I believe you; presumably, you did not know that you would do it that night". The inspector raised two fingers. "So far, two 'no's".

Braulio's fearful expression was dissolving into a look of defiance. Now he knew that his almost father in law had read his diary and had made up an idea of him which could collapse at any moment; he just needed to plant the seed of doubt.

"So, *güey*, you've come to realize that I've read your diary in detail. Don't worry, I have already thrown that piece of psychopath bullshit in the trash. You already know that you cannot judge a person twice for the same crime. And you have been absolved even though you're out of your mind". Guzmán lifted a third finger; only the thumb and little finger remained hidden and they were busy holding the little bag with the black pills. "Now for the last question. Did you murder Rita?"

Braulia looked at him with contempt.

"I will not answer that question".

The policeman closed his grip on the bag.

"Two right answers and one wrong one".

Guzmán walked towards the young man aiming his gun at him. He extended the Synchro bag. Without offering any resistance, the young man picked one of the pills.

"Swallow it", the agent ordered threateningly.

Braulio held the capsule in his hand and stared at it.

"Swallow it, I said; I want you to experience what it's like when one of those things controls your brain".

The young man swallowed the black ball, then Guzmán threw the rest of the balls inside the pen that was crammed with pigs. They hurried to eat the capsules that had fallen in their food. Guzmán opened a small door that lead into the pen. Twenty pigs moved around nervously.

"In".

"You said you'd let me go".

"I don't lie. In fact, I'm not going to kill you".

Braulio obeyed.

"Now, kiddo, take out your influencer kit and put the camera in a place where it can get a good shot of you; I guarantee you'll become famous with this video", said Guzmán, putting his gun away and bringing out his mobile phone.

Braulio seemed satisfied and became calmer; the camera made him feel like he was in his own habitat.

"They say that these animals are the closest you can get to us humans. I have read that they use pigs' hearts to experiment on people", said Guzmán, pointing at the beasts.

Braulio pressed the red recording button and stepped back to get a better shot of himself; Guzmán lifted his arm and showed him the Synchro logo on his phone's screen. He pressed the 'relax' mode. Braulio smiled sadistically; he was enjoying the challenge. After a few seconds, Braulio sat among the pigs, which did not pay any attention to the new member of their herd: it seemed strange. The camera was filming the spectacle and he was the main character of the incredible swine adventure. Guzmán looked at the scene for a moment; the pigs seemed unchanged after his selection.

Then, he searched for the wild sex mode and pressed the button again.

Suddenly, Braulio Gaytán looked transformed. He kneeled on the ground, undid his pants, and started rolling around in the manure. Then, he threw himself at a pig which dodged him in fear.

Guzmán decided that he had seen enough and left the place. Suddenly, from the other side of the door, he started hearing wild cries and squeals coming from the pen where he had just been. It sounded like a mixture of animal and human cries that blended with the background chorus of grunts.

Inside the warehouse, the animals that had ingested the black balls that manipulated emotions, were finally reacting to Synchro's electric impulses. They lifted their heads, ears pointing up, and grunted ferociously, dragging their long and rigid penises with glans the shape of corkscrews on the mud. They gathered around the young vlogger who was also screaming desperately. Meanwhile, the camera, impassible, filmed the whole atrocity.

Guzmán felt tempted to return and kill Braulio with a single shot; it was a matter of pity. But he rode his white Prius and left the place. Today, there would be no commiseration.

***

Esther Nassar and Juno Coentrao kissed after the priest pronounced, with a forced smile, the famous phrase: 'you may kiss the bride'. It was followed by a loud applause from the guests.

Anthony Somoza and his plus one, a young man with a long face who stood out because of his black leather eye patch on his right eye, held hands, brimming with emotion after the newly wed couple's kiss.

The couple left the altar among warm congratulations and walked into the mansion. They went straight to a room where the lawyers of both parts waited with their marriage contract. After three months of negotiations, the bride and groom were finally going to sign. The time had come to consolidate their relationship, and not in any spiritual manner; everything had to be well tied up. Esther and Juno drew their signatures on the two thick documents; there were no loose ends. The lawyers put the two sealed documents in their secure metal briefcases and then attached them to their wrists with handcuffs. They would take them to a strongbox. When Don Nassar walked in with his Chinese bodyguards, it had all finished already. A shudder ran down his spine at the sight of the lawyers chained to the bombproof briefcases.

The party went by with plenty of courtship, finesse, gentle music, pleasant chats, exquisite soup, and delicacies brought from every corner of the planet.

Three hours later, the couple boarded a private jet and flew to Colombia, to Hacienda Alcázar. They could not think of a better place to spend their honeymoon than that recreational fortress. The most adequate destination, considering the safety of the place and Esther Nassar's state. She had said goodbye to her father with a long and affectionate kiss on the cheek and a look that made the powerful man uneasy and full of worry. He was the alligator, the hunter, the owner of the swamp, but that kiss had turned him into a scared fawn, a prey.

Jacinto Alcázar stood waiting at the bottom of the airplane's stairs. He was the director of the fortified estate and had prepared everything for their stay, down to the smallest detail. They had booked the entire Hacienda for themselves. They wanted intimacy and no human contact other than the people who were at their service. Jacinto Alcázar had planned entertainment for each of them; Juno would do a tasting of the best wines at a winery that counted with more than ten thousand bottles of select alcohol, valued in four million dollars. Esther would enjoy testing out some of the pieces of the varied arsenal in their armory, which had at least one thousand firearms of all calibers. Her gynecologist did not say anything about not handling weapons; neither had she asked.

Ramona stayed at the party until the last of the guests left; then, she left to carry out the task that she had been given.

***

Don Nassar felt restless in his large canopied bed. He could not fall asleep, and blamed it on the emotions associated to his daughter's wedding. He was acutely aware of the softness of the mattress and felt suffocated by the white, feather duvet. He looked to his sides; the two men in their dark suits watched over his sleep, impassible, unaware of the sleeplessness that prevented Don's rest.

He could clearly hear the sounds that came from the other side of his bedroom door. Someone was talking. It sounded like they were asking for permission to get in. He opened his eyes and looked once again, lying down in the dark, at one of the bodyguards who did not understand his language. He continued to stand still, frozen.

The door opened and Ramona walked in. Behind her came the eight men of his permanent protection service, who, together with the two who kept watch at either side of his bed, completed the praetorian guard of the magnate. Don sat up in shock.

The spectacular woman walked confidently to the edge of the untouchable man's bed, where he sat, looking scared. He turned to his sides again, waiting for a reaction that would not come. Don could hardly make out the slim and powerful figure that had walked in without permission and that now stood in front of him, while the guards did nothing to prevent it.

Ramona took out a long firearm with a supplementary silencer tube, aimed it at him, and fired a dull shot at the powerful magnate's forehead.

None of the ten guards moved; they were simple spectators of a murder in cold blood, perpetrated by a beautiful woman.

Ramona Drumpf, daughter of 'The Monster', an SS officer who had fled Germany, stood staring mercilessly at Don Nassar. He had gone completely still after the shot; a metallic piece now rested deep in his skull. A red, dense, liquid flowed lazily from the hole in his forehead, and dripped down his face.

"The king has died, long live the queen", the woman whispered as she lowered her gun.

The bodyguards surrounded the bed of the dead man they were supposed to protect. Ramona nodded. The men in the dark suits, five at either side, picked up the mattress with the corpse and left the room through the open double doors. It looked like a funeral procession.

Ramona stayed at the room that was now missing a mattress; seconds later, she saw the ten men in black leave the mansion with the corpse. They walked up to a truck that was waiting outside and without hesitation, threw everything inside. The truck left the mansion's grounds. Meanwhile, its jackhammer moved, ready to compact its contents, reduce them to their minimal expression.

The men in black returned in silence to the bedroom. They followed the orders of whoever paid them, and it had been a long time since Don Nassar stopped paying the bills. The ten men, dressed elegantly, formed a perfect line. Ramona gave a thick envelope to each of them; inside, was a plane ticket and three hundred thousand dollars for them to return home as rich men and age peacefully in their own country. Their job there was done.

***

Cristina walked into the building in the Polanco area with Albi trotting at her side. She said hello to Julio, who was cleaning the hallway with earnest. They walked into the elevator and pressed the button to her floor. The doors closed.

***

Guzmán arrived home. He could hear loud music coming from Gloria's apartment. He took his sleeve to his nose and sniffed it: it stank of pig. He took it off and threw it remorselessly on the floor next to his bedroom door.

The image of his daughter Rita materialized above the AI cylinder.

"Hello, Álvaro".

"Hello, Betty".

"How was your day?" asked the artificially created image.

"It was an odd one", replied the policeman as he dropped on the sofa in front of her.

"The adjective 'odd' is very vague, could you be more explicit, please?"

Guzmán looked at the white box which was still closed.

"Betty, to what point are you trustworthy? If I tell you a secret, how do I know that you're not going to tell or that someone will get it out of you?"

"In truth, you cannot trust me; I am information, I save data, store it. My trustworthiness is of sixty percent. I am as vulnerable as any other network element. I am sorry, I cannot keep secrets".

Guzmán opened the white box where he kept his marijuana and rolled a joint calmly. He lit it with his Zippo and took a long drag, as if it were his very first time.

"Betty, play some Bruce".

***

While Juno showered after their four-hours flight, Jacinto Alcázar accompanied Esther to the room where some people waited for her. A man was speaking on the phone, sat with his back to her. In front of him was a screen with an image of Ángela Madero holding a telephone in her hand; there was a gun on the table and a greyish dog played around her. Esther stood watching Ángela.

"Is that her?"

Ambrose Levi turned to look at her.

"Yes", he replied.

***

Julián Konks told his bodyguards to go to his office and ask Matías to do several jobs for him. He was no longer Synchro's CEO, so he did not need all the protection. He was back to being a normal guy; it was what he wanted. While he walked, he thought of Box Life; that was how he would call his new idea. A project that involved banking people's lives. He was going to store their memories and generate avatars. If, by any chance, he ever had great-grandchildren, that they would be able to have a conversation with their ancestor even if he was no longer there. He quickened his pace, although he was in no hurry. He wanted to stop by Anthony's house and then he was going to meet Yalitza Torres, the anti-Synchro activist, for a chat; Ana had become a ghost in his memory.

He walked into the white, cold room that his friend had lent him. As he walked down the corridor he heard laughter coming from his host's room; he did not interrupt.

He still had his password. He accessed it from his desktop; where he kept the folder named Ana. He opened it. He was looking at Nostradamus. Anthony had created complex machinery to protect his life. If he did not introduce the password and his retina scan every twenty-four hours, Synchro would deactivate. Julián clicked twice on the folder and opened it again, like he had done a week ago, when he discovered it.

He had given Anthony everything, and in exchange, Anthony had given everything to him; he had given him the key to the secret door that guarded Synchro's source code.

Julián Konks had in front of him the on and off switch of the world's most famous app, the company with most value in pecuniary History. Anthony had given it to him out of simple friendship. Julián held, under his index finger, the trigger that determined the life or death of their creation.

Without further hesitation, Julián turned Synchro off, the system that they had created to generate fake happiness in every human.